The Fallen Persimmon

Gigi Karagoz

Chapter 1

October 1985

BROKEN GLASS LITTERED Kate's bedroom floor. I picked up the largest pieces, slammed them on top of each other in a pile of jagged edges. A few shards of shattered mirror still clung to the frame, catching the mid-afternoon light, and throwing it onto the wall in sharp patches of brightness. My fractured reflection looked back at me, and I had to turn away. Shame coloured my cheeks. With an inward breath, I stood straighter, my fingers curling into my palms. How could she? On my way to the kitchen, I side-stepped drops of blood that had soaked into the tatami matting. A crust of the same brown-red coated my little toe, and the side of my foot. The sound of glass on glass scratched the air as I whacked the pieces of mirror on the work top. When they didn't break, I was tempted to bang them down again and again, until they did. But I'd already caused enough damage.

Standing at the kitchen sink, I slowly filled a bowl with water. Outside, my bike was propped against the neighbours' wall, but not Kate's. Bitch. With a wet cloth, I scrubbed at the blood on the tatami. Damson-dark stains that wouldn't come out. Horrible reminders of a horrible night. I tutted, scrubbed harder, but they wouldn't budge. Sitting back on my heels, I looked at my watch, calculating that if Kate wanted to get to work on time, she'd have to be home soon. Unzipping my holdall, I rummaged for a clean top and threw on my grey trousers. Not bothering with make-up, I grabbed my Levi's jacket off the back of the kitchen chair and left for work early. That way, I wouldn't have to see her. Screaming matches weren't my style, but I didn't trust myself. Halfway down the road, I slowed my pace. It would cause more problems if I didn't wait for the *yakuza* car to take me to the language school. We taught our first classes at midday, and there wasn't any point in arriving early. Of course, I could always jump the next train to Osaka and leave Kate to sort her own mess out. That'd serve her right, but I couldn't leave her on her own; it wasn't safe. Our flights were booked for the day after pay day. Just five more days, and we'd be out of this nightmare.

I wanted to speak to Ryu, hear his explanation. Working out what I wanted to say, I practised out loud to get my tone right. Taking the narrow road that edged a rice field, I headed round the corner to the phone box. White, long-necked birds waded through the shallow water, barely disturbing the surface. I pulled open the phone box door with such force, the birds took flight in one synchronised movement of elegance. Ramming my phone-card into the machine, my hand trembled. I punched in his number.

'*Moshi moshi*. Hello.'

'Ryu, it's me.' I struggled to keep my voice neutral. 'Let me speak to Kate.'

'Kate? She's not here. What's up?'

'Has she gone straight to work?'

'I haven't seen her since you two left here last night – well, this morning.' His tone was distant, off-hand.

'She didn't go back to the bar?' My hand dragged at my hair, twisting it up off the back of my neck.

'No. Why would you think that?'

'Because she turned around and cycled back towards your place and I came home on my own.' I opened the folding door to let in some air, pressed my forehead against the glass wall of the phone box. Did he think I was an idiot?

'Mari, she didn't come back here.'

Chapter 2

THE TOWN OF Hitano, on the southern island of Kyushu, was nothing like I'd imagined. The modern urbanisation of chrome and glass high-rises, the technological metropolis with huge neon signs and extra-wide pedestrian crossings was a world away. The further south we travelled, the more concrete gave way to countryside, and irrigation channels ran water between Wizard of Oz green rice fields. Silver electric pylons stood sentinel at the fields' edges, the early morning sun casting angled shadows over low rise wooden houses.

Our boss's secretary, Sayuri, had met us at the airport and brought us to the apartment where Kate and I would stay, rent-free, as part of our teaching contract. We walked down the side of the building to the front door. Kate smiled at me and my solar plexus twisted. Trying to compose myself, I dug around in my cloth shoulder bag, found a velvet scrunchie, and dragged my hair into a high ponytail. Of all the girls who must have applied for the job, why did I get paired up with one who looked like my dead sister? I didn't need reminders. It wasn't likely that I'd ever forget. The memory was burned into my mind and soul; an invisible scar that pulled and twisted, making my heart ache with the missing of her, and my belly flip-flap with shame for

5

what I'd done.

Following Sayuri's lead, we left our shoes just inside the door and stepped up into the kitchen. She slid open a solid, wide partition on the other side of the kitchen and another step took us into a room with pale golden tatami flooring, fitted wall to wall. I bent to touch the soft matting, breathing in the creamy-mild smell of late summer. A sliding partition separated the room from another, smaller room. It was narrow, with a dark blue carpet. One side of the room was made up of fitted wardrobes, and the other had an opaque glass door and window.

'Marianna? Do you mind if I have this room?' Kate said. She opened the door outwards and stepped onto a narrow balcony. 'I can have a ciggy.'

'Sure.' I smiled: that suited me. I wanted to sleep on the tatami; it was more authentic, more Japanese. 'Call me Mari. Marianna's too much of a mouthful,' I said.

Sliding open one of the wardrobes, I turned to face Kate, trying to temper my reaction to one of mild surprise rather than shock. Kate moved the hangers along the rails, inspecting the brightly coloured clothes that hung there. My stomach pitched. There were times when I just knew things, and this was one of them. I couldn't put my finger on it, but something wasn't right. Sayuri stood in the doorway, like a choirgirl, her hands folded in front of her. There was no expression on her face. Blank. Bland.

'They will collect,' she said.

'But whose clothes are these?' I said.

'Previous tenant,' she said. 'They will collect soon, okay?'

'She's got awful taste, whoever she is,' said Kate, pulling the skirt of a red satin dress out. 'Good storage space, but it's all a bit... well, you know, not what I expected. And so small.' She picked at the cream laminate that peeled off one corner of a small cabinet. A full-length white framed mirror hung above it and Kate pouted at her reflection. 'It's a bit grotty. Look at the walls.'

'It's not so bad,' I said.

Scuff marks on the white painted walls didn't matter to me;

it was a rent-free apartment. I'd been sleeping on a friend's sofa for the last month. All I wanted was my own room.

'Is that coffee table all the furniture there is?' Kate's voice got shriller as it got louder. She put her hands on her hips. 'This is hardly the furnished apartment I was promised. And beds… where on earth are the beds?'

I couldn't help but laugh at her. Kate lit a cigarette, her long pink nails clacking on the plastic lighter as she dropped it back into her bag. I fanned the smoke away, moving towards the tatami room. At around five-feet-five, she had an athletic look about her. Her short Lycra skirt showed off her toned legs, and it looked like she had spent all of Australia's summer and autumn on a beach.

'Please, Kate,' Sayuri said. 'No smoking inside house.' She opened a kitchen cupboard and gave Kate a small square ashtray.

Kate moved to the front door and after a quick puff, she stabbed out her cigarette, leaving the ashtray on top of the acid-green washing machine plumbed into the wall outside. Her yawn was loud. She covered her mouth with her hand and came back inside.

'I hadn't even noticed the lack of furniture, I must be jet-lagged or something,' I said. 'A bed would be good, though.'

Sayuri opened a cupboard in the tatami room and showed us folded futons and bedding. We pulled them out and arranged one in each room. Although they were single size, they took up a lot of the floor space. That explained the need for sliding doors everywhere. In the kitchen, Kate and I pushed the small table against the open partition. We wouldn't be able to close it, but it gave us more room to move. The two chairs, we placed on either side of the table. The sink was full of dirty plates, bowls, and chopsticks. I looked past my reflection and out onto the parking space at the front of the building. Why had the girl who lived here before left in such a hurry?

'Mari, all these packets are opened,' said Kate, rummaging in the cupboards.

'Sayuri? What's going on?' I said and took off my Levi's jacket, hanging it on the back of a chair.

'Don't worry about previous tenant, okay? You must know, there is much structure in Japanese life,' Sayuri said. 'Maybe hard for you to understand. Please, ask if you have questions.' She bowed, eyes down. Tiny, she moved with the gracefulness of a ballerina: every gestured flowed and ebbed from her like part of a dance.

I squashed down the bubbles of unease and stepped up into what was now my room. I unzipped my holdall. Unpacking didn't take long, and I put my things in the cupboard where the futons had been. The dozen or so items of clothing I'd brought fitted nicely in two neat piles on the top shelf, my toiletries on the middle one. Undies would need boxes or baskets to keep them tidy, but for now, I chucked them on the lower shelf. I left my Tarot cards in my holdall, put it on the cupboard floor, and closed the door. I stood for a moment, my palms against the white painted wood. Okay. Hello, new life. And by the looks of it, hello new friend.

Kate and I had met for the first time at Sydney airport's information desk. I was a bit nervous, so it was good to have some company on the overnight flight via Singapore. We arrived in Japan red-eyed and numb-brained. The train journey from Osaka to Hitano had been a long one, and I knew Kate was as tired as I was. Hoping for time to grab a shower and a coffee, I was disappointed when Sayuri said we needed to go to the English Institute, and that classes were scheduled for the afternoon. Of course, Japan's disciplined work-ethic had turned them into a world economy to be reckoned with, especially during the last decade. I shouldn't have been surprised.

Hitano was a small town by Japanese standards, but large enough to have its own train station. Billboards advertised cosmetics and clothing with models as perfect as the products they sold. The universal ideal of a perfect life that was easier to aspire to than achieve. Not that I expected a perfect life; I didn't deserve one, not after what I'd done. Anyone who'd all but killed their own sister would say the same.

Sayuri walked ahead, leading us past row upon row of bicycles parked in metal stands under a tin roof, and into the narrow, cobbled streets of the old town. A three-wheeler motorbike pulling a trailer filled with crates of beer slowed down behind us, and we stood with our backs against a shopfront to let it pass. My foot rested on a manhole cover and I moved my toe over the embossed cherry tree that decorated it. I liked the idea of taking something functional and ugly, and making it into a work of art.

The alley opened onto a vegetable market, edged on three sides by small wooden buildings that housed shops, restaurants, and bars. Outside each shoji screen entrance, long vertical flags flapped in the breeze. Their black Japanese lettering was a barbed wire of sharply angled lines that somehow softened in movement. Shoppers pushed their bicycles, baskets filled with bags of produce. The air twittered with chatter and bike bells. Vendors and shoppers alike stopped what they were doing to stare at Kate and me.

'I keep smiling, but no one is smiling back,' said Kate.

'It's a hugely different culture,' I said. That was exactly why I'd come to Japan. I needed to move forward and distance myself from everything I knew. Moving from London to Madrid, and finally to Sydney in the last few years hadn't helped. Maybe exposure to somewhere as unique as Japan would. From what I'd seen so far, I liked it. There was a quietness, an elegance about everything.

Outside a shopfront, two men dressed head to toe in white spoke with an elderly man. The harshness of their tone made me think it might be an argument, and something in their body language was menacing. By the time we were level with the two men in white, the altercation was over. One of them pocketed the envelope the elderly man had given him. They turned and bowed at Sayuri. She said something in that quiet voice of hers. The men stared at Kate and me, bowed again and walked away. What had I just witnessed?

Sayuri led us to a flight of stairs in the middle of a concrete row of shops on the far side of the market, and we followed her up to the entrance hall of the English Institute.

Sayuri introduced the owner, Ueno-san, who waited at the top of the stairs. Short and tubby, his kindly smile was spoilt by smokers' yellow teeth. We walked across the square hall, surrounded on three sides by glass-walled classrooms, two in front of us, one on either side. The frosted glass doors of the classrooms matched the bottom portion of the walls which faded to transparent glass at shoulder height. They reminded me of goldfish bowls. A jolt of recognition ran through me. *Glass.* Memories of the nightmare I'd had in Sydney crashed in. Breaking glass falling around me while a woman cried. I'd woken breathless and terrified, clawing at my throat, fighting off invisible hands.

In the staffroom next to Ueno-san's office, Sayuri offered us coffee. I looked down at the market from the window, watching everyday life go on as it probably had for decades. What gossip had been exchanged down there? Maybe people traded secrets along with their vegetables. I knew all about secrets. They didn't exist, because someone always found out whatever you were trying to hide

'We finish at five on Fridays and Saturdays,' Kate said. She knelt on the yellow corduroy sofa, looking at our schedule written on a whiteboard attached to the wall above it. 'Seven the rest of the week. I forgot we only get Sundays off. Only one day off a week. My friend Jack works in Tokyo and I was hoping, you know, for a chance to go and see him.'

'It's not so bad. We don't start 'til midday. Who's this Jack then?' I said.

'He's not my boyfriend but, you know, we were together for a while last summer. We met at a backpackers' hostel in Cairns while he was on holiday and we did a PADI dive instructor's course together. He went back to his job in Tokyo, and I carried on travelling around Australia.'

'How long were you there?'

'I had a six-month working visa. You?'

'Same.' There was no point in telling her that I'd overstayed my visa by two years because I couldn't face going back to England, and I had nowhere else to go.

'Ladies, I must ask for your passports. For registration with local authorities. They will be returned soon.' Kate and I fished them out of our bags and handed them to Sayuri. It was only a flash of apprehension, but it was there. 'Thank you,' she said, closing the door on her way out. Voices spoke in staccato-rhythm Japanese just outside the door. Sayuri came back into the room, and I saw a hefty man in a dark suit walking away. 'All arranged.'

'Shall we check out the nightlife this weekend?' I said. 'I'd love a few beers.'

Sayuri placed her hand gently on my arm, leaned forward so slightly, it was as though she'd hardly moved. 'No, ladies not go out drinking. Not good for you. Not good for school. Night-time dangerous for you.'

'Dangerous? How?' I said. Hadn't I read that Japan was one of the safest countries in the world, with one of the lowest crime rates?

'You are foreigners, something can happen.'

'Like getting lost or something? Not being able to ask for directions. Is that what you mean?' Kate said. She must have been around the same age as me but she seemed a bit younger. I put her at about twenty, maybe twenty-one.

'Many things can happen,' Sayuri said.

'Sayuri, the woman who lived in our apartment, did something happen to her?' I said. Something inside me turned icy and sharp. 'Why'd she leave everything behind like that?' She didn't need to answer. I knew they'd forced her to leave, dragged out of there. But I didn't know why.

'Nothing happened. She went away. Her things are collected today.'

'What – '

'That is all I can tell you. But you must know, we have rules you must follow,' said Sayuri. She unfolded two pieces of paper that she took out of her bag and placed them on the table. 'This is the map to your apartment. Take only this route. And please read the rules. And comply. Then everything is fine.'

Ueno-san knocked on the door and came inside, two men followed behind.

'May I introduce Mr Ohayo,' he said.

Kate and I stood. Ohayo bowed and we bowed back, and then he spoke to Ueno-san and Sayuri. Standing a few feet away, Ohayo watched us, his lips pressed into a thin line. When he spoke over his shoulder to the other man, who looked straight at me, it was obvious what they were talking about. My stomach coiled and I folded my arms across myself, turning my shoulder towards him.

'Ladies, I have arranged for you to come. I am your boss.' Reaching inside his jacket pocket, he withdrew a thin silver case. Taking business cards out of it, he handed one with both hands to Kate, and gave a sharp bow. He turned to me and bowed, and I took the card from him. Coloured tattoos flashed at his wrists and I smiled, but he pulled down his cuffs, and stared straight back at me.

'*Onishi Exotic Fruit Imports.*' I read the flip side of the business card, written in English. 'You're not part of the English Institute?'

'Onishi is large organisation, many different business,' he said 'Property, seafood export, fruit import, entertainment, Pachinko, other gaming arcade. English Institute is only associated business.' He flicked his hand toward the larger man behind him. 'This is Mr Washan. He is my… assistant.'

'Thanks for coming to meet us,' I said.

'I never saw a woman so tall, but you have a nice body. Very feminine. Hair is good colour too. Natural?' His eyes swept over me, then Kate. He nodded in approval. 'Nice.'

At almost five-foot-ten, I was used to people mentioning my height and my conker-coloured hair. But boss or not, Ohayo's comment about my body was too personal, pervy even, and my skin crawled.

'Cheeky beggar,' Kate whispered.

'I'm sure he meant it nicely,' I said. But it didn't feel like that.

'There are many students for you, excited to learn to pronounce the English way from English speakers. We never saw Europeans in Hitano. Follow what Ms Sayuri has told you. I leave you now.'

The arrogance in his walk and the way Washan followed two steps behind, made me think Ohayo was somehow superior. But what did I know about Japanese businessmen? Ueno-san and Sayuri bowed from the waist until Ohayo's shoes stopped echoing across the hall, and he descended the stairs.

'Okay, it's almost time,' said Ueno-san. 'Your students will be arriving. Enjoy your first class at English Institute,' he said. 'Mari, you're in room two. Kate, room four. Every lesson, every day.'

'That's it? No training?' I said, my eyes flicking from him to Sayuri and back.

'None needed,' said Ueno-san. 'They're conversation classes. Just follow the format in the teaching textbooks you'll find on your desks.'

'Are you ready?' said Sayuri. 'Don't be nervous.'

'I'll give it my best shot and if I mess up, you can always send me back to Sydney.' I ran my hands over my hips and shook out the fabric of my sunflower patterned skirt, enjoying the little rush of air around my ankles

'Not go back to Sydney.'

'But things might not work out. And I might be rubbish at teaching.'

'Your contract is for one year. If things not good, we send you another place, find someone to buy your contract. This is nice job for you, best job. Better than job for Filipinas. So, *gambate*. Please try your best.'

WE ONLY HAD two classes that day, thank God. I was so jet-lagged, I couldn't see straight. When classes finished, Kate and I had a bowl of noodles at one of the few market stalls still open. We sat on low stools at folding tables set out on the cobbles. The smell of cooking hung in the air like a hungry man's dream, intoxicating with the promise of a delicious meal. I heard a sizzle and turned to see a woman in a floral apron throw thick yellow noodles into a cast-iron wok and add handfuls of sliced vegetables. She stirred the noodles with giant chopsticks, and I could almost taste the ginger and garlic, and something else, something sweet. Behind her, a woman in another floral apron gave the men in white an envelope. It must be rent collection day.

'Against nuclear arms, are we?' Kate pointed to the CND logo embroidered on my bag. I nodded and placed it between us on a child-sized stool. 'I suppose we all should be. What with Reagan and Gorbachev, and the Cold War.' She sounded so middle class, whereas my accent veered somewhere between West London and Sydney. Dad had been an executive chef for Hilton Hotels, and we'd moved from London to Madrid, on to Sydney, and then back to London. All by the time I was fifteen.

'There's something funny going on.' I told Kate what Sayuri had said.

'We signed a year's contract, so we are tied in for a year. That's normal isn't it?'

'But it was the way she said they'd find someone to buy our contract and send us somewhere else.' The apron-lady placed two bowls of yakisoba fried noodles on our table. 'That's not normal. And who is Filipinas?'

'I could ring Jack. He'll know.'

'I think we're caught up in something here, Kate. And we've just handed over our passports.'

'I think you're being a tad over-dramatic, don't you?'

Maybe she was right. Lack of sleep probably added to my overactive imagination.

Walking home, we turned onto the main road by the station and carried on up the hill, aiming for the house with blue flowerpots on its wall; a landmark on our map. That house was on the corner with the road that cut through the rice fields and led to our street. There wasn't much traffic, but a square fronted white car drove past slowly. I glanced sideways and caught a glimpse of the driver. Slicked back hair hung below the collar of his white shirt. He glanced at me, his eyes moving over my body, and the tinted window slid closed. My heart pounded in my chest and the knots tightened in my stomach when, a few hundred metres up the road, the car turned around. Time slowed and the car crawled its way back down the hill towards us.

'Kate, I think they're following us,' I said, and grabbed her hand.

'Honestly, you're paranoid. It's probably just some guys who've never seen foreigners before.'

The car got closer, and by the time it drew to a halt on the other side of the road, I was walking so fast that Kate struggled to keep up with me. We drew level with the car, and the driver's window began a slow descent. Too scared to check over my shoulder, I waited to hear a car door open, to hear footsteps running after us, to feel a hand grab my shoulder.

We didn't slow down until we reached the house with the blue flowerpots. I pulled Kate around the corner and we stopped. Bending double with my hands on my knees, I waited for my breathing to get back to normal. Kate leaned back against the wall, lit a cigarette. Peering round the wall, we looked back down the road. The car had gone.

'What's wrong with you?' she said, between puffs. 'I'm sure they were just trying to be friendly. Perhaps they wanted to ask us to go for a drink or something. Although I'm too tired to go.'

'You're probably right, Kate. Let's just go home.'

But I peeped around the corner one last time, and my heart froze. The white car waited at the side of the road, facing up the hill.

Chapter 3

KATE AND I squashed into the phone box, and she angled the receiver between our ears, so that I could listen in.

'Japanese mafia?' she said. We looked at each other, and I moved in closer, not daring to breathe.

'The *yakuza* are basically organised crime gangs,' said Jack in Tokyo. 'They get their fingers in all the pies. From the corner shop to big corporations. They're big in the entertainment industry and bring women over from the Philippines to work in the bars.'

'Filipinas? I said.

'Yes. Mostly they work as hostesses, just serving drinks and chatting,' Jack said, the Dublin in his accent as warm and mellow as sunlight. 'Respect and hospitality are a huge part of Japanese culture. Then there's singers and dancers. It does get a bit seedier, depending on the club or bar, and then there's the strip clubs and so on.'

'Thank goodness we're only here to teach,' said Kate.

'If this Ohayo has nothing to do with the school but has arranged to bring you here, then it sounds like his organisation are moving into the foreign language teaching market. I was one of the first English teachers when I came here a year ago, but there are loads of us all over Tokyo now. Someone's making a lot of money out of bringing us over. Your man may have got someone keeping an eye on you. You'll be a novelty down there in the countryside.'

'So, he's making sure we don't get any unwanted attention maybe?' Kate nodded, and looked at me.

'Maybe. Look, I'm a *gaijin*, a foreigner, so I only know a bit about it. But don't think violin cases and machine guns like in films. The *yakuza* are semi-legal and mostly business oriented. I'm pretty sure my teaching contract is with them as well. They'll be skimming a ton of money off what the school charges, and that's about the limit of their involvement.'

'So, we don't need to worry, it's all normal?'

'Yeah, *yakuza* are part of everyday life here and at this level, it's nothing to worry about. You'll be fine.'

'They've given us this list of rules to follow,' said Kate, and I nodded in encouragement. 'We can't do this and that or the other, but the main one is that we can't go out.'

The list of rules included the usual tenancy rules: no smoking in the apartment, no dogs, or cats. Usefully, there were instructions on how to handle utility bills. We weren't allowed to hang our underwear on the washing line outside our apartment. Imagining there was some knicker thief around made me smile. Perhaps he was a spotty adolescent who wasn't sure how to deal with his awakening sexuality, or a bored husband, who liked his wife to wear other women's undies. Maybe he wore them himself.

'Reputation is everything here,' Jack said. 'There's a whole load of etiquette to follow so that no one loses face, which basically means no one gets embarrassed. It's tricky at first, but you'll get the hang of it. Just play along.'

Leaving them to chat in private for a bit, I ducked out of the phone box, and took a dozen or so paces towards the house with blue flowerpots. Slung along the street, one and two-storey wooden houses skulked under slate-tiled roofs. Low eaves frowned over small windows, and narrow doors opened directly onto the pavement-less street. I turned and ambled back, the tightness in my chest and shoulders loosening. Standing with my back to the houses, I played with the flat metal buttons on my faded Levi's jacket and looked across the fields. Lines of polytunnels lay between large greenhouses with thick opaque plastic stretched over their metal frames. Greenery softened the narrow concrete embankments that split the rice fields into a tidy patchwork. The order of everything, the simple beauty of it all, was soothing. Further away, foothills and forested mountains rolled up into the milky-blue May sky.

Breathing out, I relaxed. Our contracts were on English Institute headed paper, so even if the *yakuza* were getting a kick-back, we were still employed by the school. Kate was right; I was being over-dramatic and paranoid.

'Feel better now?' Kate said. 'If Jack says it's nothing to worry about, I believe him.'

'Yeah. It's hard to know how things work. But mafia, Kate? That can't be a good thing.'

'You just heard it for yourself. Business is run that way here.' We reached the corner, and Kate stuck her head around the wall. 'Oh, no white car today. See? Jack's right.'

LATER, WHEN WE'D finished work, I stood outside the school entrance at the bottom of the stairs, waiting for Kate to finish her class. The food stalls were gone, and the shops closed. An old man rode slowly past on a creaking bike, his trousers pulled tightly around his thin ankles, and held in place with bicycle clips. Apart from one lady, the last of the vegetable sellers, the market was deserted. She loaded boxes of vegetables onto a wooden handcart. Footsteps clattered down the stairs, and Kate's students spilled out of the doorway. There was no sign of Kate. I tutted and looked at my watch, wishing she would hurry up.

'*Konbanwa,*' the students said in unison, bowing briefly.

'*Konbanwa.* Good evening,' I replied.

Kate appeared, closely followed by the last of her students. They shot each other a look, one that made me think something was going on.

She watched him waltz off, flicking her fringe out of her eyes. 'Cute bum. It's so funny,' she said. 'They can't say 'Kate', so they call me *Kato*. Hey, you look fed up. What's wrong?'

'I feel as if I'm caught out all the time. We've only been here a week and I'm baffled by all the...' I waved my hands around, searching for the word. 'By everything. The *yakuza*. Sayuri and her silly rules. Half of my student won't even speak, and it's a conversation class. I don't know if I want to be here. Something told me not to come and I didn't listen.'

Kate tilted her head to one side. 'It's horribly restrictive and I'm not sure I like it either. Like Jack said, let's just keep our heads down and do the job. Just think of the dosh.'

'Kate, I've got this older student. A businessman, about fifty, I suppose. Well, he offered me money for sex.'

'What? Shocking.' She tried to suppress a giggle but failed. 'You're very exotic, with all that chestnut hair. He's probably curious, you know, whether the rug matches the curtains.'

Laughter bubbled from me, the absurdity of the situation thinning out the insult.

'He was so angry when I refused. As if I'd insulted him, not the other way 'round. Anyway, I'm starting Japanese lessons with Ueno-san on Monday.' I was good at languages, had studied French and Italian to 'A' Level. And with Mum being Spanish, I'd grown up speaking that. 'I'll have to be at school an hour earlier every day.'

'I'll come with you.' Kate said. 'I can always go shopping or something, I know it's only a twenty-minute walk but I'd rather not do it on my own.'

'Actually, I'm glad you said that.'

A chill skittered the length of my spine. I looked up through the tangle of overhead telephone wires and electric cables that spanned the street like slack tightropes. A three-quarter moon hung low in the sky, glowing warm and golden from the light of the just-set sun. Neon signs outside the bars and restaurants flickered into life, harsh in the mellow half-light of evening. Kate walked ahead of me, through quietening, narrow streets without pavements, along foot-wide concrete slabs that covered deep gutters. Every now and then, a slab wobbled under my feet, making a dull concrete on concrete sound which echoed in the belly of the empty space below.

'Shall we find somewhere to have a drink or something?' I said. 'I don't feel like going home.'

'Good idea. Oh, guess what? I've got a date tomorrow with one of my students.'

'You move fast. The one you came down the stairs with?'

'Seiji. He's only nineteen but he's dishy,' Kate said.

'I knew it!' I laughed. 'Just be careful. This AIDS thing is really spreading, it's scary.'

'I know. I read in the paper last month that there are cases in every country now. They're even starting to screen blood donors. Don't worry. I might have a few one-night stands, but I'm not stupid. I brought condoms with me.'

'And you're breaking one of the rules,' I said. 'No fraternising with the students.'

Kate looked back over her shoulder and shrugged. 'It's only a bit of fun. At least I'm not breaking the rule about men in our apartment. I'll make sure we go to a love hotel that's on the list.'

'Tell me what it's like, the love hotel, I mean. It sounds sleazy, like a brothel.'

'It's what they do here. Apparently, couples only have sex at home when they get married. Before that, they go to these love hotels for an hour, or a night. Shag-pad-extraordinaire. Better than the back seat of a car.'

'Or a grope behind the proverbial bike-shed,' I said. I wouldn't be going to any love hotel with anyone.

We laughed but a flicker of regret pinched at my heart. I didn't want to think about my ex, Joe, with his blue eyes and too-long hair. Joe, the musician, who wrote songs for me and played his guitar for me. Joe, the rat-bastard who cheated on me. Twice. Guys were all the same. Funny how the word *boyfriend* and *bastard* both start with the same letter. I always chose the wrong guy, and my heart was a slow learner. My mother said I was cursed and didn't deserve to be loved. She said a lot of other things too.

And she was right; it was all my own fault. Payback.

Friday night was busy in Hitano's entertainment district. People flowed along the narrow streets, buoyed by beer and sake. A group of men sprawled out of a doorway framed by two elongated red lanterns. They were as large as punch-bags, their black lettering stark against the soft glow of the lights inside them. One of the men bumped into me, dropping his jacket. He muttered something I couldn't understand, gestured at me, and bent to pick up his jacket. His friends cat-catcalled and jeered. Kate and I moved away. We meandered down the alleys, the unfamiliar but mouth-watering aromas of food making me hungry.

An alleyway led to half a dozen wide steps, and wound on around the corner. I ran my foot over the smooth cobbles. They looked centuries old, as did the buildings. I touched the short curtain hanging on a bamboo pole across a shoji doorway. All the restaurants had them; plain pieces of fabric with two or three vertical splits from the bottom, so that they moved in the breeze. I wished I could read the Japanese characters that read left to right across them. And those that ran top to bottom on the tall thin flags that stood beside the doors. At the bottom of the steps, Kate chose a place because of a large ceramic raccoon that stood by the entrance.

Around me, I sensed history. I imagined other lives lived in a time when samurai walked down these steps, the end of their curved katana swords clinking against the cobbles. A noblewoman emerging from an ornate sedan chair, carried by servants, would have held her kimono up so as not to sully the hem in the dirt of the street. And geisha would have stood chatting under the light of softly glowing paper lanterns. All emotion was here. Every joy and sorrow resonated from the buildings, and the air itself. The mixture was as rich and heady as a rum cocktail.

'Mari? Mari! What are you staring at? Are you coming in or what? Come on, I'm hungry,' said Kate.

She slid open the bamboo door of the yakitori grill restaurant. Everything and everyone stopped for a second; food held in chopsticks half-way to half-open mouths, beer glasses paused, half raised. A moment of silence while everyone stared, and then the chatter started up again.

'*Irashaimasse*.' A man shouted the welcome, smiling under his moustache. A flat drum hung on the wall and he beat it three times with a wooden stick. '*Irashaimasse*.'

'That's what I call making an entrance,' said Kate. I laughed, trying not to make any noise. 'Blimey.'

The man stood behind a refrigerated glass cabinet. It ran the length of a polished wood counter, and was filled with skewers of various marinated meats. Being a vegetarian, I was relieved to see vegetables and tofu too. He turned and took glasses from shelves stacked with small bowls and oblong plates, sake flasks, and tiny cups. At the far end, next to the doorway to a small kitchen, a charcoal grill sat beneath a huge extractor fan.

With all five tables taken, we sat on stools at the counter, squeezing in alongside other diners. Kate chose a few skewers. The man slapped them onto the grill, and they sizzled and spat. Ceramic bowls of pickled vegetables were like little works of art with flower-shaped pieces of radish and flourishes of grated carrot. Tiny dishes of soy sauce and bright green wasabi paste came with bowls of rice, spooned out from two huge rice cookers at the end of the counter.

After pouring cold beer into glass tankards, I took disposable chopsticks from an upright wooden box and tipped them out of their paper wrapper.

'These hashi are stuck together.' I ran my finger down the indentation between them.

The next pair I tried were the same. Kate and I looked at each other, giggling. We tried several pairs until the man behind the counter discreetly pulled some apart. He put them down on the counter without making eye contact. He hadn't wanted us to lose face. I laughed louder then and ordered more beer. Kate ate everything: chicken, duck, pork, and beef. She refused the chicken intestines, though.

Fumbling with the chopsticks, I tried to eat the rice. I dropped more than I ate until the man silently slid soup spoons towards me, while he looked the other way, grinning.

'Masta.' He said, tapping his chest. 'You?'

Kate and I said our names and Masta smiled.

We laughed and I ordered more skewers, amazed at how delicious the sticky soy-drenched aubergine and tofu was, spiked with hints of ginger. Masta placed a large bottle of Asahi Dry beer and two frosty-iced glasses on the counter in front of us, and pointed to two men seated at a table. Kate turned and thanked them, smiling. She simpered and batted her eyelashes. I cringed inwardly, wishing she wasn't so obvious.

'IT FEELS LIKE a million years since I've had any fun,' Kate said, linking my arm as we walked home later.

'Tell me about it. That food! We must go back there again. Soon.'

'They can't stop us going out. I hate those stupid rules. Who is that Sayuri anyway? She's just an office girl, she's not the boss.'

We reached the station and walked on, past the bike stand. None of the bikes had locks to secure them to their stands. I stopped, looked along the rows and lifted a bike out of its metal supports.

'What are you doing?' Kate said.

'Borrowing this bike.' I straddled a large-wheeled red bike with a basket on the front. 'All this walking to school every day… if we borrow a couple of these, it'll be much easier. These bikes never move, they're always here.'

'We can't!'

Then she pulled a white bike with pale blue and pink streamers on the handlebars out of its stand. We wobbled off on stolen bikes, screaming with laughter. Two minutes later, we were caught in car headlights that shone past us and lit up the road ahead. Gaining speed, we didn't look back until we realised the car was keeping a measured distance behind us and driving way too slowly.

Chapter 4

DAWN'S EARLY LIGHT seeped under my eyelids to wake me as usual. Arms full of washing, I struggled to open the front door. Keeping washing machines outside tickled me. They sat like plump frogs on apartment balconies, plumbed into the side of houses under corrugated plastic roofs, even under carports. Dropping my clothes to the ground, I reached for the lid of the machine. Someone had left two origami butterflies on it. Russet-red and gold patterned paper folded here and there to reveal the plain reverse side in splashes of bright green on the edges of the swallow-tail wings. The other butterfly, beige and sky-blue, had a simpler, less flamboyant shape. Holding the red butterfly, I admired the structure, the detail, wondering who'd made them, and why they'd been left there. As gently as if they were real, I put them on top of the breezeblock wall between our building and the house next door. Clothes stuffed into the washing machine, I sprinkled washing powder over them, and closed the lid. I turned the dial and the machine chugged into life. Footsteps chimed on the metal staircase above me and I said good morning. The young woman bowed, and smiled shyly, but didn't stop. I went back inside.

With a mug of coffee beside me on the tatami, I peered round the sliding partition that divided my room from Kate's. She was still sleeping. Lying with her back to the balcony door, she held a plush blue elephant in her hand. She'd crept in sometime in the early hours after her date, and I'd pretended to be asleep. No doubt she'd tell me all about it when she woke up.

She and I came from different backgrounds, had different views on life, but we got on well together. We were becoming friends. I was glad, especially as there were just the two of us. I didn't want to make the same mistake I'd made a few times in the last five years. Making friends was easy enough, and once I felt I could trust someone, I told them about Elena. Then things changed. Maybe they could see I was to blame, or maybe they couldn't deal with the emotional burden, but the friendship was ruined either way.

I took my Tarot cards out from under a pile of folded clothes on the low table next to my futon. Closing my eyes, I shuffled the cards and spread them face down in an arc on the floor. I took one from the middle and knew before I turned it over, that it echoed my unease. The Ten of Wands. At face value, the card indicated overwhelming burdens, both physical and emotional. On a deeper level, it warned of being trapped and not having control over things. The next card I picked was the High Priestess. That told me to trust my instincts, and that things were not as they appeared. The feathered turban the High Priestess wore reminded me of India.

That was it. I'd stick it out in Hitano for six months and save as much money as I could. Then I'd travel to India, fulfil a long-standing ambition to visit Dharamshala where the Dalai Lama lived in exile from Tibet. I'd been a fan of the Dalai Lama's teachings for ages, and all things Buddhist appealed to me. The whole concept of karma and reincarnation resonated with me. It meant that we got a second chance to live a better, kinder life. Or a third chance, or maybe even a hundredth. Doing good in the next life to make up for misdeeds in the previous one sounded right to me.

So, my decision was made. The teaching job was well paid and six months' savings would probably fund a year's travelling in India.

'Ooh, are they Tarot cards?' Kate said, her sleepy face peering round the partition.

'Yes.' I gathered them together, waiting for a barbed remark, a snitty comment. People were always so judgemental about Tarot.

'You are such a hippy. Wild hair, don't eat meat, long skirts.' She padded to the kitchen, rattling around, making herself coffee. 'Are you psychic, then?'

'A bit. Sometimes I just know things. I've always been like that.'

'Witchy-woo.'

I laughed. I'd expected worse. Like when my mother said I was cursed.

LATER, AS WE cycled towards the station, the white car cruised past. The rows of parked bikes (now minus two) reminded me that there were so few cars in town. Seeing the same one again and again must be inevitable. If Jack was right and it was the *yakuza*, it probably had nothing to do with us. They were probably just doing whatever it was that *yakuza* did. Gun running and corruption seemed far-fetched for small-town Hitano, so maybe they just lived here and did their shady business elsewhere. Not looking where I was going, I nearly collided with a woman as she backed her bike out from under the shelter. Even though it was my fault, she bowed an apology before she cycled off. I'd landed in an alien world where everything was back to front. Nothing was as it seemed, but somehow it was easy to put it all down to my over-active imagination.

'THANK GOD FOR the air conditioning. This humidity is killing me,' I said, dragging my wavy hair, which was now double its size, off the back of my neck and into a ponytail.

'It's so long. You should cut it. It'd be cooler.'

'Nothing would ever make me cut my hair,' I said. 'It's my one vanity.'

'That and your green eyes. So, ready for another fun afternoon of teaching?' said Kate as we went upstairs to school. 'It's so dull.'

We crossed the hallway to the staff room and I looked around to make sure Ueno-san wasn't close by. I shot Kate a sideways look.

'What?' she said.

'I'm probably going to get into trouble, but I'm not using the textbooks. I ask the students what they want to talk about,' I said in a quiet voice. 'It's much easier. Yesterday one lot wanted to talk about music. There's one guy who's a huge Style Council and Tears for Fears fan. He's going to bring me a tape. Some superstar called Yazawa. Another class were fascinated on what I thought of our Prime Minister. Although they called her 'Maggie Tatcha'.'

'You'd better hope Ueno-san doesn't find out.'

'What? About Maggie Thatcher?' I said. Kate rolled her eyes. 'It gets worse. What Ueno-san teaches me is very formal, so I use my dictionary in class and the students are teaching me more colloquial stuff.'

'Cheeky cow! Good for you. I'm not even going to try and learn, it's too difficult. But you're learning lots, Mari, so I won't have to.'

Later that afternoon, between lessons, two earthenware bowls of noodles had just been delivered to the staff room from a stall in the market. Kate tried to fish out the long thin inoki mushrooms that floated in miso soup with brown soba noodles and sliced shitake. Cubes of silken tofu, a slice of carrot shaped like a five-petalled flower and a sprinkling of chopped spring onion brightened the dish visually. Ginger and garlic brightened it for the taste buds. The smells and sounds of the market trickled into the room from the open windows.

'I shan't be home tonight,' said Kate. 'Hope you don't mind.'

'I've got a ton of study to do. Ueno-san's set me an exam on what I've learned so far. Who is it this time? Seiji?' I couldn't remember the other guys she'd been to a love hotel with.

'Actually, it's one of your students. Calls himself Micky.'

'I saw you flirting with him in the hall the other day. God, Kate, slow down. By the time we leave, you'll have shagged the whole school.'

It just came out of my mouth; I hadn't meant to be bitchy. Her ability not to get attached, her nonchalant attitude towards men and sex, amazed me. With me, the lines between sex and love always blurred. If I let a man into my body, he always found his way into my heart. Just as I was about to apologise to Kate, Sayuri came into the room with Ohayo and Washan.

'Please stand. Boss wants to speak to you,' said Sayuri, her face expressionless, like a kabuki mask. 'And you must bow.'

We did as we were told. They must have found out about us stealing the bikes. My stomach squirmed with the humiliation of being made to stand and bow, and the embarrassment of being caught out. Like a naughty child, my face was hot, and I knew my cheeks flushed pink.

'You must obey the rules,' said Ohayo. 'Do not go out at night.'

'*Naze,* why?' I said.

'Don't question.' Ohayo's voice was loud, and he snarled as he spoke. He turned and spoke to Sayuri instead. She stood, hands clasped in front of her, eyes downcast.

'Ohayo-san say you make him angry when you ask question. He say, it is forbidden. So. It is forbidden. It is dangerous for you because maybe someone can kidnap you. You must not go out. Please, read again the rules. Stay home, be quiet.'

'Kidnap? My parents aren't that rich, they wouldn't be able to get much ransom money,' said Kate. I could've added that my parents wouldn't pay even one yen for me.

'Please, not make problem,' Sayuri said.

'Not make problem?' Kate's voice was more pinched than usual. 'Well, I *am* making a problem. You can't stop us; we have the right to –'

'It's okay, let's hear them out,' I said and put my hand on her arm. 'Let's hear what they have to say.'

Ohayo looked at me, his eyes skimming my body. Trying to keep my face impassive wasn't easy. I wanted to knee him in the balls. He fingered the button of his single-breasted suit jacket and adjusted his tie before turning away.

'Sayuri, please tell him that it's not easy for us, we have no friends here. We just want to go out and relax with other people for company. We'd like a bit of a social life, that's all,' I said, my bangles rattling as I moved my hands. 'That would be alright, wouldn't it?'

Ohayo spoke in rapid Japanese and Sayuri translated for him. 'He understands life is different for you. Maybe difficult for you in Japan, but you accept to come here. You must accept our instruction.' Sayuri moved her hands apart and glanced at Ohayo. 'Please, Mari and please, Kate. Do as we ask.'

Kate tutted and flicked her fringe out of her eyes. I moved in closer, bent my head to her ear.

'Say yes and then do what we want,' I whispered.

Ohayo's head snapped round, and he looked straight at me. He couldn't have heard, but he glared at me, his eyes hard.

'You!' Ohayo pointed at me. 'Don't you know I am your boss? You must be respectful. Do as I say.'

It wasn't his words that sent the icy chill across my skin, but something intangible. I caught a glimpse of the colourful tattoo that showed at his wrist as his arm moved downwards. He looked at me, his arrogant smirk almost daring me to say something. But why? If tattoos weren't acceptable, why have them? Turning on his heel, Ohayo walked briskly out of the staffroom, quickly followed by Washan and Sayuri. Sitting back at the table, Kate and I looked at each other, across our bowls of cooling noodles.

'I can't believe they didn't even mention the bikes,' I said after a few minutes when I was sure they'd gone. 'Maybe this losing face etiquette can be a good thing. I don't see why we can't go out, though. It's a pretty quiet town.'

'Oh, she's back.' Kate nodded toward the door.

Sayuri stepped silently into the room.

'Ohayo-san has opportunity for you.' She smiled. I dropped my noodles back into the bowl. 'He understands you like to be social. Kujaku Club is very famous in Hitano and customers all nice businessman,' she said. 'They like to speak English with nice lady. They go for relaxing and drinking import whisky. You can be hostess, serve the guest. Give drinks and light cigarette. You can speak with them. You can sing karaoke.'

'Hostess? I'm not sure. It sounds a bit sleazy,' I said. The wet noodles kept slipping through my chopsticks, so I took a fork from the drawer.

'Hostess,' Sayuri said, 'is Japanese tradition to offer hospitality. Nice job for you.'

'She's right. Remember what Jack told me, it depends on the establishment, but mostly it's all above board,' Kate said. 'The girls just serve drinks and sing songs.'

'So,' I frowned. 'we stay in the club, serve drinks and sing karaoke? Nothing else?'

'Yes, Mari. Like waitress only. Some places girls do stripping or sexy business, but not here!' She raised her small hands.

'No sexy business,' said Kate.

She nudged me and I had to bite my lip, look away before I laughed.

'Look, I don't want to be a hostess,' I said.

'But Ohayo-san has decided,' Sayuri said, looking from me to Kate and back again. 'You must do. Every Friday and Saturday evening, from seven thirty o'clock.'

'We might as well,' said Kate. 'Beats sitting in that apartment all evening.'

'Mr Ohayo has decided,' I said. 'But I haven't. Sayuri, what if I refuse?'

'You cannot refuse. You have contract with us. So, you have no choice.'

Chapter 5

WAKING EARLIER THAN usual, I realised that Kate wasn't home. She told me she was going on a date but I didn't ask who with. Instead of tackling the Japanese homework Ueno-san had given me, I left the apartment just as dawn finished breaking the day in, pink and peach. On either side of our building, unpainted breezeblock walls lined the street and behind them, bushy trees hid modern houses. Perhaps they needed so much privacy because they had their own secrets to hide.

Wandering inland, I headed towards the hills, past vegetable fields and greenhouses. A few farmers in straw hats tended their crops in the cool of morning before the heat of the day struck. The black lines of electric cables and telephone wires looked ugly and harsh in comparison to the greenery around me in the soft, quiet light of early morning. It was my favourite time of day. There was something so clean and hopeful about a new day and the gentle anticipation of good things to come. Not for me the sad melancholy of sunsets, as a tired golden evening lost itself to night's darkness. But now, sunrise reminded me of Joe. He'd called me his Sunrise Girl, even written a song about me. Maybe was still with her, the one he'd left me for. Maybe he'd cheated on her too. Rat-bastard.

Back-tracking round the rice fields, I headed to the konbini, the convenience store on the hill road. It sold all sorts: shampoo and bags of rice, instant noodles, chocolate, and sando sandwiches made with cotton wool bread, processed cheese, and overly pink ham. I took a warm steamed bun out of the heated glass cabinet. I bit into the pillow of fluffy rice flour dough, tasting something savoury in the centre. Looking closely at the small red beans of the filling, I was relieved it wasn't meat. From one of the vending machines outside the konbini, I chose a can of iced Suntori coffee, and got another one for Kate.

Wanting to explore a bit more, I walked home another way, drinking my coffee, dropping a packet of butter biscuits into my bag. Crossing a metal bridge over a wide, concrete canal, I stopped. I leaned over the side and the weather-worn paint of the handrail was rough under my fingers. Fronds of greenery grew in the cracks and crevices of the sloped canal sides and a trickle of water snaked along the base. Scruffy old houses perched along the edge. Vertical wooden planks made up the bottom half of their walls, the top half whitewashed plaster that flaked and peeled. Pipes stuck out of the canal wall underneath every house; it might originally have been a drain, or an open sewer. These weren't the dwellings of the affluent. The contrast and paradoxes of Japan constantly fascinated me and I was happy to be able to experience this side of Japan, rather than a big city. It felt more real, more authentic than the much-hyped neon metropolis of Tokyo with its extra wide zebra crossings and 24 hour nightlife.

I went back the way I'd come, then deliberately took a wrong turn. On the corner of a dirt track that made a plumb line through fields, was a ramshackle, single storey wooden building. It looked like somewhere to keep animals, or farming equipment. Under the low eaves, shutters closed over the windows, and a few roof tiles were missing. At the side of the house stood a persimmon tree. We'd had one in our garden in Madrid, and I remembered my grandmother peeling the fat plum shaped fruit and slicing them into wedges. I touched the glossy dark leaves and the small bell-shaped flowers. A tiny blonde puppy ran up to me. Its fluffy tail wagged so fast that the pup almost fell over. I picked it up, moving my face out of reach as it tried to lick me. Presuming the pup belonged to whoever lived there, I walked towards the shack. The puppy squirmed as I put it down and it ran inside, dodging a piece of hessian that hung in the doorway. I rested my hand on the battered door that leaned back against the outer wall, attached by one hinge.

'*Sumimasen,*' I called. *Excuse me.* But no one answered.

Taking the packet of biscuits out of my bag, I pushed the hessian aside. It took a moment as I stood in the doorway for my eyes to adjust to the darkness. Slivers of light shone through cracks and chinks in the wood, and the gaps around the shutters. Dust motes danced silver in the air that drifted through and I heard the gentle tinkling of a windchime somewhere close by. A tap dripped into a sink unit, and the sound of water on metal pinged around the room. Across the colourless lino floor, I could make out a futon, folded neatly, its bedding on top. A small, cast-iron wood burner sat in the middle of the room, battered pots and pans stacked beside it. I looked upwards to where the chimney stretched through the low roof, next to a bare lightbulb that hung on a length of cable. On the floor by the wall opposite the door, the chrome handle of a shiny white rice cooker reflected the light. Who lived here? Like this?

Then I saw them. I crouched and picked up two origami butterflies, the same ones that I'd found outside our apartment. One was all russet and green flamboyance, the other simpler, beige and baby blue. And I understood. Someone had made those mini works of art based on Kate's and my colouring. To whoever lived here, we were like two exotic butterflies. I placed them back on the floor, although I really wanted to take them.

Turning to leave, I gasped as I bumped into a white-haired man in a battered army jacket. He adjusted the pair of flying goggles that he wore strapped across his forehead. He stared at me and I avoided his gaze. His jacket was stained with what looked like years of wear, and the cuffs and collar were frayed. Embarrassed that I'd snooped in his house, I laughed, a false, high-pitched laugh that wasn't my own.

The old man stood his ground as I tried to move past him, running his hand across his buzz-cut hair. The puppy, glad to see its master, yapped and ran in circles. It jumped up, forelegs on my shin, trying to get at the packet of biscuits in my hand. I inched towards the door.

'For the puppy,' I said, holding out the biscuits.

He looked at me blankly, so I pointed at the dog. The man smiled crookedly, his lower jaw out of alignment with the upper, but his teeth perfect-pearl-white. The dog ran in circles, barking. The man reached down and patted its back, blocking my exit. My heart thudded as I tried to go around him. He cocked his head to one side and frowned. There was something sad about his rheumy old eyes, and my nervousness disappeared as I sensed his loneliness.

'*Kurutta*,' he said and took the packet of biscuits from me. '*Inu*.' He opened it, gave me a handful, and motioned to his puppy. '*Kurutta*.'

'*So desuka*?' *Is it?* I said, having no idea what he was saying.

'*Hai. Kurutta. Inu*' Piece by piece, I fed the puppy as the man repeated the words.' *Kurutta. Inu*.'

'*Kurutta. Inu*,' I said.

The man laughed as we broke up the biscuits and put them on the floor. I stood, my hand reaching to move the hessian aside, and I stepped out into daylight. The old man followed me but I kept moving. He waved, a big smile on his face. Glancing at my watch, I couldn't believe it was already ten o'clock. There was just enough time to go home and get ready for my Japanese lesson and work.

As I turned onto the street, the white car cruised past me. I turned and watched as the driver got out and opened the boot. He looked at me and inclined his head towards me, then carried a large bag of what looked like rice into the shack.

Relief flooded through me. Jack had been wrong; no one was keeping an eye on us. It really was just a coincidence that we kept seeing the same car. And the hostessing thing sounded quite easy. Kate had explained it more and I relaxed. India could wait a few more months, until I'd saved enough money. Things would be okay.

While I walked home, I looked up the two words the old man had said in my dictionary. Crazy and dog.

Back at the apartment block I picked up an origami turtle from the washing machine. The green geometric pattern on the paper enhanced the contours of its shell. Its tiny feet fascinated me; how had the old man managed to fold something so small?

'Morning,' said Kate, opening the front door. 'Where've you been so early?'

'Just to get some iced coffee.'

'I'm off to phone Jack, I'll have mine when I get back.'

Quickly, I dropped the turtle into my bag. I didn't feel good about hiding it from Kate, but she wouldn't understand. The old man was a misfit, and I knew how that felt. We misfits had to stick together. Don't ask me why I didn't show Kate the origami figure, because I can't answer. Maybe it was because I was used to keeping secrets.

Chapter 6

SAYURI ARRANGED FOR two of the Filipinas who worked in Kujaku to take us shopping in Kitakyushu. Imee was all smiles, asking questions about my family, which I evaded. Melody wasn't quite so friendly; she seemed resentful. Maybe she hadn't wanted to give up her morning off.

The department store bookshop had the clean, papery smell of new books and the hush of a library. In the travel section, I scanned the neat shelves and found a few coffee-table books with sumptuous photos. I browsed, finding a rack of guidebooks. A bright yellow cover caught my eye - *Asia on a Shoestring*. It covered all the countries I eventually wanted to travel through and more, listing accommodation, things to do and how to get from one place to the next. And it included India. Perfect. I moved to the language section, picked up a Japanese language book and a few children's activity books to help me learn to read and write two of the three Japanese alphabets. The third, kanji, was based on Chinese symbols, so I wasn't even going to try that for now. After paying for my books, I headed down to the food hall to meet up with the others.

'Look what I bought.' Kate held up a zebra stripe and jungle print t-shirt. 'There's more, I'll show you when we get home.'

What else could I do but smile at her awful choice? But Imee and Melody 'oohed' and 'aahed'.

At the sweet counter, I chose a selection of pastel coloured confections shaped like flowers. The assistant wrapped each one in translucent white tissue paper decorated with delicate pink cherry blossoms. She placed them in a similarly decorated rectangular box, tying white and pink ribbons around it. Bowing, she handed me a mini paper carrier bag covered in gold and pink cherry blossoms.

'Blimey, all that for ten sweets,' I said. 'Look at this packaging, it's gorgeous.'

'I'm looking forward to seeing the real thing next spring,' said Kate, pursing her lips as she ran her fingers over the raised flowers. 'It's the main reason I came to Japan.'

Opening the packet of sweets, I offered them around. Only Kate accepted. My face contorted as I took a bite of the pale green confection. The sugar and pounded rice outer casing gave way to grainy, sour bean paste inside. Kate didn't like it either. The other girls laughed.

'Let's go and find some coffee,' I said.

'Oh, yes please.' Kate said. 'But I'll meet you in the café, I need the loo. Here, would you take my bags for me?'

MELODY AND IMEE told me about the Philippines, about the great seafood and the small towns they came from on equally small islands. They spoke of aqua coloured seas and forested mountains, frenetic cites and a thousand churches. It sounded beautiful and I liked the idea of travelling there. Mentally, I added it to my list.

In the café, I paid for our drinks and carried the tray with four coffees and a plateful of cookies to an empty table. I sat opposite the Filipinas, turning to hang my bag over the back of my chair. Imee smiled and pulled her chair nearer the table, tucking her slender legs underneath. An intelligent girl, she was saving enough money to get herself through nursing college after she returned to Manila. She'd been in Hitano for almost a year and a half. With a blunt fringe above her almond-shaped eyes, she looked more Japanese than Filipina.

'Imee? Melody? Can I ask you something?' I said. They nodded. 'Why do they say it's dangerous to go out at night? And all the rules. I don't get it.'

'I don't know what to tell you,' Imee said and exchanged a look with Melody.

'What?' My wooden bangles clattered down my arm as I rested my elbow on the table.

'We should tell her,' Imee said. She made herself busy, reapplying her rich red lipstick. Melody shrugged and looked away. Whatever Imee was about to say probably wasn't good, but I kept smiling, waiting for her to continue. Eventually, she checked her reflection in her compact, put it away. 'The import company is a lie,' she said in a quiet voice. 'It's a front and the people who own it, they own you now. At least for your one-year contract.'

It wasn't a surprise. '*Yakuza*,' I said.

'Oh, you already know. Well, they make big money from you and that's why they expect you to work a lot.'

Cutlery scraped on plates and the background noise of chatter grated on my nerves. A woman accidentally kicked the leg of my chair as she walked past. She bowed her apology and I bowed back in response.

'You'll work for free at Kujaku right? It's the *yakuza* – not nice people,' Melody said, and Imee shushed her, put her forefinger to her lips, and looked around like some character in a comedy film, all exaggerated eyes. 'The school borrowed big money from them to bring you here. You think a small school like that can pay to bring two foreign teachers? They have a debt to the *yakuza* now, so you work hard.'

'All bars work with *yakuza*, so it was easy for them to sell you as hostesses when they see you like to go out,' said Imee. 'You played right into their hands. Now they make more money out of you. From the school and now also from the bar. Do you understand?'

'I knew there was a *yakuza* connection, but I didn't really understand it.' I said.

'Onishi Imports is *yakuza*. You and Kato, you're *yakuza* property,' said Melody. 'Just do what you are here to do, make your money and go home when the year is up. What's the expression you have in English? Don't rock the boat? Well, don't. They are dangerous.'

'*Yakuza*.' I said. 'Kate's friend in Tokyo didn't say they're dangerous.'

'It's organised crime.' Imee shrugged. 'China has the Triads; Japan has gangs of *yakuza*. Sometimes they fight each other over territories. It can get nasty, especially in the big cities. Nothing to do with us though. If a club changes hands, they just keep the same staff.'

'I keep seeing a white car. I think it's following us, but it could be anyone, couldn't it?'

'Probably *yakuza*. If something happens to you, the school can't pay them back, the bar won't pay them, and they lose money,' said Imee. 'It cost a lot just to bring you here. Plane ticket, apartment, salary, utilities, visas.'

I leaned back in my chair and ran my fingers over my forehead. What the hell had I got myself into? Sounds of slurping came from the table next to ours and I wanted to push the man's face into his coffee cup.

'When we moved into our apartment, it looked like a woman had left suddenly. All her clothes were still there and food in the fridge There were even dirty dishes in the sink.'

'Cherry. She was with a *yakuza*, Ohayo-san, for some time. She's in Sapporo now,' said Imee. 'I heard she cheated on him, and he sent her away.'

'You know Ohayo?' I said, my heart jumping.

'We all know Ohayo-san,' said Melody, pulling a face. 'He's not such a powerful man. Not yet, but he has ambition. Gives nice presents too. I was with him a few times before he decided on Cherry.'

'We hope Cherry is in Sapporo, but we actually don't know,' said Imee. 'One day she was here, the next she was gone.'

'Without her clothes and stuff?' I imagined a dark-haired girl being dragged from the apartment, bundled into a car, and driven somewhere remote. And then I stopped, didn't want to take my imagination further. I knew something bad had happened to her.

'She caused Ohayo-san to lose face. Sometimes girls just disappear.' Imee shrugged. 'There are stories from other towns and from the cities. We don't know for sure. Mama, she owns Shima, threatens us all the time, says she will send us back to Philippines with no money. She fines us for everything, like being one minute late, or not getting the customer to spend enough. She works with the *yakuza*, something outside Shima, but we don't know what.'

'What's Shima?' I said.

'The bar underneath Kujaku. We work in both.' Melody nodded, a half smile on her lips. 'Sometimes, some of the low-ranking *yakuza* come to Shima. They wear see-through shirts to show off their irezumi tattoos, all down their arms. You can't miss it, it's on their back too. It's harder to see them on the higher-ranking *yakuza*. Like Ohayo-san. His whole back is covered in a big tattoo of a samurai warrior.'

'It's not so bad if you obey the rules. Like you, we must go home after work, no chance for any fun. Daytime, it's okay, we can do what we want, like now, having coffee with you. But we must stay close to Hitano and Kitakyushu. And we must tell Mama where we are going. And she asked us to tell her if we know where you are going. Sorry, Mari.'

'We never go anywhere or do anything, so it doesn't matter. I still don't understand what could happen to us?' I said, sliding my hands under my thighs, my coffee untouched.

'Maybe another syndicate could steal you. A few years ago, a girl hanged herself in our rooms. Everyone had to pretend they didn't know her, that she had never worked here. It was all hushed up,' Melody said. She broke her cookie in two, wrapped one half in a paper napkin and put it in her handbag. 'She was stupid and gave her married boyfriend all her money – he gambled and then made her borrow from another *yakuza* syndicate. To save face, our *yakuza* sold her contract to them and they wanted her to sell herself so she could pay them back. She had no way out.'

'Why didn't she go to the police?'

'The *yakuza* do what they want, and the police allow it. And for us Filipinas, problem is that if we break our contract, we need to pay back all plane ticket and visa money. So, she hanged herself before she was sent away. I hear she haunts Kujaku and our rooms, although I've never seen her. I wish I could so I could ask her things about the after-life.'

'I have,' said Imee. 'I was too scared to speak to her. I hid under the blanket.'

I looked from Imee to Melody and back, biting my lip. Kate bustled over to our table, another carrier bag in her hand.

'We believe in these things. Spirits, magic, ghosts. And God,' Melody said.

'I read Tarot cards. And sometimes, I just know things,' I said.

'Ooh,' they said at the same time.

'Yes, she's a bit of a freaky hippie, but in the nicest way,' said Kate.

Melody stared at her, frowning.

'You are gifted, Mari.' said Imee. 'Please, read for us one day.' She put her hand on mine.

'I will. You know, I had some strange nightmares before I came to Japan. There was one where lots of glass broke and I woke up feeling like I was being choked. That was the worst one. The other dream was about black lace-up shoes. You know the ones; shiny black brogues that have those punched holes in the shape of a widow's peak and three lines of narrow shoelaces that tie across the bridge. Ridiculous, I know, but I woke up terrified. I thought something was telling me not to come to Japan.'

'Dreams usually tell you something. You're here now but don't think to leave,' said Melody. She took my arm and looked at my carved wooden bangles. I took one off and gave it to her to try on, but she put it straight into her handbag. I didn't mind, I had plenty.

'To stop us running away, the *yakuza* keep our passports,' said Imee. I covered my face with my hands, forgetting to breathe out. 'Are you okay, Mari?'

'They've got ours too,' I said from behind my fingers. 'They said it was to register us with the authorities.' As the world tilted and the realisation that we were trapped formed a solid lump in my stomach, I sat back. 'I don't believe this. It's got to be illegal.'

'Can't we go to the police?' said Kate.

'You signed a contract, right? They're legally binding. Now, *yakuza* own you. Don't think it's any different for you just because you're Europeans. They still won't let you leave, and if you cause trouble, they might sell you somewhere else.'

My coffee was suddenly revolting; the smell of it turning my stomach. The pounding in my head matched my heartbeat and pressure built behind my eyes as the walls closed in. I rubbed my temples. We had to get our passports back. But how?

Chapter 7

A STRONG WIND disturbed the night. Lying on my futon, I heard it whistle and moan around the trees and sing softly, hauntingly, through the rice fields. It kept me awake through the early hours, dancing with itself down our street. Every now and then it quietened, only to draw its breath and blow louder, fiercer. Once it was daylight, I got up to make coffee. I opened the front door, wanting to bring my clothes in off the washing line, and found an origami figure on the washing machine. I couldn't believe that it hadn't been blown away. Intricately folded black paper created the rounded body of a cat in a sitting position. Cleverly, the ears and the nose were tiny white triangles where the reverse side of the paper had been folded inwards. What would the old man leave me tomorrow? Slipping the paper cat into the pocket of my jeans, I battled the wind for my clothes and went inside.

LATER, ON THE way home from shopping in town, and as it was Sunday lunchtime, we bought beer from a vending machine near the house with the blue flower pots. I pushed the yen notes into the slot, pressed various buttons and large brown bottles of Asahi beer popped out at the bottom. My fingers stuck to the thin film of ice that coated the glass. As I stood, my arms full of bottles, the white car approached, slower than it needed to. I looked at the driver through the open window but he ignored me as he drove past. Frowning, I wiped a wet hand on my jeans.

Maybe he lived nearby.

'Let's get some more and get blotto. My treat,' said Kate.

We piled the clanking, dripping bottles into our bags and walked home.

'I HAD TO buy the one with the cherry blossom on,' said Kate as we put on our new yukatas. 'That aqua really suits you.'

'Thank you, I love sea colours,' I said. Twirling, I held my arms out to let the long rectangular sleeves of the summer kimono hang down. I admired the pattern of flowers and ribbons, tied the sash at the back, and looked at myself in Kate's mirror. She moved behind me, wanting to check her reflection, so I moved aside, stepping onto something soft and squidgy. Picking Kate's blue elephant off the floor, I dropped it onto her futon. 'It's a bit like a dressing gown; nice to float around in now that the days are so hot. It's only May. God knows what it'll be like in August,' I said.

'We are slowly becoming Japanese,' she said.

We bowed at each other at the same time and laughed. With the doors and windows open and the electric fans switched on, a delicious breeze of cool air moved through the apartment. Kate opened the first beers and I slotted a mix tape of Japanese pop into the player. We sat on the tatami, wearing our yukatas, chatting and singing. By early evening, a row of empties stood lined up along the wall like little brown soldiers on parade.

'I'm leaving and I am going overland to India,' I said with that specific certainty and confidence that I only ever found in myself when I'd had a drink.

'India, really?'

'I kid you not, Kato.' I wagged my finger.

'When did you decide that? Hang on, when are you planning to leave?'

'I don't think I can stay here another eleven months and see out the contract. I know it's a once in a lifetime chance and all that, but I'm not enjoying it here. I'm giving it five more months and I'll ask the school if I can leave at the end of October. But to be honest even if they don't agree, I'll go anyway.' I grinned, excited to share my plan, to speak about it out loud. 'I want to go overland all the way from Singapore, up through Malaysia, and up through Thailand, into Burma, and all the way to India. Then everywhere in India.' I made a circle in the air with my bottle. 'Oh, it's empty.'

I took the last two beers out of the fridge, opened them on the work top by the sink. Our upstairs neighbour walked across the parking area and I waved through the window, but she looked at the ground. Oh well. Dancing my way back to the living room, I handed a bottle to Kate, still sitting on the floor.

'You *are* inviting me to come as well?' Kate stretched up to touch my arm. 'Don't leave me here on my own. I don't like it either.'

'Yes, come with me. We could go to the Philippines; it sounds wonderful. You can go diving there. We should keep it quiet though, so don't say anything to Melody and Imee and don't tell Sayuri or the bosses. Not yet anyway.' I wagged my finger. The tape finished and I pushed my Japanese language books out of the way, looking for the new cassette tape one of my students had given me. I clicked the play button and upped the volume. Japanese superstars Anzen Chitai's music filled the apartment and I danced around the room. Bugger the neighbours.

Kate bobbed her head in time to the music, and then swigged her beer. 'I won't tell a soul, promise.'

'I just think they might get nasty. Remember what Sayuri said about sending us somewhere else? I don't want to end up in Outer Mongolia or somewhere.' I laughed. 'God, am I being melodramatic?'

'Yes, but that's just you. Maybe you are right, especially after what the Filipinas said. But does it have to be October? That means we won't be here for spring and the sakura.'

'I know, but there are other things worth seeing that might just be better than cherry blossom, like the Rajasthan desert, a

Burmese temple, the islands of Thailand.'

'You're right, Mari. I've always wanted to go diving in Thailand.'

The song ended and I plopped down next to Kate. 'Shit. Oh, shit.'

'What?'

'Why is it taking so long to register us? They should have given us our passports back by now.'

'Well, they'll have to give them back when we leave, won't they? I'm sure it's fine, and Jack said it was.'

Anxiety hid behind hope, but I didn't want to voice it. That would make it more real.

Chapter 8

STILL IN NEED of clothes to wear to Kujaku, Kate and I went to the divinely air-conditioned shopping mall near the station. I didn't want to park the bikes in the stands there in case the real owners saw them, so we left them by the school and walked the rest of the way. The mall was newly built and the glass atrium rose through three storeys, spilling light down the escalators to reflect off the mirrored water fountain in the centre of the ground floor.

The cosmetic shop gave us make-overs and the assistants complimented me on my pale skin. The foundation they recommended made me paler still but the assistant assured me it was "*Japanese beauty*." I looked too pale, too much like a geisha, but I liked the way she had done my eyes; with subtle shades of bronze that made them look greengage green. She'd wanted to pluck my eyebrows thin like Kate's, but I preferred mine natural.

Kate and I browsed the clothing section for something dressy and glamorous. The Peter Pan collars and school-girl-like fashions of short pleated skirts and preppy jumpers left me in despair. And my height meant everything was short on me. I managed to find a few glitzy tops but had to resort to the men's department for trousers.

Hitano's mall fascinated me. Plastic sandals hung on racks, and cheap t-shirts were piled onto display units next door to designer clothing shops. Golf accessories rubbed shoulders with plastic kitchenware. I looked up at advertising banners and signs that hung from the domed, see-through roof. Thin vertical flags stood at doorways and yet more advertising filled the windows and the walls. Inside the shops, even the air was used as advertising space as little signs dangled from ceilings and fluttered in the air conditioning. A few of the lower hanging ones bumped my head, and I laughed. The bold lettering of slogans and offers I couldn't understand, zig-zagged and writhed across brightly coloured banners. I wanted to learn to read and write Japanese, as well as speak it.

A French patisserie, called *"Paris"* with a pink and black striped awning, lured me in with the smell of freshly ground coffee. A black stencil of the Eiffel Tower decorated the window, and a round wrought iron table with two ornate chairs stood outside.

'*Tarte tatin* and real coffee,' I said as the waiter brought it over. 'What a treat.'

'Have you seen the price, Mari? It's almost four times what I'd pay at home.' She looked shocked, her blue eyes wide. That Elena look.

'My shout. It's worth it. Good coffee's always worth it. And I'm so hung over from all that beer we drank last night.'

After I paid, we headed back into the mall. Sitting with her back to the wall between shop windows, a little girl cried. People just walked past her and I looked round to see if her mother or someone was near. The child made whimpering noises as her chin wobbled and tears wet her cheeks. I crouched beside her, and smiled.

'Where is mother?' I said in Japanese.

The girl pointed towards the fountain. Crowds of people milled about, but no one claimed the child. I took her little hand and she stood. She stopped crying and looked up at me.

'Kate, let's take her to the police.'

'What? No, I'm sure her mother will appear in a minute. Leave her.'

'I can't just leave her; she can't be more than about three.'

'Not really our problem is it?' Kate pushed open a shop door. 'You take her if you want. I'll be in here.'

'Kate!' I yelled, but she'd gone inside.

Shaking my head, I hooked my carrier bags over one arm and picked up the child. As I straightened her pink and white Minnie Mouse t-shirt, her arm went around my neck and her other hand held on to my hair. She stared at me.

'Come on then, little'un. Let's put you somewhere safe. They'll help find your mummy, yes?' The child probably didn't understand English, but I hoped my tone was soothing. How could Kate be so heartless?

I carried the girl on my hip, expecting her mother to appear at any moment. People stopped, stared, and then looked away. The koban was at the other end of the shopping street outside the mall, near the station. A small concrete and steel construction, nothing more than a double glass door, three walls and a flat roof, I understood why it was called a police box. A red light shone above the door, under the police insignia. Hindered by full arms, I used my shoulder to push the koban door open. A woman in a lilac flowered tent-dress held her pregnant belly with one hand as she spoke to two uniformed officers behind the wooden desk. All three of them stopped speaking as I walked in, and the woman stepped towards me, smiled, and took the child from my arms.

'*Arigato gozaimas*,' *Thank you,* she said. The woman bowed awkwardly, then bowed again, and I touched her arm. All this bowing was too much, especially over a baby-belly. '*Arigato.*'

Once she'd left and I waved goodbye to the little girl, an idea came into my head.

'Do you speak English?' I said. My dictionary at the ready, I wanted to ask about registration and passports. 'English?'

Behind the desk, the officer said something to his colleague. Their eyes slid over my body before they stared at my face, with that look I'd seen before.

Chapter 9

On the Friday evening we dressed up. Kate acted like we were getting ready for a night out. Singing and jiggling to the music while she checked herself in front of the full-length mirror on the back wall of her room. We had plenty of time between finishing school at five and starting in Kujaku at seven thirty.

I opened my cupboard and took out the two-tier black lacquered bento box I used to store my makeup in, careful not to disturb the growing collection of origami figures. Carrying the box in one hand and a small make-up mirror in the other, I sat on the tatami just in front of the doorway between our rooms. Sitting on her futon, her blue elephant beside her, Kate blew on her nails, trying to dry the dark coral-red varnish. Her gold signet ring caught the light as she waved her hands around. It didn't take long to put my make-up on; I didn't use a lot. With nail scissors, I snipped the shoulder pads out of my new black, sequinned jacket, careful not to catch the peacock blue lining. It might be a bit Liberace, but I loved it, loved anything glittery. Luck had been on my side when I found some men's skinny trousers in the same shade of blue-green. Twisting my hair up into a messy French pleat, I secured it with hair grips. A few wispy waves hung around my face and I spiked up most of my short fringe, using a ton of hairspray to hold it in place.

Glancing at my watch, I slipped my shoes on at the door and ushered Kate outside.

'How am I going to cycle in this dress?' Kate tied the straps of her brown leather bag to her bike's basket, hindered by her long nails.

'You should've worn a longer one,' I said and locked the front door.

An origami peacock sat proudly on top of the washing machine. I picked up the paper bird, its turquoise body in beautiful contrast with the gold and green of its crisply folded fan tail. If Kate and I were the butterflies, who or what was the peacock? I must remember to take the old man some more biscuits. I dropped the origami figure into my bag and grabbed the bike handles. Riding off, I shouted over my shoulder, 'Come on, slow coach.'

'Hey, wait for me!' said Kate, gingerly perching on the bike saddle.

I stopped at the corner, waiting for her to catch up, and we rode side by side. A few streets on, we passed the old man. He rummaged in the greenery at the side of the road, picking leaves. Standing straight as we passed, he saluted and I raised my hand in a brief wave.

'*Kurutta! Inu! Kurutta. Inu!*'

'What on earth is he saying?' Kate said.

'Crazy. Dog,' I said.

'Dirty old loony more like.'

'Don't be so harsh. I feel sorry for him. Anyway, he's harmless. Crazy Dog.'

Kate had to stop every few minutes to pull down the hem of her dress as we rode down the hill. While she went into the department store to buy some opaque tights, I bought some biscuits and some sencha green tea for Crazy Dog. Hiding them in my big cloth bag, I planned to take them to him the next morning, while Kate slept.

Kujaku Club wasn't far from the steps near the yakitori we'd gone to the night we'd stolen the bikes. It still amazed me that nothing had been said about that, and I didn't feel too guilty. I planned to put the bike back before I left Japan. So, if I was only borrowing it, I hadn't stolen it.

We left the bikes near the bins in the cobbled alley behind the kitchen that served Kujaku and its sister bar, Shima. Sayuri met us, took us through the kitchen where a man in chefs' whites prepped food, and we exited onto the pedestrianised street. Neon advertising signs lined both sides of the narrow street that even at seven-thirty was already busy with people out for the evening. Sandwich boards and flashing signs showed opening times and cover charges. At least numbers were legible. Shops no bigger than a doorway offered take-away fast food.

Two women in satin dresses and heavy make-up stopped in front of me, exchanged a glance and whispered to each other before they went into one of the bars further down the street. Although they were Asian, they didn't look Japanese.

In single file, we climbed the narrow, carpeted staircase next to the entrance to Shima Bar. From the small landing, more stairs led to an upper floor that was blocked off by a door.

'Kujaku, means peacock,' said Sayuri. She tapped her finger on the carving that graced a heavy wooden door and then pushed it open. A blast of cool air hit me and I put my jacket on, rolling the sleeves back to reveal the lining. 'You wear peacock colour, Mari.'

The origami peacock. I didn't believe in coincidences. Everything was linked, happened as part of something else, while the synergy played out. So, Crazy Dog knew things too, he had his own curse. Maybe that was why I connected with him.

'Wow,' said Kate. 'This is rather nice.'

I smiled and said to Kate, 'It's much nicer than I expected. Smaller too.'

Yoshinori, the manager, stood by his desk near the entrance, buttoning his blue and gold brocade waistcoat. Sayuri introduced us. She had to leave, she said; something about taking her mother somewhere. Kate and I sat in one of the five horseshoe-shaped booths that lined the longest wall. Yoshinori brought us warm oshiburi on a small tray. Just big enough to clean my hands with, the wet towelling square smelt of jasmine. He took the used towels away and returned with glasses of ocha, placing them on the smoked glass table in the centre of the booth. Sitting on a plush stool on the other side of the table, Yoshinori cleared his throat. I sipped at the cold green tea. Too strong and acidic, it made my tongue dry.

'This is members' club. Guest buys bottles of whisky or brandy.' He pointed to the shelves opposite that were lined with cut-glass decanters full of gold-amber liquids. They sported little silver chains with numbered medallions hanging proudly like Olympic winners' medals. 'They come and sit here, maybe one or maybe eight. Please, never sit next to guest, okay? Always opposite, like me. Easy to change ashtray and get ice or menu.' He adjusted the over-sized glasses that completed his snooker player look. 'I sign out their bottle and you bring soda, cola or ocha and look after them, okay? Smile, talk, sing and be respectful,' Yoshinori said. 'Always give drink with two hands and never cross your legs. Never cross your arms. It is not respectful. Please remember, this is class place. No arranging sex, understand?'

Squirming, I wondered why Japanese men thought foreign women were easy. I got the impression that sex was misogynous and dirty and that it floated somewhere in a murky sublayer of life. Hopefully, no one here would find out about Kate and her lover-boy-students. The way she was going, she'd prove them right. To be honest, I didn't want anyone to think like that about me. I wasn't perfect, and I'd had my fair share of boyfriends. Maybe it was lapsed Catholic guilt, but I didn't want to be taken for a slapper.

'These ladies don't speak English.' He turned towards a group of four very elegant Japanese women, probably about my age, although some might have been a little older. They smiled, inclining their heads, but continued to talk amongst themselves. 'You stay with Imee and Melody, okay? They can teach you. Also, you call me Yoshi-san.'

He waved the two Filipinas over, bowed and went back to his desk. A group of customers arrived, quickly followed by a couple of businessmen who we all welcomed with bows and high-pitched cries of *'Irashaimasse'*. Kate followed Melody as she led the businessmen to the furthest booth and took oshiburi from the glass-doored heater near the kitchen at the back of the room. I stayed with Imee, following her lead. It wasn't rocket science. Put ice in a glass, pour the drink and hand it over with two hands, all politeness, and sweet smiles. Imee emptied the ashtray and lit the customers' cigarettes. I fanned the smoke away. There was a lot of formality, which surprised me. I'd expected a more relaxed atmosphere in a bar. Japan, despite her beauty was very structured and complicated.

As my customers left, Yoshi-san picked up an empty sake flask from Kate's table and came to speak to me again.

'Sometimes, when men drink too much, they get sukebe. I mean they want sex. Please refuse their attentions. Again, I tell you, this is class place. And remember, no alcohol for you.'

'I haven't had any, Yoshi-san,' said Imee.

Their conversation continued but I watched Kate giggle and simper, leaning in close to her departing customer as she walked him to the door.

'Mari, did you hear? Kato, please come here,' said Yoshi-san. Kate came over and stood behind me, her hand on my shoulder, as Imee cleared the table. 'Alcohol forbidden,' warned Yoshi-san with a paternal frown. 'But you say *'Itadekimas'* and you get ocha or soda okay. Get many, customer pay and I give tea money.' His frown continued to crease his face as he walked back to his desk.

'What's tea money?' I asked Imee.

'About one US dollar per glass. It's commission; you respectfully ask the customer and he buys it for you.' She smiled, her raspberry-red lipstick making her mouth look jammy. 'The glasses are small, if you can manage to drink six or eight glasses every night, the money adds up. They pay us each Friday. We keep count of how many we drink, especially downstairs in Shima Bar. Mama sometime make mistakes.'

'Come tonight,' said Melody. 'We can be your hostesses.'

'Yes, once we close here, come down with us,' said Imee. She took a lipstick and compact out of her small evening bag and touched up her lips. 'It's more fun down there. We call it "Shima Time." It's not a members' bar like here. It's an izakaya. Customers still have their bottle of drink, and they pay a cover charge. Then extra for soda, snacks, karaoke. It's good fun. We sing and dance a lot down there.'

'I do a half hour cabaret twice a night,' said Melody. 'You should come and watch. I sing, but not like karaoke.' She fluffed up her bleached hair. She may have been aiming for blonde, but had only got as far as light brown. 'I have great costumes, one of them from Taiwan.'

KUJAKU ATTRACTED MATURE businessmen who came to relax wearing suits and carrying briefcases, even on Saturdays. Serious discussions between customers made the atmosphere stuffy, and I hated the American songs I was asked to sing. Old 1960's and 70's hits were popular; 'I left my Heart in San Francisco' or 'Yesterday.' The traditional slow Japanese enka songs of war and challenging times that the men liked to sing were interesting rather than entertaining. Accompanying videos showed scenes of farmers in the snow, or rivers flowing through autumnal mountains. My favourite video was of a glorious temple with a roof that curled upwards to the sky, like hands reaching to the gods. There was so much to learn about this intriguing, beautiful country.

A group of lawyers arrived and Yoshi-san sent me, on my own, to be their hostess. They stared at me. One of them looked at my breasts and said something to the others. They all looked at my breasts. There wasn't much to see, but I pulled the edges of my jacket together over my vest top. As I served the drinks, they carried on talking about me.

'You are too tall,' said one of the men. 'Too big. You must have vagina like an ice-bucket.'

His companions laughed. I bristled, imagining how good it would feel to chuck the ice all over them. The still solid ice cubes would melt inside their collars, and the water from the bottom of the bucket would fill their noses and mouths so that they spluttered and coughed. Instead, I smiled as an idea came to me.

'Me,' I said, pointing to the ice-bucket. 'You.' I pointed at the tongs and then threw them back into the ice-bucket with a satisfying clatter.

After a split second of silence, when I thought I'd done the wrong thing in throwing their insult back at them, they all roared with laughter. One of them poured some brandy into my glass of ocha. Raising my glass, I gestured to Kate in the next booth. She didn't see me. She lit her customer's cigarette, her hand holding his for much longer than she needed to while he stared at her legs. Oh, God. She was such a flirt.

A little alcohol gave me the courage to sing a modern Japanese ballad, '*Tsugenai*,' a song about a broken love. Imee encouraged me and helped me write the words down phonetically, and we sang it together a few times. Watching the little dot dance over the words on the karaoke screen, I sang along, and began to recognise a few of the Japanese characters I was learning to write.

'LOVE THE FACT that we can put brandy in that horrible cold tea,' I said. It was closing time and we helped with the clearing up. 'Makes being called an ice-bucket more bearable.'

'One of them asked me if I was an ice-bucket, too. Is that a Japanese joke or something?'

'Well, yes and no. They think because we're European, we have huge vaginas, like ice-buckets.'

Kate's eyes widened with shock and then she giggled, reminding me of Elena. It was getting easier to deal with, but every now and then my stomach twisted with guilt as memories crashed in. Sometimes it was good to hurt. It meant that I hadn't forgotten.

Watching Kate laugh was infectious. We laughed until we could hardly stand up. Holding on to each other, we stopped, taking in breaths. Kate glanced at me, and we started again. I laughed until my sides ached and I had to dab my eyes with an oshiburi. The

Filipinas looked at each other, shaking their heads as they left.

On our way down the stairs, we heard music coming from Shima. Kate looked at me, her body moving to the beat.

'What do you think? We could go in for a little "Shima Time",' she said.

'Come on then.' I pushed the door open.

We walked into a dark red, open plan lounge, misty with cigarette smoke. Someone sang badly on a large raised stage that took up half the room, while his friends and hostesses shouted '*ah soreh soreh*' and cheered him on. Filipina hostesses chatted to groups of customers who sat on maroon, leatherette banquettes along the wall, facing the stage. I looked around the room, but there was no sign of Melody or Imee. The place was loud with laughter and music. The customers were younger, and the atmosphere more relaxed than upstairs. I wanted to stay but couldn't remember Melody's explanation of how it all worked. A woman in her mid-forties with a Bonnie Tyler hairdo bowed at me from behind the cashier's desk right next to the entrance. I bowed back. Another woman approached. Short and fat, with broken veins across her cheeks, and her hair dyed so black that it looked like spray-paint, or maybe a wig. Her floral dress stretched tight across her belly and it looked as though her pudgy feet had been forced into shoes too small for her, Ugly Sister style. She didn't smile but asked if we wanted to *drinku beeru*. Yoshi-san followed us in and spoke at length to her, but she looked at us with such contempt, that I was sure we'd be asked to leave.

'You must go home,' said Yoshi-san. 'This is no place for you. Good women do not drink alone.'

'Can't we just stay and have one beer? Please, Yoshi-san. We want to see Melody sing.' Kate held onto his arm.

He moved away, speaking again to the large woman.

'I invite you – *dozo* – please, come drink with my friends and me,' said a male voice. 'I am Koji.'

I turned to see a guy in a red baseball jacket. He bowed and Yoshi-san bowed back. A brief discussion in Japanese and then

Yoshi-san nodded. Kate sauntered off to the guy's table and smiled over her shoulder at me.

'One time. You stay for one drink, then go home.' Eyebrows drawn together, he wagged a finger at me. 'One drink, okay. See you tomorrow.'

When Yoshi-san left, I joined Kate and her new friend at his table near the door. His two friends made room for us; the older looking one moved to the stool on the other side of the table. Kate squeezed in next to Koji, pulling the hem of her dress down as she sat. I perched at the end, glad to stretch my legs out after sitting folded up on a low stool all evening. At the other end of the banquette, a Filipina cuddled up to another man. She left the table for a minute and came back with fragrant, warm oshiburi for Kate and me.

'I am Koji.' He tapped the capital 'K' on his baseball jacket. 'I am single, twenty-six. My father and I own supply company. Steel and electrical cables for construction. I have company truck and live close by, in the hills outside Hitano,' he said in one breath. I smiled, tried to be encouraging. His earnest and obviously much practiced introduction was sweet. He pushed his metal-rimmed glasses up onto the bridge of his nose. 'I like cooking.' He patted his flat belly. His haircut was untidy and he had a round-faced, cheeky grin that made him look a lot younger than twenty-six. 'I am glad to meet you.'

Hiroshi, Koji's "besto-friendo", had a long face, like a horse. He worked for an electronics company and lived locally. He sat with an arm round the hostess's shoulders. He kept nuzzling her neck, whispering into her ear and didn't say a lot to anyone else. Koji explained that Hiroshi couldn't speak English and I felt bad for thinking he was just rude. The hostess, Myla, disengaged herself from Hiroshi and served us all brandy and soda.

'Melody sister,' she said. 'No good English.'

'Yes, you look like her,' I said, but I don't think she understood.

Ice clinked in the glasses as we all said *kampai*, cheers. Myla smiled as she lit Kate's cigarette. I glanced at the stage where

Imee was singing a duet with a customer, and waved. She waved back with so much enthusiasm, her customer waved too.

The third of the group, Junichi, was a bit older than the others. He ran a firm of accountants and spent a lot of time working away in Osaka. He opened his wallet and proudly showed us photos of his two teenaged daughters.

'You sound American,' I said. 'Did you learn from an American teacher?'

'Most Japanese learn English grammar at school and pronunciation from American films, but I lived in New York for five years before I got married. You could say America taught me my English. Are you learning any Japanese?' He tucked his wallet into his back pocket.

'I have an hour's lesson every day and then there's homework too. I'm lucky; the customers upstairs and my students help me a lot.' I took my bag off the floor, knocked my knee against the table and pulled out my dictionary. 'I take this everywhere, and I practise whenever I can.'

'Good for you. How are you finding the cultural differences? I know it can be tough.' He flicked ash from his cigarette into a big square ashtray just in front of me. I pushed it away slowly, into the middle of the table.

'Just when I think I understand Japan, something happens and I realise I don't. But then, we've been here less than a month.' As I swirled my glass, the ice-cubes and my bangles tinkled. 'I'm glad I'm not here on my own, though.'

'Watch how you go here,' he warned. 'Japan is difficult for foreigners, especially women. But if you play by the rules and remember that you're not in your home country, you'll be okay. Don't get too involved with Mama.' He pointed discreetly at the overweight woman who had been talking to Yoshi-san earlier. She spoke to one of the hostesses, the red end of her cigarette dancing like a rabid ladybird. 'I'm not always around, but these guys,' he continued, 'Yeah, you'll be okay with them.' He gestured to his two friends.

'Why, what's wrong with Mama?'

'She's a bitch. And she was a gangster's moll, back in the day.'

'And she's still *yakuza*?' I said.

A tipsy man on his way out stumbled and leaned heavily against Junichi, causing him to spill his drink. Junichi put his glass on the table, stood and spoke quietly to the man who bowed his apology, held the position, his eyes downcast. Then the lights went on, signalling closing time. Kate and I followed the guys outside and we stood chatting for a while longer.

'Great to meet you, I gotta run,' said Junichi. 'See you around.'

'Have you tried takoyaki?' said Koji, 'I can buy some for you.'

He walked over to the window of a fast-food place and came back with two little cardboard trays, each with six bite-sized deep-fried buns made of rice flour, a sprinkling of chopped spring onion and dark ribbons of sauce across each one.

'Is there anything inside?' said Kate.

She stood close to him, her hand on his arm. Her red fingernails matched his jacket.

'Octopus.'

Trying not to laugh, I stood a few steps away from them. Octopus. Yep, Kate certainly had the ability to latch on. Hiroshi looked up at a small open window above Kujaku, where Myla blew kisses. Kate giggled and simpered as Koji fed her the takoyaki. Poor guy, he'd end up as just another notch on her bedpost.

THE NEXT EVENING, Yoshi-san and Mama offered us the chance to work as hostesses in Shima. Yoshi-san did the talking while she looked us up and down. If she wanted us to work there, why was she so hostile? As well as tea-money, they paid ten dollars for working a few hours. Once Kujaku shut we went to Shima and stayed until closing at around two in the morning.

'I love it,' I said. 'Being paid to socialise, and we'll be able to save even more money.'

'It's much better than Kujaku, at least we can have some fun,' said Kate. 'And the customers are better looking.'

Chapter 10

KATE SPOKE TO Koji about our passport situation, and he had an English-speaking friend who owned a bar. If, like Imee said, all bars worked with the *yakuza,* maybe this guy could help us. We needed someone who knew how they really operated, someone who wasn't involved in paying the Onishi company back-handers to employ us.

Kate and I did what we were told, for a while. We rarely saw the white car these days and decided that we'd go and see Koji's friend at his bar that evening.

Koji picked us up from home and we sat three-up in the front of his truck. On the edge of town, he pulled into a small car park in front of a two-storey concrete building. Surrounded by fields, the bar looked out of place. A blue and white neon sign hung above the doorway, next to the Coca-Cola sign. The evening air chilled my skin and I shrugged on my Levi's jacket, pulling my hair out of its scrunchie so that it fell loosely down my back.

'You'll be glad to meet my friend Ryu, Mari,' said Koji. 'His grandfather was American and he's twenty-seven.'

Koji pushed open the door of the izakaya, and a blast of music and smoke hit us. Hiroshi was already there, an ice-bucket and two bottles of soda on the opaque ice-blue bar in front of him. He raised a hand as we came inside and we joined him. A few empty stools separated us from three men in business suits who stared for a moment before looking away.

The metal legs of the barstool scraped on the stone tiled floor as I moved it and climbed up. Koji fussed around Kate, getting her rice crackers and an ashtray.

Koji introduced us and Ryu shook my hand, holding on to it for a little too long. His eyes held mine a fraction longer. I blushed, aware of my heartbeat. I was flooded with that knowing feeling that he and I would be together, but I had other things to focus on. He gave Koji a white marker pen which he used to write his name across the front of a brandy bottle while Hiroshi put ice into glasses.

'I will pay.' Koji dug out his Superdry wallet from his jacket pocket.

Ryu took a tray of drinks to customers who sat on a blue three-seater sofa at the far end of the room. It filled the wall opposite a doorway to a small kitchen, and another to the bathroom. I liked the casual atmosphere; the place was modern and energetic. And there were no hostesses.

I walked the length of the crescent shaped bar on my way to the loo at the back of the narrow room. With only ten stools at the bar, it didn't take long, but I dawdled, looking at the unframed canvases that covered the dove grey walls. Some larger than others, many were in the same style, but each one distinct. Swathes of muted colours with blurred edges merged with bold geometric lines and streaks of textured paint. So that's why the izakaya's blue neon sign said '*Art Bar*'.

On my way back to my stool, I watched Ryu move without rushing as he served drinks and chatted to his customers. There was something relaxed about him and he seemed comfortable with himself. As he bent to lift a plastic tub from a shelf under the bar, his hair fell forwards. He took the lid off and scooped rice crackers into small glass bowls, round at the bottom, square at the top. His hands fascinated me. Slim, elegant fingers moved in a way that made me think of sex. So did his thick hair. Long, just past the top of his shoulders, it shone so black it was almost blue. I wanted to run my fingers through the almost-waves that stopped it being dead-straight.

Oh, God. That wasn't what we were there for. But Ryu and I caught each other's eye several times as the evening went on. When he smiled it was slow, and it set off a reaction that made me very aware of being female.

'This could be interesting, Kato. He's got to be six feet tall and look at his hair. I love a man with long hair.' I rested my elbow on the bar, my chin on the back of my fingers.

'Nice arse, but he's a bit too slim-built for me,' she said.

'You like him?' Koji said.

Ryu looked back at me from the other end of the bar. We both smiled, as if we shared a secret.

'He likes you too,' said Koji. 'I told him he would.'

'What did you tell him?' I bit my lip, feeling like a teenager.

'That you are a woman who would like a man like him,' said Koji. He adjusted his glasses. 'And he is a man who would like a woman like you.'

I laughed. Koji grinned his cheeky-face grin. He took off his baseball jacket, hung it on the back of Kate's stool and the white satin sleeves dangled like deflated balloons.

'For God's sake, Mari, let's not forget the reason we are here,' said Kate.

'Sorry,' I said. 'You're right.'

'Koji, you shouldn't be matchmaking either.'

Her long nails picked at the label on her second bottle of Asahi Dry. Koji offered her a cigarette and lit it for her before he turned to speak to Hiroshi.

'You shouldn't be so hard on Koji. He's besotted with you,' I said. 'Take him to a love hotel, put him out of his misery.'

'Oh, God. No. Don't fancy him in the slightest,' she said. 'He's a bit goofy. I think he's nice to have as a friend. And that's all.'

'Look at Handsome Boy over there,' I said. Kate and I watched Ryu roll up the sleeves of his black shirt, revealing the olive-gold skin of his forearms. I shifted on my stool. 'I'd definitely say yes, but it'd only be a bit of fun.' Who was I kidding? It was never just a bit of fun. Maybe I was trying to be like Kate. But watching Ryu, I felt things I shouldn't be feeling. Not there, not then.

A while later, Koji and Kate sang a karaoke duet on the tiny stage in the corner by the door, the words displayed on a wall-mounted TV screen. After I took a sneaky photo of them with my camera, I put it back into my bag. Ryu came to the end of the bar, sat beside me, and poured brandy into my glass. I felt an emotional pull so strong, it was almost physical, and I held my breath. He put an ice-cube into my glass and it clinked as he added another. Then another.

'It's nice to meet you,' he said. His accent was American. 'Koji's quite taken with Kate, isn't he?'

'He's nuts about her. Look at them.' I inclined my head, but my eyes didn't leave his face. I stared at his mouth, craving the feel of his full lips, the taste of his tongue.

A group at the other end of the bar called to Ryu.

'Wait a minute, I'll be back,' he said.

He got their drinks, chatted to them, but glanced at me. A lot. I looked at him every now and then from under my lashes, a half smile on my lips. Hiroshi chatted to someone sitting on the other side of him and I was glad I didn't need to make small talk. When Kate and Koji finished their second song, I wouldn't let Koji have his stool back.

Ryu smiled and touched my arm as he passed by to open the door behind me. 'Fresh air,' he said. 'It's getting way too smoky in here.'

I glimpsed his bare ankle as he kicked a wedge of wood under the heavy door with the toe of his brown leather deck shoe. He took a handful of my hair, pulled it gently and let it fall through his fingers as he walked away. It felt intimate. Familiar. The back of my neck tingled and goose-bumps shimmied down my back. My eyes widened as I looked at Kate.

'I can see the attraction,' said Kate. 'He definitely likes you. But can Koji have his seat back now? Your guy's busy so he won't be needing it.'

I laughed, then cleared my throat as Ryu leaned in beside me. He smelt good close up. Subtle aftershave, something woody. Leaning on the bar, he tapped out a cigarette from a soft pack of Seven Star and offered me one before he lit his own. I was disappointed that he smoked.

'I'm not too busy. How are you enjoying Hitano?' he said.

A customer on his way out said something to Ryu. He laughed and patted the man on the back as he walked him to the open door.

'He said you're pretty.' Ryu pulled up a vacant stool, positioned it at the end of the bar, at right angles to me. 'I agreed.' He shrugged. 'So, Hitano?'

His smile unsettled me and the heat of a blush crept up my neck. I fiddled with the silver bugle beads that edged the off-the-shoulder neckline of my silky top. The way he looked at me made me feel more than pretty.

'I am enjoy Hitano absolutely.' My Japanese wasn't perfect, I knew that. I practised as much as possible anyway, but right then, I wanted to impress him. 'Japan is interesting.'

'Mari. Showing off as usual,' said Kate. 'I want to learn as well. Ryu, maybe you can teach me some Japanese.'

'Maybe,' he said over his shoulder as he collected empty glasses and went back behind the bar. 'But I think it's better you ask Koji.'

The last customers left and Koji spoke at length to Ryu, explaining that we needed to get our passports back. He nodded now and then, ran his finger down the high bridge of his nose, letting it settle across his lips.

'I'm not sure I can help,' he said. 'But I'll ask around, see what I can find out. Leave it with me.'

Chapter 11

On Sunday, Koji picked Kate and me up and took us to the park by the river. Ryu walked over from where he'd left his car. His knees bent outwards slightly as he sauntered towards us. It gave him a swagger that on another man might have seemed arrogant, but it made him dead sexy. As he reached us, the sun gave up its battle with the clouds and disappeared. Above us, the sky darkened as a bank of purple-grey clouds rolled in.

'Looks like we're in for a summer storm,' he said. 'Let's go to the teahouse. We can talk there.'

Kate and Koji walked ahead, Ryu and I following. He smiled, the back of his fingers grazing mine as we walked down the narrow path of uneven stepping-stones that led towards the river. His touch didn't come across as cheeky or presumptuous and I knew we'd fast-forwarded to somewhere the other side of strangers. My insides fluttered and I glanced at him. He took my hand and moving ahead, led me along the stones. The teahouse was tucked into a clearing shaded by trees. Rounded pewter-coloured tiles that matched the sky formed the roof, and eaves curled skywards at the edges. The teahouse had been there for hundreds of years, and I sensed its history. Half on stilts in the water, the other half of the building squatted on the riverbank. The outside doors were pushed back, an unspoken welcome for customers.

Over the years, so many people's lives must have been changed by meetings in this tea house. My imagination conjured up shady business dealings, lovers' trysts, and marriage negotiations. I imagined a noblewoman, the sheen of her silk kimono brought out by the glow of the lanterns, as she bribed the teahouse owner with a jade hairpin for some privacy with her samurai lover. Perhaps she was betrayed and her husband found out. Had a father cried in his heart when he sold his beloved daughter in marriage to pay off a debt? Maybe a vengeful trader had paid an assassin with a bag of gold to rid him of a troublesome competitor. I doubted the *yakuza* conducted their shady dealings here nowadays, but ronin and samurai would have done. Stories, this place had so many stories.

'Wait a second,' I said, and fished my instamatic camera out of my bag. I took a snap of the teahouse, and the ratchety sound as I wound the film on was harsh in such gentle surroundings.

We slipped off our shoes and stepped up onto the tatami of a room facing the river. Ryu and Koji moved the two low tables end to end. We sat in a line so that everyone enjoyed the view. The muted daylight diffused through the screen to the side and we sat in silence, looking out across the river. A bird sang nearby, a gentle lullaby. It was peaceful and the humidity made me feel dreamy as I watched a blue dragonfly skim the water. Ryu's arm brushed mine as moody light played on the surface of the water, turning the river into satin.

The waiter brought barley tea, served in tactile blue and grey mottled earthenware pots with bamboo handles. Matching tea bowls, just big enough to hold in the palm of one hand, sat alongside a flat dish of small rice cookies.

'So,' said Ryu. 'I spoke to my... a friend's uncle who has close dealings with the Hitano branch of the Yamaguchi-gumi. Looks like you're going to have to see out your contracts before you get your passports back.'

'I thought you'd say that,' I said. 'Thanks for trying.' It didn't feel like the end of the world, but it didn't feel right either. We had our return tickets, so it wasn't like we could never leave.

'Yama what?' said Kate.

'Yamaguchi-gumi. Most big *yakuza* syndicate. Do your work and everything is okay,' said Koji from the end of the table.

'Exactly. My friend's uncle said that it's pretty much standard practice for them to hold on to gaijin women's passports as security. You'll get them back when your contracts are up. But, if there are strong reasons why you need to leave early, like a family emergency or something, they'll ask you to pay back their expenses.'

'We heard as much from our friends,' I said.

'To be honest, it's all about honour. In Japanese culture if you agree to something you have to follow it through. And *yakuza* like to intimidate, show off their power.'

'And your friend's uncle said all this?' I said.

'In so many words, yes.'

We stayed in that teahouse for the whole afternoon. Koji picked my camera off the table and took a photo of Ryu and me and asked me to take one of him and Kate. Ryu poured tea for me while Koji and Kate went for a walk, after borrowing two red umbrellas ready to protect them from the threatened deluge.

'Is it your own bar?' I wanted to say that his English was so perfect, why was he wasting it in a bar, but it'd sound rude. And I wanted him to like me.

'I'm just fooling around for a while before I...'He paused to sip his tea. 'It was my father's restaurant. When I finished university, he retired and handed it over to me. It's a tradition that the oldest son takes over the family business. I don't cook so well, so I turned it into a bar. I've had a great time for the last coupla years but my parents want me to use my business degree. I will, soon. But not yet.'

'My dad's a chef, too.' My heart pinched. Of all my family, I missed my dad most. He always had my back, always stuck up for me against my mum, always hugged it better. Funny how he, an Englishman, had more emotion in him, showed me more love and kindness than my Spanish mother. 'He runs his own restaurant. *Randall's* in Chiswick, West London.' I presumed

Dad still had it, but five years on since mum threw me out, how would I know?

Someone came to clear away the dishes and place the bill on the table. I tapped my fingers, not sure if I should offer to pay something towards it. Ryu took my hand and turned it over in his, moving his thumb slowly along my palm, down to my fingertip. I held my breath and dropped my gaze as colour and heat flushed my face. A smear of blue paint or something ran along the outside of his hand and part of his little finger. He turned my hand and grazed his fingers along the back of mine. My pulse raced, and pleasure darted through me. I imagined his hands on my body, and what they'd do to me. It had been so long since anyone had touched me, and I felt my own heat.

'Do you live upstairs with your parents?' I said.

Love hotels filled my mind and I stared at his hands as I played with his fingers. Our fingers twined and linked as we traced each other's palms, turning, stroking. Finger dancing.

'They moved away, up to the mountains, growing fruit and keeping bees.'

After he paid, we walked along the river, towards the carpark to meet Kate and Koji. Raindrops pit-patted, creating a polka-dot pattern on the stones. Ryu pulled me into the space behind the dripping garlands of a willow tree that leaned towards the river. He pressed me against the narrow trunk with his body, one hand on the tree, just above my shoulder, the other moving my hair back from my face. My breath caught and I literally trembled. His almond-shaped eyes crinkled at the corners as he smiled. Hidden by long streamers of new willow leaves and surrounded by that summer-green river smell, he kissed me, slowly at first. I had to break away to catch my breath. He kissed my neck, and I pulled his head up so I could have more of his mouth. My fingers moved through his hair. It felt exactly as I'd known it would.

'I've wanted to do that since the minute I saw you. Come to my place? Tomorrow evening. We'll eat something, just you and me, before the customers arrive.' His ink-dark eyes searched my face. 'Plan on staying over, Mari.'

'But the *yakuza*...'

'Leave them to me.'

Chapter 12

Between classes, Kate and I met in the staff room with just enough time to have a quick coffee. I waited for the kettle to boil while Kate smoked out of the window, the smell of Seven Star cigarettes wafting into the room.

'I'm not sure if I'm nervous or excited about seeing Ryu,' I said. 'It's a bit soon to stay over.' It wasn't as if I was an angel, but I wasn't one to sleep with someone so quickly. Ryu made me feel different, in that random, unidentifiable way that dissolved my morals and had me wearing my skimpiest knickers.

'Don't go,' said Kate, leaning out of the window with her cigarette. 'I don't want to go to Koji's on my own. I know he said he'd drop you at Ryu's, but come with us instead.'

Before I had a chance to reply, Washan opened the door and Ohayo walked in. Kate dropped her ciggy and we both bowed briefly. Ohayo stared at Kate's bare legs and I wondered how on earth Melody could sleep with him. It made my skin crawl. Kate tugged at the hem of her short denim skirt and pulled it down an inch.

'I have told you before, do not go out night-time,' said Ohayo in English. 'It is not safe for gaijin women.'

'We're never alone, we're always with our friends,' I said, trying to keep my voice level and keep my face relaxed. My fingers curled into my palms and I dropped my gaze.

'Your friends okay, daytime... not night-time. Next time, I will find appropriate response.'

Ohayo and Washan left as abruptly as they'd arrived.

'Maybe they'll fine us or stop our pay.' I rattled around, making coffee. 'What else could appropriate response mean?'

'You probably shouldn't go tonight,' said Kate, flopping on the yellow sofa, crossing her feet at the ankles, and lying back. 'They'll be cross.'

'If all I'm facing is a fine, I'm not going to pass up the chance of seeing Ryu because Ohayo says so. Anyway, you're going to Koji's, so whats the difference?'

'I still don't understand, you know, why they say it isn't safe?' Kate flicked her fringe out of her eyes, her long nails a flash of neon pink.

'Intimidation, Ryu said.' I handed Kate a mug, spilling a little. 'Sorry.'

'This is all stupid.' Kate pursed her lips and pulled at her green and black paisley scarf, tied cowboy style around her neck. 'Stupid idiots. I hate it here.'

'We have to stick it out. Neither of us can afford to pay the *yakuza* back. Maybe we can talk to them in six months, invent some family emergency if we have to, see how the land lies. That fits our plan of saving to go to India. Six months isn't that long.'

THE REST OF the afternoon dragged itself into early evening. Letting my students talk about whatever they wanted was just laziness; I found it hard to concentrate. I got ready during breaks between classes. My sea-green jersey dress with three-quarter length sleeves flattered my figure. I loved the way it showed off my waist and how the soft fabric slid over my hips. With my makeup subtle, I felt gorgeous, sexy even. My stomach was tight with anticipation as I slipped on my flat silver sandals. I stood up and twirled; the fabric flaring out just above my ankles.

I WAVED GOODBYE to Kate and Koji as they dropped me off. Looking up at the blue and white neon sign, I pushed the door open. I stepped into the dim light of the empty bar. Ryu smiled that slow smile of his, left his cigarette burning in the ashtray and came out from behind the bar. He kissed my lips and led me to the sofa at the back corner of the room.

'You look lovely.' His eyes moved over me. I wished they were his hands, and I squirmed in my seat.

'Tell me about your family.' I hoped he'd do the talking while I pulled myself together. The anticipation of what was to come was like a sweet endorphin. 'Which part of the States was your grandad from? How did he meet your grandmother?'

'Boston. He worked at the US Embassy in Tokyo.' Ryu opened a bottle of Coke, slowly pouring the dark liquid over ice in tall glasses. 'They met at a teahouse one summer.'

'Romantic. A teahouse.' I could add this to my imagined stories. The handsome American wearing a grey suit, smoothed his shirt collar absentmindedly, his eyes fixed on the beautiful lady in her pale blue kimono. She wouldn't look at him directly; she was modest, well raised. And when they passed each other in the doorway, they both knew.

'Yes, it was love at first sight for them both. She turned her back on her family so she could be with him. Marriage to a foreigner is unusual nowadays, but back then it was pretty scandalous. Mom was five when America entered the war, and my grandpa was sent home.'

'Did he come back?'

'No. Sometimes, love is not enough and circumstance takes over.' The back of his fingers stroked my face, and my heart turned over. 'He was in the US Army by then. He sent money regularly so Mom would have a good education. Remember, Grandma was alone, no family around to help her raise a half American kid. One day, the bank called to tell her that a large amount of money had been deposited. She learned years later that he'd died in the Pacific conflict and left a huge amount of money, and a townhouse in Boston to her.'

'That's a sad story. Can't have been easy for anyone.' I sipped my Coke.

'You have no idea.' Ryu went to the kitchen and brought out a flat earthenware plate of sushi and the inari rolls I loved. 'I'll tell you another time. Anyway, Mom went to the American School in Osaka and then University in Boston. She raised me speaking English first, then Japanese.'

'In case you'd want to go to America?'

'I guess. Not sure I'd belong there. It's hard enough here. I'm only half Japanese. My dad's mother's family is Korean. They were brought over here during the Japanese annexation of Korea. So, my grandma is what's called zainichi, Japanese born but never a Japanese citizen.' I frowned, confused. 'I know, right? Zainichi live, work, pay taxes etc like Japanese citizens, but can't call themselves Japanese as they have no Japanese blood.'

It didn't matter to me what his blood was or wasn't, but the way he said it made me think there was some disadvantage in being only half Japanese. Such a baffling, beautiful country.

He cupped my chin in one hand, his eyes intense. Waiting for his kiss, I opened my mouth a little. My heart raced. Instead, he held an inari roll to my lips, tantalising me with the savoury-sweet smell of the golden fried tofu casing. Just as I opened my mouth fully, he popped the food into his own.

'Tease.' My desire for him was overwhelming, urgent. I leaned towards him.

He kissed me. Just as his tongue touched mine the door opened and a group of customers walked in. We moved apart, glancing at each other, and laughing.

While he worked, I did my Japanese homework, conjugating a few new verbs, learning new vocabulary, and practising writing characters in the activity book. When Kate and Koji arrived, Ryu was sitting with me on the sofa, his hand and mine joined, finger dancing. The customers who sat further along the curved bar, near the entrance, called him over.

I moved to the bar to join Kate. 'How was your meal?'

'Fine,' Kate said.

She sounded pissed off and I wondered if something had

happened at Koji's. Ryu got a drink for his friend, then hand-washed a few glasses in the sink behind the bar.

'What did he cook for you?' I asked her.

'I made fried tofu with eggplant and red pepper. She liked it,' said Koji.

'Sounds right up my street. I'd like to have that recipe.'

Taped music played, something mellow, as Ryu reached for a Perspex ice-bucket which he filled with ice. He placed it next to two glasses in front of me. Kate drank her beer and Koji moved away to talk to someone he knew.

'I've got something for you,' Ryu said, and pointed to a bottle of Hennessy brandy on the shelf behind him. My name was written in white marker pen across the front.

He turned and reached for the bottle, and I caught his eye in the mirror that backed the shelving unit. We smiled at each other. Kate didn't know I could see her reflection. Her thin top lip curled in a sneer, and she looked as though she had trodden in something nasty. Shock and confusion twisted sourly as I tried to work out whether Kate's expression was aimed at me, or at Ryu. Or both of us. It annoyed me to think she was jealous; she'd had plenty of male attention already and it looked as though Koji was nuts about her.

'Kate,' I said. 'Did the white car follow you?'

'Nope.' She breathed out cigarette smoke and I fanned it away from my face. She flicked the ash into the ashtray Ryu had just put down, and her short skirt rode up as she crossed her legs.

'Yeah, I think we're okay. Apart from Ohayo nagging us. Kate, Ryu is—'

She cut me off with a tutting noise.

'What's wrong?' I leaned forward and put my hand on her arm, trying to catch her eye but she wouldn't look at me. 'Tell me.'

'Nothing. It's late anyway. Can we go, Koji?' She fiddled with her signet ring.

'Okaaay...' Koji drew the word out. Frowning, he stuffed his hands into his jacket pockets. 'If you really want to leave.'

'Just take me home.' She stood up, waiting for him to open the door for her.

I didn't want to leave, didn't want my evening with Ryu to end. I looked at him and shrugged.

He shook his head. 'Mari's staying,' he said. His hand slid under my hair, onto the back of my neck.

I shivered. Kate didn't say goodbye. Whatever she was sulking about could wait until tomorrow. I had other things to think about.

It felt like ages until the last customers left. Ryu locked the door and looked at me. His slow smile pulled at my belly. He switched off the lights and without either of us saying a word, he took me by the hand and led me through the kitchen to the back door. Outside, the noise of cicadas filled the air as we walked up the metal staircase to his apartment. We left our shoes just inside the door, next to his flip-flops and a pair of black lace-ups. I followed him into an open-plan room. An intricately carved cherrywood screen topped a hip-height solid partition, creating a sleeping area separate from the rest of the room. I ran my hand over the smoothly carved scrolls and curves. My fingers traced the grooves of the petals and the square key designs at the corners. A double-sized futon lay behind the screen, navy blue sheets folded neatly across it. With the windows open, the breeze blew through and there was no need for a fan. Ryu leaned up against the kitchen cupboards by the door, watching me. I felt his gaze, looked over my shoulder, and smiled at him. I wanted to rip his clothes off, but at the same time I didn't want to rush it.

A beaten-up brown leather sofa faced a TV, dividing the rest of the space from the kitchen. Windows took up the top half of the wall at the front of the room and I peeked out at the bar's carpark. At the side, another window had a tree so close to it, there was no need for curtains. I touched the leaves of the tree through the open window and laughed.

'It's like a tree house.'

The wooden floor creaked under my feet and I loved the old

feel of the place. I looked through a pile of videotapes on top of a shoulder-height shelf unit with books crammed into every space. Not that I could read the Japanese titles yet.

'I keep meaning to alphabetize them,' he said. 'I can never find anything when I want it, but then I think, what the heck.'

Ryu's art filled the room. Different-sized canvases were propped up against each other along the wall under the window and in the corner by the screen. I stood in front of a large canvas, mesmerised by daubs of light green that swept down from the top right-hand corner in symmetrical patterns, highlighted with pale, yellowish-white and flecks of gold.

'You did all these?' I said. I stepped carefully amongst half-empty tubes of paint and earthenware pots filled with paint brushes on the floor in front of the canvas. Pastels, crayons, and charcoals lay scattered, and paint-stained cloths smelled of oil and turpentine. 'They're lovely.'

'It's a hobby, nothing more.' He smiled. 'I'm glad you like them.'

Crouching to look at a painting head-on, the skirt of my dress scattered some paintbrushes and I scrabbled to pick them up. The wooden ends felt warm under my fingertips as I put them back in the clay pot. Looking over my shoulder at Ryu, my heart tip-tapped out of synch for a second. I barely knew him, but it didn't matter, I knew this would be something special. And it might just make being stuck in Japan for six months more bearable.

'Come over here, I want to show you something,' Ryu said from the kitchen end of the room, the smoke from his cigarette undulating upwards.

I bit my lip, moving slowly towards him. Staring at my mouth, he took an inward breath. Quickly, he turned me round, positioning me in front of him and walking me towards the door. Laughing, he manoeuvred me outside into the night. We stood on the top step, the metal cool under my feet and the night air fragrant and soft.

'See?' He pointed out into the darkness. He kissed the back of my neck, his lips hot. 'Can you see them?'

I gasped. Hundreds of golden dots flickered across the fields. They danced, then vanished, only to magically reappear in bursts of tiny twinkling light. Thinking of fairies and water-sprites, I smiled.

'What are they?'

'Fireflies. They flash...looking for a mate.'

I laughed when he walked backwards into the kitchen, taking me with him. My heart skipped as he moved my hair aside. I closed my eyes. He unzipped the back of my dress and kissed my bare shoulders. A deep sigh escaped me as my dress slipped to the floor. When I turned, he kissed my breast, his lips gently sucking my nipple. His hand moved between my legs, and I had to hold on to him. Unbuttoning his shirt, I stepped back and looked into his eyes. He smiled as I put my hands on the smooth firmness of his chest. I pushed his shirt off his shoulders, relieved there were no tattoos. My fingers trailed from nipple to nipple and down his belly and I unbuckled his belt. He pulled me to him, his hands in my hair, kissing me hard. Pushing me against the cherrywood screen, he took off his jeans and then half-pushed, half-carried me to the futon, not losing my kiss.

Chapter 13

WHEN I WOKE in Ryu's arms the next morning, the world was a wonderful place. It was light and carefree and beautiful. There were no hard edges in me; everything had softened and blurred. I couldn't remember feeling so alive, and Ohayo and the *yakuza* faded away. Turning me onto my back, Ryu moved over me and his hair flopped forward across his eyes. I brushed it away and he turned his face to kiss my palm, moving my legs apart with his knee. Dark eyes stared into mine and my heart and body opened like a rose.

'IT WAS A great night,' he said later when he dropped me home. 'I really enjoyed it.'

'Good, me too,' I said, leaning in through the car window to kiss him.

'Can't wait to see you again.' He smiled, pulling at a lock of my hair. 'Soon, okay?'

Waving him off, I went inside and watered the plants, singing softly to myself. Kate woke when I flopped next to her on her futon.

'Budge up,' I said.

'And?' Kate yawned as she scooched across. She opened the balcony door a few inches and reached for her pack of Seven Star cigarettes. 'Have a good time?'

'Wonderful. God, Kate,' I stretched my arms above my head.

'he's so… I really, really like him. Oh, and he told me Ryu means 'Dragon'. Isn't that fabulous? Dragon.' I sighed. 'I've always wanted a dragon.'

'Mari, look, I have something to tell you.' She sat up and adjusted her pillow behind her back. I moved to sit cross- legged on the floor, smoothing the fabric of my dress over my knees, I expected her to tell about whatever had been bothering her last night. 'Don't have a paddy.' She took a deep breath. 'Okay, here goes. Koji told me your dragon boy has a girlfriend.'

'No way.' Standing up, I placed one hand on the wardrobe door. She wouldn't lie to me, would she? 'I can see you're trying not to smile. You're kidding me.'

'I'm not. She's an art lecturer at Osaka University but she's been at Padua University in Italy since March, so that's why we haven't seen her.'

Anger bubbled, bursting before it surfaced. There'd be an explanation as to why he hadn't mentioned a girlfriend. There could be a million reasons.

'Maybe he's already finished with her, and Koji doesn't know.'

I didn't want it to be a one-night-stand; it was more than just physical attraction. Love at first sight might sound corny, but I believed in it, in that sensation that floods through you when you first meet someone. I believed in soul mates, in endless love, in perfect, fairy tale endings.

'Look, I know you like him, but it gets worse.' She pulled her cotton yukata around her, and stood opposite me, blocking my pacing. 'Listen to me.' She took hold of my arms just above the elbows. 'They're getting officially engaged soon and the wedding is planned for next sakura season.'

I moved away from Kate and sat on my futon, knocking my bangles off the table. 'My God. He never said a word.'

Kate walked through to the kitchen. 'Remember you said it would only be a bit of fun? You should be like me, just love' em and leave 'em. It's no good getting involved with them. Their culture is too different.'

'That doesn't matter if two people really…' I stopped talking when Kate rolled her eyes.

Stepping down into the kitchen, I rubbed away silent tears of disappointment with the back of my hand. In the bathroom, I turned on the tap and cried. The gushing water drowned out the sound but did nothing to dilute my frustration. It didn't make sense. How could he be so tender, how could he look at me like that if he was engaged?

The bathroom door opened and Kate leaned against it. She pushed her fringe away from her face. Her eyes were filled with that honest expression, so like Elena's.

'God, I didn't realise you liked him that much. I do feel bad telling you,' Kate said. 'But you know, better you find out now, right? He's sexy enough, I'd shag him. But that American accent is rather irritating. And he works in a bar! You can do better than that.'

'I slept with him, Kate. I more than just like him. I know it's stupid but I can't help it. Why is nothing as it seems here?'

'There's something else too. That Sayuri came earlier. She wasn't happy that you weren't home. I said you went to get iced coffee.'

'What did she want now?'

'Don't know, but your Japanese lesson is cancelled and so are our classes for the rest of the week.'

'Ohayo's appropriate response. They'll stop our money. Sorry, Kate.'

'She knew I'd been out as well. Even told me where I'd been.'

Chapter 14

MELODY POPPED THE cash she'd asked to borrow from me into her bag, and then shuffled the cards. I took them from her and spread them into an arc on the table, moving the ashtray out of the way. She leaned forward on her elbows as Imee, Kate and a few of the Japanese hostesses crowded into the booth with us.

'Be quick, ladies,' said Yoshi-san. 'Customers may arrive soon.'

Reading Tarot came as naturally to me as breathing. Once the person I was reading for had shuffled the cards, I looked at them and started talking. I didn't hear voices or see visions, I just spoke of the things I suddenly knew as fact, or things I could sense. I felt their emotions, their hopes and dreams, fears, and problems. I'd sense the nitty-gritty of their life. Sometimes there were physical feelings too. A fleeting sensation of pain somewhere in my body which hinted at illnesses. It wasn't easy to explain how or why I could read Tarot and I didn't need to know. It was the only part of myself that I found easy to accept.

'You have a little boy?' I said to Melody, surprised that she'd never mentioned him before. 'He's learning to read already.'

'I came here for him, to make money for his schooling. It's difficult in Luzon to get a good education. If I save a lot, I can send him to Manila.'

'You never even talk about him,' said Kate. 'Must have been hard to leave him behind.'

'He is with his grandparents and cousins, so it's okay. We

look after family.'

'A bit like my mum's side of the family,' I said. 'She's Spanish, and all the cousins and second cousins know each other and everyone helps each other.'

'Philippines was Spanish long ago. And so, we're Catholic. Church, and community are important, but family is everything.'

Family. My Uncle Saturnino was our lynchpin. He was the only one who'd spoken to me after my sister died. He said didn't blame me, but he was lying, I could see it in his eyes. I envied Melody and Imee's culture, the warmth of their family ties. Pushing away the thought, I focused on Melody's cards.

'Poor kid,' said Kate. 'I couldn't leave my child like that.'

I looked from one girl to the other, weighed up whether to intervene. The others moved away as the atmosphere tightened. Melody stared at Kate, her eyes hard and angry. Kate's stared back, defiant.

'That's true,' Melody said, 'but you wouldn't have to, not with your rich mummy and daddy. And you can always hire a nanny.' She walked towards the kitchen area to get the ice-buckets ready.

'I think that's appalling. What sort of woman leaves her child?'

'Don't be so judgemental, Kate. They've come here to work because they need to,' I said. 'People go from Britain to Dubai to make big money for a few years, don't they? There's no difference. You should apologise to Melody.'

'I won't.'

'Okay, let me do a reading for you.' Anything to diffuse the tension. 'You know the drill, shuffle the cards to put your energy into them, then put the pack in front of me.'

When she finished, she handed me the cards. I turned up three cards, frowned and handed the pack back, asked her to shuffle again. The next three cards were the same.

'What do you see?' she said. 'Is it good or bad?'

'I can't see anything. Maybe you have no future.' There was no surge of knowing, I felt nothing.

'Serves her right,' Melody said under her breath and placed

another ashtray on the table, harder than she needed to.

IT WAS NO surprise when Ryu walked into Shima just after midnight. He looked good in his jeans and black t-shirt under a white linen jacket. Junichi was with him and they sat at the last booth at the far end of the room. Trying to hide my smile wasn't easy. I was never one to hide my feelings; I wasn't blessed with artifice enough to play it cool. My heart bounced as I waited at the kitchen hatch for more ice for the customers I was with. I undid another button on my rose-pink, oversized shirt so that it revealed more of the black lace camisole underneath.

Mama smirked and shooed me in Ryu's direction. I walked slowly, the parachute-silk shirt clinging to me like water. I didn't bother to bow or say '*Irashaimasse*' but I touched his hand briefly.

'Koji told Kate, so I guess she told you. *Gomen*, I'm sorry. I didn't tell you because I knew it was wrong.'

'You should've been honest, Ryu.'

He avoided my eye, his hands between his knees, his head bowed. I sat on the stool opposite and angled my legs sideways. Ryu stared at the space between my black footless tights and my sling-back shoes. Junichi fiddled with the menu, said something under his breath to Ryu who nodded.

'You should know, I've come to speak on his behalf.' Junichi spoke with the air of an older brother looking out for his sibling. 'This is a troublesome situation – you and him – it's not possible. Love isn't going to triumph here. I know you don't fully understand how things work, but in our culture, dating isn't casual. It leads to marriage, and he's committed elsewhere. There is no future for your relationship, so whatever you think you feel, stay away from each other. This needs to end now, okay?'

'But that's for him and me to decide, isn't it?' I directed the question at Ryu, but he stared at the table and wouldn't look at me.

'It's not as straightforward as that, believe me. He has to honour his promise to my niece.' Junichi glanced at his watch, got up from the table and patted my hand. 'I gotta leave. Look,

Mari, he has no choice, so make it easier for him and walk away.'

The lights flashed and a fanfare of music announced Melody's cabaret. She opened with a Whitney Houston power ballad, the sequins on her red evening dress sparkling under the lights.

'Ryu.' I shouted above the music. 'Look, I think you feel the same way I do. If not... we're still *tomodachi*. Friends, okay?'

That was a lie; I never stayed friends with an ex-boyfriend, and I didn't want to be just friends with Ryu. I knew it wasn't over for either of us, whatever Junichi said. Glancing back over my shoulder as I walked away from the table, I watched Ryu push back his jacket sleeves and reach for his packet of Seven Star cigarettes. He looked up at me and half-smiled, that slow smile of his catching my heart. We locked eyes, and the bond tightened, as if we shared a secret. It was wrong, I knew, but I didn't care about a fiancée somewhere, making wedding plans. I'd done worse things after all, hadn't I? Funny how everything led back to when my sister died.

Hiroshi and Koji walked in. As I drew level with them, Koji looked everywhere except at me, his shoulders hunched in his jacket.

'I'm sorry, Mari,' he said. 'I should not have introduced you.'

'Mari.' Mama's voice cut through the room. Koji went to sit with Ryu and Hiroshi.

She waved me over, the fat of her arm wobbling. A newly arrived customer sat in the middle booth, which gave the best view of the stage. She told me to hostess for the man. Stocky, in his early thirties, his head sported stubble. Maybe he had decided on the shortest of short haircuts, or he was re-growing his shaved-off hair. He wore tight, white trousers and a vest underneath a semi-see-through white shirt that hardly disguised the colourful tattoos visible down both his arms. Gold chains adorned his thick neck and wrists, and the rings on his fingers glinted in the soft lighting. *Yakuza*.

Mama watched me with narrowed eyes. My palms felt clammy. The best thing was to act normally, so I took a deep breath and smiled, bowed a welcome. Following the rules of etiquette, I offered the customer his drink and asked for my own. The customer raised his glass. '*Kampai*.' He sat back, appraised me with narrowed eyes. He wore that expression I'd seen in men's eyes so many times before. Was he imagining me naked, with my feet on the table, my legs spread open? I cringed, folded my arms across myself and looked away. Mr *Yakuza*'s mouth pulled into a derisive snarl and I felt my skin prickle. Once Melody finished her cabaret, I offered the menu and the list of karaoke songs, speaking Japanese, as I would with any customer. He laughed, like I was the funniest thing he'd ever seen.

Uncomfortable, I went to the kitchen to get more ice and my eyes drifted to meet Ryu's at the back of the room. He rose from his seat but Koji said something to him, he quickly sat down and looked away. The evening dragged on and although I focused on my customer, I noticed the glances and hushed conversations around me. Mama sat at the bar, her eyes constantly on me and Mr *Yakuza*. He talked about motorbikes and cars. I stifled a yawn, fiddled with my bangles. Then I noticed the top half of his left little finger was missing.

'What happened?' I asked, gesturing towards his hand.

'Dog bite – hungry dog.' He laughed. So did I.

After bowing to Mr *Yakuza* as he left, I breathed out, smoothing down my shirt. I turned to Ryu and the others as they headed towards the exit.

'Here.' Mama cornered me, gave me a cloth to clean the tables with.

'I just want to say goodbye to my friends,' I said, but she blocked my way. Mama took my arm and dragged me to the kitchen. 'You're hurting me.' I tried to shake her off, looking behind me, but Ryu had left.

'You,' she said. 'Stupid girl.'

Imagining slapping her fat face gave me no satisfaction. Then, my imaginary slap turned into a punch that sent her flying against the wall. Her spray-paint-wig slid sideways, and she hurried to straighten it as everyone laughed at her, pointing and jeering. If only.

Imee and Kate chatted as they piled empty glasses onto trays. Imee put hers down on a table near the kitchen. She turned to me, linking my arm.

'Are you okay? I heard a little of what Junichi said. They love foreigners for their foreignness, but they never marry them. By the way, you handled that *yakuza* guy well.'

'Who was he?' I said.

'Low ranking. Remember I told you about the white shirts? We haven't seen him before so we think he's from another syndicate.'

Imee walked away and I stood for a moment. A cold wave of dread came over me. The same feeling I'd had back in Sydney. The same one I'd managed to squash down and deny over and over again since I'd arrived in Hitano. I dismissed it again. Nothing bad had happened. *Yakuza* or not, he was just a man who came into a bar for a drink. And I was too preoccupied with Ryu.

When we got home, Ryu's blue Toyota Celica was parked outside our apartment block. He leant against the side, one sockless foot crossed over the other, the sleeves of his white linen jacket pushed halfway up his forearms. He looked like a dark-haired version of Crockett from *Miami Vice*.

'I knew it!' I said.

Pushing a strand of my hair behind my ear, I waited as Kate took ages to untie the straps of her bag from her bike's basket. Finally, she went inside, leaving me and Ryu alone in the velvet warmth of the summer night. He pulled me to him, and his arms enfolded me. He rested his face on the side of my head for a moment, then lifted my chin to look in my eyes. Kissing me briefly, his hands slid down from my waist, pulling my hips to his. Silently, he moved away and opened the car door for me.

'Let me tell Kate,' I said and stuck my head round the open front door.

'I just hope you know what you're doing,' said Kate, handing me my toothbrush.

Chapter 15

RYU AND I spent every possible moment together. We both knew our time was limited. Deep down, I hoped things would change, hoped that he'd somehow love me enough to call things off with what's-her-face. I stayed at his place every night and whenever guilt raised its ugly head, I'd smother it with the love-lust that had brought me alive. He was my salvation. It wasn't just the great sex, although there was plenty of that. He proved that I was loveable, desirable, and that my mother was wrong. If anything, I felt he'd broken my curse, and the sense of freedom that gave me was the strongest aphrodisiac. We never went for lunch, or coffee, or back to the teahouse, and I wondered if, for him, our relationship was just sexual. And then he showed me a painting, the one that caught my eye the first night I'd stayed there. It was finished now and I could see it was a willow tree. And he'd named it *First Kiss*.

UENO-SAN HAD CANCELLED my Japanese lesson due to a meeting he had with the bank, and as we had an extra hour, Kate and I stopped for a very early lunch on our way to school. The white car passed us as usual, but we didn't even bother to comment on it. After we parked the bikes in stands outside, I slid open the door, and ducked under the short blue and white curtain of the sushi restaurant. Narrow and long, the place seated about a dozen people on high legged stools at the counter. Edging past the other diners, we got the last two seats at the far end, by the back door. We sat on the stools and turned to hang our bags on the hooks in the wall behind us. By the time we turned back, warm oshiburi waited on a bamboo tray in front of us. Across a foot-high glass partition, three chefs worked. Watching them prepare edible works of art in seconds was one of my favourite things. It amazed me how their white linen aprons stayed so clean. I tended to stick to inari rolls and vegetable sushi, but that day I felt brave, reckless, and tried some maguro tuna. Picking it up with chopsticks, I admired the delicate sheen of the dark red fish before I ate it. The balanced flavours of fish, rice, ginger, and wasabi unlayered themselves in my mouth.

'Some vegetarian you are! Shall we grab some noodles before you go to Ryu's?' said Kate, as she pulled down the hem of her short skirt.

'Okay, I'll call him and tell him to pick me up a bit later. I love that he leaves his customers to look after themselves so he can come and get me.' I watched the quick flashes of silver as the sushi knives worked. 'And it saves all that cycling back and forth. It's too hot now it's mid-summer.'

A couple of businessmen came in and put their suit jackets on the coat hangers that hung on the hooks in the wall behind newly vacated stools. The men squeezed in next to us and I had to move my stool, but Kate wouldn't. She tutted and gave them a filthy look.

The chef placed a small oblong plate of inari rolls in front of me and I picked one up with my chopsticks, ready to eat.

'I've got a hot date myself.' She grinned and then frowned. 'You won't approve. It's another first date.'

'Is it the thrill of the chase?' I said, closing my eyes for a second as I took a bite of the sweet-savoury rice.

'A bit.'

'I can't imagine ever being with anyone but Ryu.'

'That would bore me. I like variety. It's the only thing that makes this place bearable.' She speared a piece of sushi with a single chopstick. Grains of rice dropped as she tried to pick it up. The chef said something about 'gaijin' and I tried not to laugh. 'Did he say "*gaijin*"?' said Kate. She looked straight at the chef. 'Idiot.'

'Kate!' I looked at her, shook my head. 'You can be so… what if he's *yakuza*?'

'They don't seem to be a problem anymore, do they? I mean, Ohayo hasn't even come to tell you off for going out every night, and he must know I go to love hotels. What was all that *oh you can't go out at night* rubbish about in the beginning?'

'They just like people to do what they tell them.' I shrugged.

The chef placed a square of green-black nori seaweed on a mat made of matchstick-thin bamboo and pressed sticky rice onto it. He spooned fish roe, glistening like orange pearls, down the centre and used the mat to roll the rice into shape. With a fat knife, he sliced the roll into sections creating perfectly uniform pieces of sushi, a thin orange spiral through each one.

'Mari, you do know you're going to get your heart broken?' Kate tapped a chopstick in the soy sauce dish.

'Maybe, Kate. I didn't plan this, you know.'

'Does he ever talk about the other woman?'

Laughter came from a group of older men who sat further along the counter, nearer the door. They poured sake from an earthenware flask into each other's tiny cups. One of them stared at me and I looked away. When I glanced back, he still stared, looking me up and down. I slapped my chopsticks on the counter, wishing I could slap his head.

'I asked him once. They met at university in Osaka and have been friends for years. They started going out two years ago. Apparently, their families say that marriage is the next logical step.'

'He's more Japanese than he seems then.'

'He's true to his culture; it's who he is, and I respect that.' I picked at a sliver of pink pickled ginger. 'She'll be back in October, staying with his parents for a while before the academic year starts.' The guilt I felt being with someone else's man was pushed aside, hidden behind a flimsy veneer of belief that love would conquer all.

'Sounds like he's still planning on getting engaged to her. Lucky girl. I think he's hot. I'd give him a –'

'Kate!' I half-laughed. 'You know what? I'm just going to enjoy being with him and what happens in October can wait 'til October.'

'We are still going to leave then, aren't we? You know, travelling, like you said.'

'Yes, of course. We can start planning nearer the time.'

Deep down I hoped Ryu would ask me to stay. And I would. Ashamed I was lying to Kate, I signalled for the bill.

'Already taken care of, Miss,' said the cashier. 'And they left a note for you.'

I unfolded the small piece of paper and read the English writing.

You've had your fun. Now, stop seeing Tamaki Ryu

'Who left this?' I asked the cashier

'Yamaguchi-gumi.'

Chapter 16

Classes were over for the day and I gathered up my pens and notebook, piled them on top of the still-unused textbook. I needed to get changed quickly; Ryu was picking me up. On my way to the staff room, I saw Kate through the glass wall of her classroom. She stood at the side of the table, her back to the door. One of her students whispered something in her ear as she held on to his arm. He turned her to him, about to kiss her and I cleared my throat as I passed the door.

'Mari, you know Mickey?' she said.

'Hi, Mickey.' I smiled. He bowed and then left, followed by Kate.

'I'll see you tomorrow,' she said over her shoulder.

'Have fun.' She must really like him; this was a second date. It could be a third or fourth. I wasn't around to monitor her love hotel outings.

Ueno-san knocked on the staff room door just as I'd finished changing. 'Can I have a word?'

My first thought was that he might be cancelling my Japanese lesson tomorrow. Then I wondered if he'd found out that I was winging it, and not using the textbook. And then it occurred to me that we were constantly breaking the rules, so it might be anything. 'Of course, Ueno-san.'

'Please come to my office.'

I followed him in and sat opposite him at his desk. He cleared his throat. Oh no, I was in for a telling off. He must have found out about the bikes we'd stolen.

'Mari, excuse me but I must ask. Is it correct that you've been seeing Mr Tamaki for the last few months?'

'Sorry?'

'Ryu, isn't it?'

'My personal life isn't really your business.' I frowned as I spoke. 'It's nothing to do with my teaching.'

'So, it's true. Then I request that you stay away from Mr Tamaki, for your own good. Also, the school's reputation is at stake. Mari-chan, the *yakuza* don't like it.'

'The *yakuza*? Yes, they sent me a note. What's it got to do with them?'

'I can't answer that. Just understand, when the *yakuza* don't like something, they usually do something about it. Mari-chan, please take my advice.'

THE NEXT MORNING, Ryu and I drank coffee, entwined and naked on the sofa. The breeze rustled the tree outside the window, and the summer's new leaves that draped inside the apartment danced a little. The sun turned everything into a heat haze of liquid gold and I believed it was just for us. The future didn't matter. I had the present.

'I didn't know it could be like this,' said Ryu. 'You've changed everything.' He ran his thumb over my lips. 'You have a perfect mouth. Cupid's bow, full bottom lip. I adore you.'

'It's the same for me. The first second I saw you, I knew. That feeling that you'll be with someone.'

'We have an expression for that. *Koi no yokan*. It translates as something like the prediction of love.'

'Tell me more about your grandparents They had *koi no yokan*, didn't they? It sounds like a sad story.'

Ryu moved his arm from my shoulders, looking at the ceiling. 'My Grandma was a strong woman, but she had it tough. She died when I was young, but Mom tells stories of her being spat at in the street and having rotten fish thrown at her.'

'What?' I sat up, pulling my hair over my shoulder, twisting it into a thick plait. 'Why?'

'Mari, hatred towards the US after the bombs dropped on Hiroshima and Nagasaki was pretty strong. Other cities were destroyed too. Japan was in ruins and people were starving. Grandma was okay, she had money and managed to buy food. Many others weren't so lucky, especially the women and children.'

'No husbands and fathers around?'

'Killed. Wounded. Missing.' Ryu shrugged. 'People slowly tried to rebuild their lives. Mom had always been taunted for being half gaijin, but after the bombs, it got worse. Can you imagine how it was for her, watching her mother being beaten by a group of women? Grandma was called a whore, a collaborator, a traitor.'

'That's awful. Poor woman.' My hand reached for Ryu's but he moved it away, ran his fingers across his jaw.

'They moved around, trying to find a safe place, and eventually came to Osaka. Grandma pushed Mom to study, figuring she'd never make a good marriage. There weren't many options in Japan for a half-American woman.'

'Is that why she went to the States?'

'Yeah. She went to seek out her Dad's family, but they didn't want to know. And it was worse for her there as a half-Japanese woman.'

'So, she came back here?'

'And was introduced to my dad by a matchmaker. Two half-bloods with not many marriage options. And that's it really.'

'But it's a happy ending.' I smiled, wishing there'd be one for us.

I stood, grabbed the sheet from the futon and wrapping it around me, I walked to the window overlooking the empty car park and stood in the sun. Ryu stood naked, behind me, pulling my hair through his fingers.

'In the sun your hair's like dragon breath. Red and gold.'

'Ryu means dragon.' I turned to touch his face. 'I think there really were dragons, a long time ago. And maybe I was a geisha, and you were a samurai. We met secretly in a teahouse and you had to leave your sword outside. You gave money to the owner so he wouldn't disturb us, and we made love right there on the tatami.'

'Crazy girl,' He laughed and pulled me closer, his fingers running down my back. 'how does your mind work? There's so much about you I don't know.'

That was an understatement. I wanted to tell him about the Tarot and my intuition, wanted him to know everything about me. I wanted to tell him that when Elena had been born, I kept saying the word *dead*. I was two and a half years old. When she died, because of me, my mother said I was cursed, evil. She said I was a horrible person and didn't deserve anything but misery. But I was scared to tell Ryu all that. What if it changed the way he looked at me?

'But just think, if I was a lady in a silk kimono and you were a samurai. How fun would that be?'

'A samurai?' Ryu laughed, took one end of the sheet, and dragged me across the room. 'Come here, my geisha woman.'

He pulled the sheet off me, pushed me down onto the futon. His long hair moved as he bent to kiss my breasts. I pulled his head up and his mouth was on mine, his kisses hot and hungry. He sat back on his heels, his fingers trailing up my thighs. My heart pounded and I parted my knees. For a moment, he just looked at me laying there, exposed. He made a noise, deep in his throat and bent to kiss my belly, running his tongue further down. With my hands in his hair, I let his mouth open me until my back arched. Kneeling back, he took my wrists and pulled me onto his lap. I guided him inside me then, and his eyes didn't leave mine. We moved together slowly, gently. The air was hot with thick, somnolent, heat that made everything heavy and each movement slower. Ryu watched me, smiling. A sheen of sweat covered us and he licked one of my nipples and then the other. He lay me down and moved over me, pulling my legs around him.

Our rhythm increased its speed, and our breathing quickened. I gripped his shoulders, and cried out, my body shuddering. A few seconds later, it was the same for him.

I WOKE ALONE. By the banging and clanking coming from downstairs, Ryu was putting a delivery away. After I showered, I wrapped a towel around me and pottered around the apartment. Coffee mugs washed and Ryu's clothes tidied, I straightened the shoes by the front door, wiping a thin film of dust off his black lace-ups.

When Ryu came back, I was crouched by the open window, picking up leaves that had dropped from the tree. He grabbed the towel off me with one hand and unzipped his jeans with the other.

'Time for one more,' he said and pulled me to him. I kissed his neck while his fingers worked their magic between my thighs.

'Ueno-sa said the *yakuza* don't like us seeing each other,' I said. Ryu stopped what he was doing and looked at me. 'And someone paid for our lunch, then left me a note saying I should stop seeing you.'

'Who? Who was the note from?'

'Yamaguchi-gumi.'

Ryu moved away from me, so quickly, as if my skin burned him like acid.

Chapter 17

I NEEDED TO get home, get ready for my Japanese lesson and work. After so much sex, it was easier to push rather than ride the bike. Above me, sparrows twittered, perched on the criss-cross of overhead wires. I stopped at the supermarket and bought a whole chicken and another bag of rice, a toothbrush to leave at Ryu's, and a couple of cans of iced coffee. Piling it all into the bike's basket, I headed off to see Crazy Dog. He wasn't home, but he must have known I'd visit because he'd left an origami love-heart on his bench. Folds upon folds created the curves and a sharp crease formed the pointed bottom.

I sat and waited a while, admiring the persimmon tree's black branches and the small nubs of dark green that would ripen into orange fruit in the late summer. Crazy Dog didn't appear, so I left the food inside the door. Placing the red heart in my pocket, I cycled the short distance home through sticky summer rain. The white car passed me. I hadn't seen it in a while and the way it slowed to a snail's pace as it passed rattled me. I waited for a hand to appear out of the window to push me off my bike or something. Instead, it sped away.

KATE SAT AT the kitchen table, reading a letter I presumed was from home. She'd left the front door open and warm air swept through, making my room's curtains flutter. A mix tape Ryu had given me filled the apartment with the beat of an Anzen Chitai rock-pop anthem.

'You're back then,' said Kate.

'Morning.' I opened a can of coffee, handed it to her. 'I'll have a quick shower and I've still got to do my Japanese homework. Would you pop my washing through the machine when you get in tonight? Then it'll be ready for me to hang out tomorrow morning when I get back. And you couldn't give the kitchen a going-over, could you? It's looking a bit grimy.'

Kate said nothing but by the look on her face, I knew I'd said the wrong thing.

'I'm not coming home tonight,' said Kate. 'I'm going to Koji's. He wants to watch the highlights of that concert in London last week, you know, that Live Aid thing. Bob Geldof organised it for famine relief or something.' She opened a bottle of bubble gum pink nail varnish. 'Anyway, you don't exactly do much housekeeping anymore, so why should I? I'm not your servant.'

'Housekeeping?' I swallowed a laugh. 'I water the plants and I've done most of the cleaning and all the cooking since we arrived. I'm hardly ever here.' I pushed my hair back over my shoulders. 'I'm just asking you to take your turn, that's all.'

'To be honest, you are doing my head in. All I hear is "Ryu this, Ryu that," and I'm left here on my own all the time.'

Something twisted and rose in my belly. I dragged my dirty washing from my room, stormed outside and thrust it into the washing machine. Powder flew everywhere as I waved my arm at her round the door.

'Alone? Don't be so bloody childish. I see you at school and at the bars. I'm just not sleeping here, that's all. And you've had, what, half a dozen little flings, so what's the problem?'

'I don't have anyone to talk to.' Kate pouted, actually pouted, and started painting her nails.

'What about the Filipinas?'

'They're not like us.' The smell of nail varnish was acrid.

'So? They're still our friends.'

'You're deluded. They're not our friends. You lend them

clothes, make-up, even money, which they never give back. Melody just uses you for what she can get. You are the only one who understands how I feel here, how much I hate this place. You come back from Ryu's and rush to get to your Japanese lesson. And now you ask me to do your washing while you're off shagging Ryu.'

'You're so judgemental, you have no idea what it's like for them, or how privileged you are. You always turn everything round to being all about you. And believe me, everyone knows you hate it here, you don't exactly hide the fact. Why do you begrudge someone else some happiness? Ryu and I are in love, we're – '

'Ryu and you? There is no Ryu and you! He's. Getting. Married.'

My mouth open, I stood still, shocked at the venom that laced Kate's words. Opening the fridge, I took out a bottle of water, and my hand shook as I poured it into a glass.

'You're like a child. You don't know the half of it!' I said. 'I keep quiet over so many things and you have a go at me like this over some fucking washing?'

'Have you met his parents? No. Do you go out anywhere? No.'

'That doesn't mean anything. You're jealous!'

'Jealous? Yes, because every girl wants a boyfriend who's marrying someone else. It's just sex, there's no real relationship,' Kate yelled, her pinched voice as harsh as her words.

'You don't know what you're talking about. We're destined, it's meant to be.'

'You are ridiculous, you know, all your fake spirituality, hippie-drippy bullshit.'

'Kate, don't – '

'Destiny. Utter rubbish. Has he broken it off with her, then? No. Don't expect me to pick up the pieces when this all goes wrong. And it will go wrong, Mari, it will. I can see why you like him, but how could you be with him, knowing he's someone else's?'

'Don't you dare judge me! At least I haven't shagged half the school. And you treat poor Koji so badly. You lead him on and leave him hanging all the time. If you're not interested in him, leave the man alone,' I yelled back, pushing the chair back from the table with a loud scrape. I strode across the kitchen to the bathroom, resisting the urge to slap her.

'And what's that got to do with you?'

I showered in lukewarm water, trying to cool my blood. By the time I combed Wella Flex conditioner through my hair, I'd begun to calm down. At least I knew what she really thought of me. I rinsed my comb and looked in the mirror. Ryu. Everything was about Ryu. Maybe Kate had a point.

Kate sat at the table with her back to me when I came out of the bathroom. Wrapping the towel round my torso, I tucked it in just under my arm. She ignored me as I passed her on the way to my room. Cow. I couldn't even close the door, so I stood by my window, drumming my fingers on the sill. Even though the music played, the silence between Kate and me was weighty. I couldn't stand it. I shook my head, my wet hair cold on my bare back, and stepped down into the kitchen

'Let's not fight,' I said. 'I'm sorry.'

'Apology accepted.'

Twisting my hair into another towel, I waited for her to say sorry. Arguments disturbed me, and I hated the chilly silences and hurt expressions afterwards. Fights with my sisters, whoever was right or wrong, always ended with me saying sorry first, just to restore the peace. Then we hugged and cried and everything was okay again. But my dad's hugs were the best. Great enveloping bear hugs that put the world back on its axis and made me feel safe. I missed him the most.

'You said some awful things, Kate.'

'I'm not apologising. It's not my problem if you don't want to hear the truth.'

I stepped back into my room and curled my fingers into my palms. The door of my cupboard was ajar, and I whacked it shut. If I was being selfish leaving her on her own, she was selfish making me feel guilty. Guilt. I hated that feeling, had been battling it for the last five years.

Chapter 18

'KATE SPAT THE dummy about me spending every night with you,' I told Ryu later that night. He lay behind me, cuddled up and sleepy. 'She's right really. I wouldn't like it if was the other way around.' I stroked his forearm.

'She spat what?'

'The dummy. You know, before a baby starts screaming, it spits out its dummy.'

Ryu laughed. 'You mean a pacifier?'

'I forget you speak American. Pacifier. Sounds better than dummy.'

'And what now? You need to stay home at night and look after your baby sister?'

Baby sister. That stung.

'Yeah. I hate myself for giving in to her. She drives me nuts. She makes me feel so guilty. But, there's only the two of us here, we need to look out for each other.'

'She has plenty of boys to play with, Mari. Why do you always let her have her own way?'

'It's easier. I hate confrontation. She can be difficult and she's young for her age.' And because she reminded me of Elena. Letting Kate have her own way somehow made me feel less guilty about Elena.

Ryu gently pulled my hair, ran his fingers through it. I turned around to face him. 'I want you with me all the time. But we have a problem,' he said.

'The *yakuza*?'

'They came and spoke to me yesterday and said we have to end it. I asked for a little more time. They've given us two weeks.'

'No.' I pushed his shoulders onto the futon. 'That's too soon. Why do they care so much? I don't understand.'

I kissed him from his chest to his belly, following the line of fine hair. Just as he hardened in my mouth, the phone rang and his body tensed. I slid my mouth off him.

'Mari, I'm sorry, it'll be her. I have to answer.' He moved from the futon and grabbed the phone.

Sitting up, I watched him through the carved screen, drinking in the curve of his buttocks and the muscles of his legs. The planes of his shoulder blades tensed as he stood there speaking to the woman so far away in Italy. His tone was friendly, but there were no words of love. If she knew that I was in his bed; if she knew he loved me, not her, it'd probably break her heart. I didn't want to be responsible for that, but I didn't want to lose him. I imagined the woman standing with the phone in her hand, too nervous to sit. Her other hand curled and uncurled the telephone cord. She breathed in deeply, trying to be calm and composed, her voice light, not giving anything away. Then it hit me. Oh God, I wasn't imagining it. She did know about me and was waiting for Ryu to tell her. When he hung up the phone, I knew she was crying. But if she knew, why didn't she finish things with him?

'Junichi told me she'd call today,' he said. 'I'm sorry.'

'Do you love her?' I stood opposite him, twisting my hair. *Please say no, please say no.*

'I like her well enough.' He shot me a glance. 'Which is why we agreed to marry. But breaking it off isn't an option, you know that. My parents tolerate my artistic side and allow me to express my individuality. But in the end, they expect me to conform and be a dutiful son. It's a matter of honour now but that doesn't make it easy for me. What we're... no, what *I'm* doing is wrong. She doesn't deserve this.'

'So, you will marry her?' Ryu looked at me and frowned. I'd obviously asked a stupid question. 'Then we should stop this.'

'We will. And sooner than we both want to, I have to give you up but I can't, not yet.' His hand slid between my legs, his fingers making me moan. 'Let's make the most of the little time we do have.'

'RYU, WHY DON'T the *yakuza* like us being together?' I asked him later when we'd caught our breath. 'Is it because it's you, or is it because I'm an employee gaijin?'

'I'm not sure.'

But the way he wouldn't look me in the eye made me think he was lying. It wasn't the right time to tell him that my period was a week late.

Chapter 19

CROSS-LEGGED, KATE AND I sat opposite each other on a sheet of canvas, among giant spools of cables and wires, in the back of Koji's work truck. With my hand over the side of the truck buffeted by the backdraught, I smiled to myself, happy that Ryu and I were doing something together.

'It's a shame the Filipinas didn't come today,' I said. We pulled to a stop at red traffic lights and I shrugged my Levi's jacket on.

'Church in the city or a picnic at a lake in a bamboo forest. I know which one I'd choose,' Kate said. 'And it was rude to cancel there and then, after we'd gone to pick them up.'

'October the first is some big saint's day and it's important to them.' October the first was also the two-week deadline for me and Ryu. I guessed that was why we were having a big outing and I didn't want sadness to spoil the day. 'I'm glad we didn't go back to get Ryu's car. I love riding in the back of this truck.'

Ryu sat in the front with Koji and Hiroshi as we drove up into the thickly forested hills that surrounded Hitano. Wispy, transparent clouds laced an end-of-summer sky. I pulled out a bottle of water from a large red cool-box that sat between us and drank from it, spilling a little on my new trousers. Kate leaned over and I handed another bottle to her. The town slipped away as we turned at the crossroads and took the mountain road. On either side, vegetable fields with long poly-tunnel frames surrounded wooden houses, the planks of their walls already scorched so that they wouldn't catch fire. Ahead, the road started to climb into the forest, leaving the flat land behind.

A BLACK CAR followed along behind us and although I'd seen it, it wasn't until it sped up and overtook us that it registered. The driver glared through the open window as he passed, his arm resting on the rim. His short-sleeved white shirt showed arms tattooed to the wrist. My deep inward breath stopped short of my lungs and I forgot to breathe out. Two men in dark clothes sat in the back of the car, but I couldn't see their faces. Koji hit the brakes and quickly pulled over to the side of the road, under a cluster of trees. The car stopped in front and two men approached. Ryu got out. Frowning, he bit his lip as he reached over the side of the truck to stroke my face.

'Listen to me, both of you, don't speak. Do not look at these men, whatever happens. I'm serious. Don't make eye contact.'

I nodded and shuffled over to sit next to Kate as Ryu turned back to the driver's side of the truck. The two- minute discussion between Ryu and the *yakuza* was in hushed tones. Kate and I kept our heads down, not even looking at each other.

'What's going on?' she whispered.

'Shhh.' I angled my head slightly, hoping to hear but the only thing I understood was *onna gaijin* - foreign woman. This was about us. Footsteps walked away, and I risked a sideways peek. Ryu walked between two dark suited men. Holding his arms, they hurried him towards their car where the white shirted driver held the door open. Where were they taking Ryu? Koji turned the truck round and drove back towards town. And that steely-cold knot of fear, that had disappeared from my stomach of late, reappeared with a grip so strong, it stopped the blood flowing in my veins, turning it dry and dusty.

It took about twenty minutes to get back to the main crossroads. Twenty minutes that doubled their volume just to torment me. Twenty fat minutes of not knowing where Ryu was, or if he was okay. Koji braked and slowed down and I looked ahead to see Ryu standing at the side of the empty road. He ignored me and got into the front of the truck. I breathed better, easier, but my throat felt tight and my chin trembled. Ignoring Kate's questions, I looked the other way, trying to control my feeling, to let the blood in my veins flow normally again. Koji drove into town and parked at the station end of the shopping mall, near the koban where I'd taken the little girl that day. He climbed out and opened the tailgate. Kate and I jumped down. Ryu emerged from the truck and I threw my arms around his neck. He reached up, pulled my arms down and stepped away from me. The rejection stung, made me look away.

'What did they want? What happened?' I said, not daring to face him.

Ryu spoke in rapid Japanese to Hiroshi and Koji, quietly and deliberately not including me and I shivered despite the sun. A cigarette in her hand, Kate shuffled from foot to foot and neither of us spoke, waiting for things to be explained. A police car turned into the koban parking area and Ryu looked at me.

'It's okay, come on, let's go grab a bite to eat. We can talk.' He turned to Kate. 'Kato. Stay close with Koji.'

The five of us walked in strained silence through the busy pedestrianised streets. Families chatted, happy to be out for lunch. Sunday shoppers carried newly purchased items in gloriously decorated carrier bags. Music played outside a new children's clothes store, advertising a promotion, and cartoon characters danced across a screen in the window. Adults in fancy-dress handed out leaflets for the opening of the shop. Everything felt wrong, surreal, something other.

Ryu slid open the door of the yakitori that Kate and I had come to all those weeks ago and moved the curtain aside for me. The drum beat out our welcome.

'Masta, is the room at the back free?' said Ryu, lighting a cigarette.

Masta showed us to the small room reserved for private dining. I hadn't known it was there. Shoes left outside, we stepped up into the tatami floored room. We sat on two sides of the low table on the black cushions with structured high backs, like legless chairs. I couldn't work out how to get comfortable. Eventually I drew my knees up to my chest and lay my forehead against them, my hands running down my shins. My heart thumped loudly, filling my ears. The guys were silent. That worried me as much as the *yakuza* taking Ryu off somewhere. Cupping my hands over my mouth, I took in long breaths. Five large bottles of beer and ice-cold glasses straight from the freezer arrived, along with oshiburi. Masta bowed before sliding the door closed behind him. The air conditioner blew cool air and I lifted my hair off the back of my neck, enjoying the coolness.

A painting of two parts covered both the door and the wall it slid on. Charcoal lines depicted Fujiyama in the background. A cherry tree in bloom showed off its pale pink flowers in front of a pagoda with curved roofs. A long -necked bird stood in the bottom corner, looking at the view. The irony of picture postcard Japan wasn't lost on me.

'Okay, I've waited long enough.' Kate looked from Ryu to Koji and back. 'If someone doesn't tell me what's going on, I'll scream. Just explain, someone, please.'

'So?' I leaned my arm against Ryu's.

Koji chewed his bottom lip and adjusted his glasses. Ryu nodded at him.

'So,' Koji said. '*Yakuza* give you last warning.'

Hiroshi coughed and we all looked at him. He startled and mumbled something, running his hand across his long face.

Ryu started to speak but I interrupted him. 'This is stupid. They can't – '

'Listen. Mari. Listen to me.' Ryu's tone silenced me and I turned in my seat to look at him. 'Those men were messengers sent by the *wakagashira*, second boss of Hitano *yakuza*. He said you've created a problem. They told you the rules from the beginning, but you didn't listen. They kept warning you, it's dangerous. Now there's a problem and they told me to tell you,

you need to do as they say. And there's something else.'

'And what? If we don't stay home? What are they going to do, fire us, withhold our pay or something?' Kate said. 'I wouldn't mind if they asked us to leave.'

'This is serious. The problem is way bigger than that. There's interest in you from Nagasaki syndicate and to protect you from them, your contracts have been sold to Nagoya *yakuza*. You're being sent there.' He touched my cheek and tucked a strand of hair behind my ear.

'What? I don't understand,' I said.

'It's complicated.' He looked up at the ceiling for a moment, taking a deep breath. 'Hitano and Nagoya syndicates are all part of the same family, the Yamaguchi-gumi. But Hitano are in debt to Nagasaki *yakuza,* which belongs to another family and that debt needs to be paid by the end of the month. But the Nagasaki oyabun, their Godfather I guess, wants your contracts instead. You work for him in Nagasaki, the debt gets written off. Of course, Hitano's oyabun doesn't want to give your contracts away. They earn big money from you, you know that, right? The school pays, Shima pays and Kujaku pays. Gaijin women.' He shook his head. 'Today, they said that in Nagasaki…' He cleared his throat. 'There's talk of making you work like some of the Filipina girls. I'm guessing it's a lie and they just want to scare us.'

'Well, he did excellent job!' said Koji, who sat with his arm round Kate's shoulders. She said nothing, her eyes huge in her face, twisting her signet ring round her finger.

'Shit, they can't force us to do that.' My words sounded hollow as I remembered the story Imee and Melody had told me about the girl that hanged herself rather than be forced into prostitution.

Masta's cry of *'Irashaimasse'* came from the main part of the restaurant, along with the drumbeat, and the clatter of dishes and plates being washed in the kitchen echoed down the corridor. But it all sounded further away, as if it came from another dimension.

'When you go to Nagoya, Nagasaki can't touch you because

they have no issue with that syndicate. But if you stay here…'
Ryu's hand was strong and steady, as he reached down to mine. 'In
some ways, you're just a commodity to them, but they *are* trying
to protect you from the sleazier side of things. The debt can be
paid off with cash, but Nagasaki know your earning potential
and there's a certain kudos for having Europeans working for
them. Anyway, so that's why they want you.'

'This can't be real. A commodity? It's 1985 not the middle-
ages; this can't be happening.'

Ryu nodded, drinking his beer straight from the bottle.

'I'm confused. They could come to the school and take us,
or from the clubs. But they don't, so why would they take us
from anywhere else?'

My mouth tripped over words, my thoughts forming faster
than I could speak them. My head reeled and I felt sick.

'One syndicate can come into another's territory. Remember
the man in Shima with the tattoos? He wasn't local. Fukuoka and
Kitakyushu are real *yakuza* strongholds and there's been a turf
war going on for the last coupla years. There have been shootings
and all. Things are settling now so I guess they don't want to
stir things up. There is a small chance they'll make a grab for
you, and if they do, it'll be from somewhere that doesn't belong
to Hitano *yakuza*. I guess that's why they don't like you cycling
around. We have to keep you safe until you go to Nagoya.' His
voice wavered. I knew he was scared.

'Why didn't we go to the koban, then?'

'Mari, my love, you still don't get it. *Yakuza* to do their business
their way. It's accepted that they're pretty much beyond the law.'

'You were looking straight at it when we were standing outside.'

'I was looking at the *yakuza* headquarters, two doors down.
Their offices are always close to the police. That should tell you
something.'

'We thought the *yakuza* were leaving us alone,' said Kate.

'Ohayo and Hitano aren't the threat. Nagasaki are,' Ryu said,
'Keep your heads down for the next coupla weeks. Then you go

to Nagoya.' He closed his eyes for a moment.

'So, Imee was right when she said they own us. This is crap. Ryu, does this mean trouble for you too?' I watched his face storm with emotions, and the little muscle in his jaw flexed. 'Do they… did they threaten you?'

'Look, after work, just go straight home. They'll put someone outside your place to watch you… protecting their investment.' He smiled a half smile.

Reaching for my beer, I took a huge swig. I wouldn't go to Nagoya. Not now. There was a chance I might be in no condition to go to Nagoya. My period was three weeks late but I still hadn't done a test. I put down the bottle and pushed it away, reaching instead for the tall glass of water.

'But we're safe during the day, right?' said Kate.

'You are not safe at any time,' said Koji.

The boys ordered food. I lay my head against Ryu's shoulder, and he stroked my hair. Masta delivered the food and switched on the overhead light. I ate little but tasted nothing.

A while later, Koji offered to take Kate home, and Hiroshi went off to see Myla. Ryu and I stayed and ordered tea.

He turned to me, held both my shoulders, and looked into my eyes. He nodded once as he blew out a long slow breath and released me. Standing, he ran his hand through his hair, shining blue-black under the electric light.

'What?' I said to his back as he walked across the room.

'This is us. Two weeks is up.' He turned to me and shrugged. 'No more talking, no more excuses. And she's coming back early from Italy. Arrives Wednesday this week,' he said. The breath that left me was sharp, but I had no words. 'Sorry, Mari. Let's get you a cab from the station, okay?'

'I need to go home and talk to Kate.' I stood, pulling my bag onto my shoulder. 'We need to get out of here before the *yakuza* send us to Nagoya like a box of oranges.' I ran my hand over my forehead and breathed out a long sigh. 'Ryu, oh my God, they've still got our passports.'

He didn't look at me, staying silent for just a moment too long. On our way out of the yakitori, Ryu paid the bill. My heart pounded as I waited for him to speak. Outside, he tapped a cigarette out of the packet, lit it, and took a long drag. When he breathed it out, he nodded.

'You're right, the *yakuza* will do what they want with you. I'll speak to Ohayo about your passports.'

Walking to the station, I felt an out of body lightness, as if I was dreaming. He kept his distance from me, walking slightly ahead, too far away for me to reach out and touch him.

'Why would he listen to you?'

'He and I used to hang out. Leave it with me.'

'You and Ohayo are old friends? My God.' I stopped dead. He turned to face me, still two steps away.

'I am not his friend, Mari. I might be able to use some leverage, that's all. Some time back, I was seeing a girl. He wanted her and I stepped aside. Ohayo gets what he wants. He... it's complicated but he didn't treat her well. He kind of owes me a favour.'

'Cherry?' That one flash of intuition illuminated how little I knew about Ryu, and how flimsy our relationship was. It'd been built on no foundation, never destined to last, *koi no yokan* or not. Kate's comment about me never having met his parents found a deeper wound to settle in.

'It was a while ago.'

'Not that long.' He knew what happened to her. It had something to do with him, I could feel it. The thought slipped away as another one took over. If he could get our passports back, why hadn't he offered to do it before? A wet firework of anger spat and faded. It didn't matter, I wouldn't have left any earlier anyway.

'Look, we knew this was never going to be a permanent thing, you and me. We've both gotten in over our heads. Like with my grandparents, love isn't enough and circumstance takes over. I wish things were different.'

'But they're not. Please look at me, Ryu.' He didn't, just kept walking half a step ahead of me until we reached the taxi rank. My heart's fractures cracked wider. 'I want you to be happy. You'll make a good hus…' I couldn't say it.

'And you were planning to travel to India before we got together and I don't want to stop you doing that.' He opened the taxi door for me. 'See you, Mari.'

The urge to cry was hard to control, but I held it together until I got in the taxi and it drove away, leaving him standing there.

Chapter 20

MY THROAT ACHED. I traced the images looking back at me from the photos lying on the tatami, surrounded by scrunched up, damp tissues. If every picture told a story, all I saw were two people in love. I rolled onto my back, staring at the ceiling, noting every crack and bump, now as familiar to me as the contours of Ryu's face. I wanted to be fat and waddling, with Ryu standing proudly beside me as we waited for the birth of our child. I wanted to be holding a black-haired baby. I wanted Ryu to look at me adoringly as the baby grasped his little finger with her strong, tiny fist. His wedding ring, the one that matched mine, would reflect the sunlight. Our daughter would be called Elena. We'd be the perfect family. There'd be a happy ending. But then I remembered that I wasn't a princess in a fairy tale. And my mother was right; I was cursed.

Clatters and bangs came from the kitchen, and the smell of coffee and onions. I sat up and tied the sash on my yukata as Kate's face peered round the partition.

'You're not crying again are you?' she said. 'Thank God you're not pregnant. It's for the best, you know. And put those photos away, it's not doing you any good looking at him all the time. Come on, breakfast's ready'

'You cooked?' I didn't think she knew how. 'Just coffee please.'

I stacked the photos and put them back in their Fujifilm envelope. The photo Koji took of us at the teahouse, I slid between the pages of my dictionary. Padding into the bathroom, I opened the little cabinet and took out the packet of Veganin. It was the only thing that got rid of my period pain.

'You can't have a fourth day off work. That Ueno said he'd withhold the whole month's pay. And you must eat, Mari. You've hardly had anything since Sunday and you're starting to worry me. I went out while you were sleeping and bought all your favourite things.'

I stepped down into the kitchen. Kate held up a plate of steamed buns, inari rolls and cakes. She'd even made an omelette, like I'd shown her once, with fried onions and peppers and potatoes. This was the first time she'd done more than make coffee.

'Thank you.' I hugged her. 'It all looks lovely.'

'After breakfast, I'll paint your nails for you.' She pulled at a lock of my hair. 'We could try and do something different with it today if you like?'

'No, it's okay.'

'Mari, why didn't you tell me you thought you were pregnant?'

'I was going to ask you to come to the doctor with me, so I could get a test done but then we had that fight.'

'Well. You must be relieved that you're not having his baby. Haven't you heard of condoms? Honestly!'

'Well, I'm not pregnant, so it doesn't matter.' Sitting at the table, I pulled the plate of food towards me. 'Listen, Kate. We have to get out of Japan. What if we don't get to Nagoya? I'm not going to end up in some sleazy bar, working 'like the Filipinas." My fingers made air quotes. 'And neither are you. I haven't worked it out yet, but we need to escape.'

Chapter 21

THE MORNINGS BEFORE school became planning sessions as we worked out how we'd leave Japan. Pay day was on the 24th, the last Thursday in October. It made sense to wait for the money and get out a week before they planned to send us to Nagoya on the last day of the month.

'We need to find a Singapore Airlines office, or a travel agency. Let's go to Fukuoka tomorrow, see what we can do with the return portion of our tickets from Osaka to Sydney.' I said. I sat cross-legged in the middle of my room, folding clothes, and sorting things into piles. The few items I wanted to take with me went into my black holdall. 'They might let us cash it in, or change the destination and date. We could just fly as far as Singapore. Or we buy new tickets.' I pointed to the stack of yen on my futon. 'I just counted it all, there's about £2,800 worth.'

'I've got a bit less than that, 'said Kate. She put mugs and plates back into the kitchen cupboard. 'I'll count mine later.'

'You spent yours on too many love hotels.'

'Ha, ha. Very funny. I'll ring Koji later. He'll know where we can go. Or at least look it up in the phone book, which is more than I can do.' Kate stood in the doorway to the kitchen. 'It'll be nice to go to the city anyway. Do you good, you know, cheer you up a bit.'

Someone knocked on the door. I stood, stepped down into the kitchen. Kate frowned at me. The knock came again and I froze for a second. As Kate moved towards it, I grabbed her hand to stop her. I put my finger to my lips. 'Shhhhh.'

'It's Sayuri,' called a voice.

The breath I held came out as a little laugh. At least she was a friendly foe. Kate opened the door and Sayuri came inside, moving as if on water. She slipped off her shoes and stepped up into the kitchen. I pulled Kate next to me and we stood blocking the entrance to my room, hoping Sayuri wouldn't notice the obvious packing.

'I come from Onishi Imports and with message from Mr Ohayo and Ueno-san. Can you stay home, please? No work for you for three days.'

I had questions, but she worked for the *yakuza*, so it would be better not to show concern or weakness.

'Days off? Sounds good to us,' I said. 'Doesn't it, Kato?'

'Yes, super.'

'We told you. You would not comply and now there is big problem. Mari, your boyfriend explained it, I think? Now, your punishment is three days stay at home. School will not pay you. From Saturday, we send a car to take you to work and then back home. You must do as you are told until you go to Nagoya.'

Punishment? It took all my willpower not to scream at her.

'Yes, of course we will. We'll see you again on pay day, Sayuri.' I opened the front door.

We sorted out our stuff. I tried not to cry as I sang along to Paul Young's *'Everything Must Change'* and put all my Kujaku clothes into a packing box ready to ship home. Things I didn't want filled a grey bin-bag. It felt good, symbolic even, to throw things away. Just five months before, my hands had shaken while I'd packed to come to Japan. I'd arrived scared and now I was scared I wouldn't be able to leave.

Chapter 22

A MUCH BIGGER city than Kitakyushu, Fukuoka's streets were busy, and morning traffic crawled. Above us, high-rise offices stretched to the watery-grey sky. In front of the downtown buildings, throngs of people walked on wide pavements. This was more the Japan I'd imagined. After sleepy Hitano, the bustle and buzz of the traffic-filled streets was full-on. Kate linked my arm as we crossed the road on extra-wide black and white pedestrian crossings. Glitzy shop fronts offered all sorts of temptations, their illuminations reflected on the rain-wet pavements. People rushed past or stopped to look in the shop windows. Apart from the Japanese signage and the fact that everyone had black hair, we could have been on Oxford Street in London or Pitt Street in Sydney.

An hour or so later, Kate and I stepped out of the airline office and into the busy street.

'That worked out well, I didn't expect to be able to change the date without having to pay,' I said. 'Ha, *yakuza* shitheads, we're running away to Singapore on your tickets! That makes me feel so good.'

'We're really leaving, I can't believe it,' said Kate.

'Coffee. I need coffee. Eighteen days, Kato.' I waved my ticket at her, and we walked towards a café a few doors down. 'Eighteen days and we are out of here. Now we just need Ryu to get our passports back.'

'Do you trust him?'

'I have to, he's our only hope. He's got some connection with Ohayo, said he had something on him.'

'Cherry.'

'You know about that?'

'Imee told me. Ryu and Ohayo almost came to blows over her. Ryu finished with her and then Ohayo set her up where we live. Then, and this is only what Imee said, Ohayo caught her with Ryu. Not long after that, she vanished.'

'So, I was right. That's what Ryu meant when he said he had leverage; he knows what happened to Cherry.' Thinking of him with this faceless woman who'd been with Ohayo made me feel sick. It cheapened our relationship and made me feel less special. What kind of man was he? He cheated on his fiancée. Twice. I'd justified our relationship, sure that it was love. But what had it been with Cherry?

'We could go to the British Embassy and just tell them what's going on,' said Kate. 'Just in case Ryu doesn't come through. They might help us get new passports.'

'Oh my God, why didn't I think of that?' I grabbed Kate and kissed her on the cheek. 'I'm not sure it's that easy. Won't we need birth certificates? But it's worth a try.'

'Definitely. Let's find out where it is.'

Kate and I rushed to the trio of yellow phone boxes further along the street and crammed ourselves into the middle one. She hefted the phone book onto the shelf.

'What'll it be under?' she said. 'Try *Embassy.*'

I looked up the symbol for 'E' and them 'Em' but there was nothing. Next, I tried under the symbol for 'B'.

'It's here!' I said, running my finger under the capital letters *BRITISH CONSULAR OFFICE.* 'Thank God.'

Jamming my Hello Kitty phone-card into the slot, I tapped in the numbers Kate read out. There was no answer.

'Let's try again later,' said Kate, taking her red address book out of her handbag. 'I'll write the number down.'

'No, come on.' I tore the page out of the book and dashed onto the street, my hand in the air. 'Taxi!'

THE TAXI DROPPED us outside a shopping mall and we headed for the escalators. A brass plaque stated that we'd found the British Consular office. It wasn't what I'd imagined at all. No Union Jack flying atop a grand building, just this small office on the top floor of a shopping mall, next door to insurance brokers and employment agencies. Kate pushed on the door but it didn't open. I tried too, but it was locked. There was no bell to ring, nothing to tell us when someone would be there.

I asked a lone teenaged boy sitting in the office next door but he didn't know when the office opened.

'We'll try the phone later,' I said. 'It's funny that no one's here though, it's mid-morning. Normal working hours.'

'Well, maybe it's closed down or something. There can't be much call for a consular office anyway.'

'Let's come back in an hour. And if there's still no one here today, at least we know where it is.'

We filled the hour easily. Kate bought a pair of walking shoes in the camping shop, and we each got a Sony Walkman from the hi-fi shop on the ground floor.

On our second visit, the office was still closed. We phoned the number several times throughout the day but there was never an answer. Please, God, let Ryu keep his promise.

My thoughts kept turning to Ryu's association with Ohayo, and I felt uncomfortable. Thinking about him with Cherry was a whole other emotion. I had no right to jealousy; he was never mine to begin with. My imagination didn't need to run riot. I remembered the nightmare I had in Sydney, when I woke feeling like I was being choked. Had that been about Cherry? And with that thought came a heavy feeling, and I just knew. Someone had strangled her. Cherry had been murdered.

Chapter 23

THE NEXT MORNING, the *yakuza* car arrived to take us to school. Slipping on our shoes, we stepped outside, and I locked the front door.

'Where are our bikes? They've taken our bloody bikes,' Kate said.

'They're making sure we don't go anywhere on our own. Seventeen days, Kato. Just seventeen days.' I felt deflated rather than angry. My wings were clipped, and the bars of the birdcage were suddenly thicker. 'They weren't ours anyway.'

The driver dropped us at the station and we walked the last block to school. Sayuri arrived at the same time, having come from the opposite direction. We followed her upstairs. I wondered what we'd done wrong now. Could they have found out our plan to leave? I stopped at the top of the stairs, pulled Kate next to me.

'Yes, Sayuri?' I said. 'Did you want to see us?'

'Your visa will expire in fifteen days. We must get extension for you before you go to Nagoya. We will take you to Ministry of Justice in Fukuoka. Immigration office is there.'

'No, it's okay, thanks. I think we can go and do that ourselves,' I said. This was what we needed; a chance to get our hands on our passports. Kate touched my arm, left her hand there. It wasn't easy keeping my face expressionless but I daren't show any reaction. I had to play this carefully. 'So, you'll give us back our passports now?'

'Onishi Imports must apply on your behalf, so please, we will take you to Fukuoka tomorrow, and you will have new visa same day.' Sayuri bowed.

'If you tell us where we need to go, we can do it. Surely you can just give us a letter or something with our passports?'

'We go together. I must insist. Everything is arranged.'

On the way home from work, I persuaded the driver to stop at the vending machine and bought a couple of beers. Kate and I read the guidebook and planned the route to India from Thailand. We put crosses next to Philippine islands and read about the ferries between them. It was hard to concentrate on what Kate was saying, so I went to get a glass of water. There was so much to think about, and tomorrow really would be make or break as far as getting out of Japan was concerned.

'I reckon they really do have someone out there watching us. There's a car parked down the street.' I peered out of the kitchen window. 'I saw it yesterday as well, when they dropped us home. It's the same white one that used to follow us. It's mental, isn't it? We have a bloody bodyguard! A gangster bodyguard protecting us from other gangsters.'

'It's a bit like an old James Cagney movie,' said Kate. 'Or that one with Tony Curtis and Jack Lemmon.'

'"*Some Like it Hot!*" That's a great film.' I turned, my back to the sink. 'But there's nothing funny about this. Looks like Ryu came through for us though.' I didn't want to think of the reason behind it. 'If we can get our passports back tomorrow, we're in the clear. And we'll be on that plane a week before they think they're sending us to Nagoya.'

Chapter 24

Sayuri sat in the front seat of the chauffeured car as we drove to the Immigration Bureau in Fukuoka. In the back, Kate and I glanced at each other repeatedly, both of us nervous. The silence was solid, and we didn't talk for the whole journey. Not having a clue how we'd achieve it, all we knew was that we had to get our passports back.

Sayuri led us into an office on the second floor of the Ministry of Justice building. She carried a cardboard file and handed it to the official at the desk.

'What happens now?' I asked.

'They must check details, Mari. Don't worry, I speak directly with them. Onishi company will pay everything. You can sit.' Sayuri gestured to a few chairs along the wall.

'How?' I said. Kate and I sat and huddled together so we could talk without being overheard. 'Other than physically wrestling Sayuri to the floor and snatching the passports, I don't know how this is going to work.'

'I'll make a scene. You know, *I'm a British citizen, give me my passport.* That type of thing. We're here in an official building, surely that'd work?'

'Maybe. Okay, let's both make a scene; embarrass them and it might work. But once we leave here, I'm not sure how we can stop her taking them back.'

'How about we ask for a receipt or something signed, stamped?'

'Kate, the whole idea is not to give them back.'

'Oh. Yes. Sorry.'

For what seemed like hours, we sat waiting. I smoothed out the fabric of my skirt, hoping and trusting that somehow this would work.

'Miss Katherine Woodman,' the official behind the desk said.

'That's me.' She stood. 'I'm British, give me my passport.' Her plummy voice was gull-shrill as she grabbed the passport out of the poor man's hand.

At first, I cringed, thinking Sayuri would guess what we planned, step in, and snatch the passport away. When Kate slipped it into her bag, I breathed out. Half-way there!

'Miss Marianna Garcia Randall.'

Stepping towards the desk, I bowed and retrieved my passport. The gold embossed crest on the navy-blue cover had never looked so good. When I smiled at Sayuri, she didn't smile back.

In the car, on the long ride home, Kate and I chatted about everything and nothing, careful not to drop any hint about our plans to leave. Sayuri was probably listening to everything we said, so we kept our voices low.

When we arrived home, I got out of the car and rushed to the front door. My hands shook and the key wouldn't go in properly. Kate had to take it from me. She opened the door easily and we went inside, bolting the door behind us.

'I expected some white-shirted *yakuza* thug to appear from behind the washing machine and jump on us and grab our passports,' I said. 'How come Sayuri didn't take them back? This must have something to do with Ryu.'

'Don't care. And neither should you. Stop thinking everything is about him. From now on, I'm keeping this in my bag all the time,' said Kate, opening her passport. 'Not letting it out of my sight.'

'How will we manage at work? I can't imagine singing karaoke with my bag hanging off my shoulder.'

'We can take it in turns. You look after my bag, and I'll look after yours. That way, no one can sneak into them.'

Chapter 25

SHIMA HAD RUN out of ice and the chef went to find some from a neighbouring bar. I waited ages by the kitchen. Turning back to the room, I watched Kate with her new customer. Mama waved her hand around, her cigarette dangerously close to Kate's face. They were too far away for me to hear what was being said, but it looked heated. Kate looked the other way with her arms folded, and legs crossed. A big no-no.

'What's going on?' I asked Melody as she joined me, waiting for ice. 'Kate doesn't look happy.'

'She refused to sit with him but I don't know why. Mama insisted. Now, she won't serve his drink.'

My stomach roiled. This wouldn't be good. Kate turned her back to the customer and Mama pulled her off the stool. It happened so fast that I wasn't sure I'd seen it right. The customer left, followed by Mama, dragging Kate behind her.

I grabbed Kate's bag and by the time I got outside, Mama had pulled her halfway up the staircase to Kujaku. Kate was crying, trying to shake Mama off.

'Kate! What the fuck's going on?' I yelled.

'Shut up,' said Mama. 'Go back inside.'

I ran up the stairs but the door to Kujaku slammed in my face. The key turned in the lock. My fists pounded on the door, then I pressed my ear against it, hoping to hear what was going on.

'Mari,' said Melody from the bottom of the stairs. 'Come

away. You can't help her.'

'What do you mean?'

'He's a *yakuza* boss. She offended him. Come away.'

Slowly, I came down the stairs, looking back over my shoulder, waiting for the door to open. Out on the street, Melody and I stood apart, watching the stairwell as the rain splattered down. Chilled, I rubbed my bare arms as raindrops formed a pattern on the front of my green top.

'She refused to offer hospitality. You know this is a big offense, especially with him.' Melody shook her head. 'He's the *wakagashira*, Number two big boss.'

'Why didn't she show him respect? She can be so stupid. Oh, God.'

Mama clattered down the stairs, her pudgy feet awkward in her too-small shoes. 'You. Your stupid friend. Too much trouble,' she said, and spat at my feet.

Only the *wakagashira*'s appearance stopped me belting her around her fat head. He ignored us all and walked away. Mama yanked open the door to Shima and went inside. Melody followed her.

'Mari?' Kate's voice was wobbly.

I turned. She stood shivering in the rain as it turned her blonde hair darker. 'What happened?' I asked, putting my arm round her shoulders. We stepped back into the stairwell, out of the rain. 'Are you okay?'

She turned into me, her hand covering her face as she cried. I held her not knowing what to say. Shima's door opened, and a stream of customers left, zipping up jackets and opening umbrellas. They took ages to say their goodbyes and finally move away. Imee stuck her head round the door and looked around before coming outside.

'Kato, you need to say sorry,' said Imee, placing her hand on Kate's arm. 'He's the *wakagashira*, second most high up *yakuza* boss for this area. You didn't show respect, you made him lose face. He is truly angry.'

'I don't see why I should apologise. I said he was an idiot, and he is. Who does he think he is? I didn't want to sit with him in the first place.' Kate pushed herself away from me and scuffed the toe of her shoe on the cobbles.

'He's the one who sent the message about Nagoya.' I spoke to Kate as patiently as I could, my hands curled into fists as I measured out each word. 'For God's sake, you know the position we're in. You should've apologised. Being defiant isn't going to help anything.'

'Don't reproach me, please don't...' Her chin wobbled.

I put my arm round her and walked her through the pouring rain to the car that waited in the back alley to take us home.

Chapter 26

THE DAYS FELT longer than normal. They felt stretched like elastic and held a tension that could snap at any time. We had another ten days until pay day, and eleven until our flight left for Singapore. I felt the first stirrings of excitement. Or was it relief? Whatever it was, I couldn't wait to get out of there.

In the still and quiet light of dawn, I walked towards the mountains to clear my head. Somehow, it was fitting to leave Japan as the seasons turned and the shadows got longer. The autumn of late October turned the mountains from deep green to shades of copper, russet, red and gold, like a rich tapestry, all texture and detail. The mists of early morning hung around them at low levels, like opaque chiffon skirts, hiding secrets and mysteries. Walking through narrow lanes, I passed a few small houses. A crooked branch of a persimmon tree hung over a garden wall, heavy with ripe orange fruit. I stepped around one that had fallen on the ground and burst open, revealing pumpkin coloured flesh. There must have been more fallers on the other side of the wall because the air was heavy with the sickly-sweet smell of rot. It made me think of death, and I shivered. In the surrounding fields, the poly-tunnels had been peeled back, leaving skinny, metal skeletons. The vegetables were harvested, and already eaten, or pickled for winter. Even the birdsong had changed as the migratory season started. The sky seemed higher than before, and long-necked birds flew in V formations, heading for the warmth of southern winters. My mood matched theirs in needing to leave what had become familiar, even though I always knew that Japan was never going to be my home.

I huddled into myself, pulling the arms of my sloppy-joe over my hands, and moving the ripped neckline back onto my shoulder. Thoughts of Ryu shadowed across my mind as feelings came and went, rippling through my heart. But there were no more tears. The last five months had depleted my already worn out emotions.

Looking at my watch, I was surprised to see that I'd been wandering for almost two hours. Feeling cold and needing coffee, I took a different way back to our apartment, found myself looking through a grey wrought iron gate into a small garden. The grey-white pebbles swirled in wave patterns around two large lumpy rocks. Knobbly Bonsai trees sat in black ceramic pots, and a long-handled rake leaned against the stone wall.

'*Sumimasen, sumimasen*, excuse me,' called a female voice and I turned to see a woman in jeans and an oversized stripy jumper walking towards me. She bowed. 'Thank you for what you have been doing.'

Certain I didn't know her, I looked at her, puzzled.

'My mother's uncle.' She bowed again, held position for a few seconds. 'The old man who has a small yellow dog.'

'Oh, yes! No problem. I'm happy to help.'

'He was a fighter pilot. His plane got shot down in Manchuria in 1945. He returned with some damage to his brain.' She shrugged. 'We do what we can, but it isn't easy. So, thank you.'

So that was why he wore flight goggles strapped across his forehead. The woman bowed again and walked back towards her house. I thought of Ryu's grandparents, his mother, and what they'd suffered after the war. How his father's country has been annexed and plundered by Japan. My generation was blessed for not having lived through anything so horrific. We had to keep it that way, the world needed to disarm, but I didn't trust Reagan or Gorbachev.

Crazy Dog was another casualty of war, but it felt good knowing he wasn't alone.

MY LAST STUDENT left after his one-to-one class. I'd used the lesson with him to ask about hotels. The normal kind, not the love kind. He said there was a Holiday Inn in the business district. I stood at the table in the staff room, bent over a thick blue phone book. I wanted to book a room in Osaka for the night before we flew from there to Singapore. If I could find the Holiday Inn number, I could call them. They'd have a number for their sister hotel in Osaka.

'There're too many kanji symbols in with the hiragana and katagana. I just don't read well enough.'

'I'll ask Koji,' said Kate. 'He has his uses.'

Sayuri knocked on the door and I slammed the phone book closed so hard that Kate jumped. Sayuri requested that we go straight to Kujaku for a meeting.

'We'll meet you there. Give us ten minutes please,' I said and Sayuri closed the door on her way out. 'It could be about what happened on Saturday, Kate. If they ask you to say sorry, just do it.'

'Maybe they found out we're leaving. The other thing was, you know, something and nothing. Just some arrogant man throwing his weight around, and you know what I think about that.'

'I have a bad feeling. God, you might be right. If they know we're leaving, they might try and stop us. On the other hand, they might say we can go now. That wouldn't be too bad, although if they don't pay us, it's a lot of money to lose.'

'I'm not leaving until we get paid,' said Kate. 'I've earned that money.'

'I know, but we have our passports, so we could go now. Visit Kyoto and Nara on the way to Osaka. Or Tokyo. You could meet up with Jack. Seriously, I think we should leave tomorrow.'

'Let's stick to the original plan, Mari. It's only a few more days. I need this month's salary, and so do you.'

And if she didn't want to leave, I couldn't either. And what difference would a few more days make?

WE WALKED UP the stairs to Kujaku. A hand-written notice "*closed*" had been taped to the door just under the carved peacock's feet. Pushing open the door, I went in first. Ohayo and Washan stood near the karaoke machine; Mama and Imee waited by Yoshi-san's desk. A minute later, we bowed as the wakagshira walked into the club. Although I'd seen him leave Kujaku, I hadn't noticed how small and wiry he was. Not what I expected for someone so powerful. Ohayo fiddled with the knot of his tie, said I should wait outside. I hesitated but Mama pushed me out of the door and closed it. The key turned on the other side. With my ear to the peacock design, I hardly breathed. It wasn't possible to understand the muffled voices, but I heard Kate crying.

The *wakagashira* flung open the door, nearly knocking me over, and rushed down the stairs. Mama shouted at Kate, who knelt on the floor, her face red and blotchy.

'Hey.' I rushed inside, 'Don't shout at her like that.'

I crouched next to Kate and helped her up off her knees, seating her in the nearest booth. Yoshi-san brought two glasses of ocha and I looked up at him, but he wouldn't meet my eye.

'You stupid girl,' said Mama. Her eyes disappeared into thin slits in her fat cheeks, and she almost spat the words. 'You foreign women, all the same. No good for anything.'

Just before I could tell her to fuck off, she left, slamming the door behind her. Imee motioned to me from the other end of the room, and I left Kate to drink her tea.

'God, it was awful,' said Imee. 'He had her by her hair and made her kneel to apologise, but she would not. I kept telling her to look down, but she did not listen to me. She stared right back at him, with no respect. Oh, *Dios*.' She wiped a tear from her cheek. 'Now, he is very dishonoured and very angry. He came to see your bosses and Mama on Saturday to tell them at the end of this month you will move to Nagoya. He was trying to help you, but now -'

'We already know we're going to Nagoya.'

'No. He changed his mind. You'll go to Nagasaki. Mari, you should speak on Kate's behalf. Apologise for her.'

I looked at Kate. Why couldn't she just apologise? It wouldn't kill her to smooth the waters. Maybe I could say sorry for her but part of me didn't see why I should. Nagoya or Nagasaki; did it matter? We were leaving for Singapore in a few days.

'I need a proper drink but not here,' said Kate. She stood, her arms hanging by her side, her black Lycra skirt askew.

'Yoshi-san, can we just go and grab a drink at the *yakitori*?'

'Don't tell Mama, okay? I will send car to collect you in one hour, from back alleyway. You have made big problem Kato. You know who that man is. Go to eat now. One hour okay? Don't make me regret I agree for this. And please, apologise.'

Kate jutted her chin out and looked the other way.

'I'll talk to her,' I said.

KATE SLID OPEN the door and Masta greeted us in his usual way. We sat at a table at the back of the room and ordered beer. The smell of grilled meat turned my stomach but I gulped down the cold beer and signalled for another.

'At first, I was going to play along, you know, pretend I was sorry for the other night, but he was so awful. I only cried because he was pulling my hair and it hurt, not for any other reason. He should be apologising to me. He's in the wrong,' Kate said.

'Look, we only have ten days to go, so let's just keep our heads down. Imee told me the *wakagashira* said something about sending us to Nagasaki. We know we can get away from here. It might not be so easy from there.' I drank straight out of the bottle.

'I don't even know where that is.'

'Exactly, Kate. Exactly.'

'*Irashaimasse*,' cried Masta, and beat three times on the drum.

Ryu stood at the door, all smiles, a Japanese woman beside him. Her short-bobbed hair moved as she nodded to the owner.

She looked prim, dressed in a navy-blue knee length dress with a white collar. I caught Ryu's eye as his smile faded and I dropped my gaze, looked at the table.

'I need to get out of here. I'll meet you out the back. You pay the bill.' I pulled yen out of my bag as I got up. I felt his eyes on me as I walked down the corridor past the payphone and the private dining room, and out of the back door into an empty street.

I took in deep breaths of the cool night. A silky soft drizzle hung in the air like mist. With my back to the wall, I stood under the eaves of the building, twirling my hair. I couldn't put a name to my emotions, didn't know what to think or to feel. The streetlights shone, reflecting yellow and fuzzy in the puddles the rain had left in the grooves and joins of the cobbles. Music came from somewhere close, and tyres swished on the wet tarmac road at the end of the alley. I sniffed, looking up at nothing.

'You okay?' Kate came out a few minutes later.

'Did you see them? He seemed happy with her. She looks nice, I'm glad.' My eyes blinked rapidly. 'What a bloody night.'

'He introduced me to her and asked how you are.'

Someone emerged out of a doorway across the street. Fear flicked through me, caught rock-solid in my chest as I recognised him.

'If he asks you to apologise, do it. Don't look at him, be respectful.' I grabbed Kate's hand and pulled her arm down, taut. One of her nails dug into my palm. 'For God's sake, bow, and don't look at him.'

Footsteps rang out on the cobbles as he walked towards us. My heart slammed against my ribs and I stared at the ground, my breath shallow.

The *wakagashira* stopped in front of us. His shiny black brogues were decorated with punched holes in the shape of a widow's peak. Three lines of narrow shoelaces tied in a neat bow across the bridge of his foot. Shoes from my nightmare. My heart pounded harder.

'*Konbanwa,* good evening,' I said.

He didn't answer. I stared at his shoes and prayed that Kate was doing the same. Time didn't move. Instead it clung to my fear, making itself slower still. Then, the *wakagashira* dropped his cigarette end, crushing it into the ground with his toe. He slowly walked away. I didn't look up until I heard the echo of his heels recede a long way down the alley. Our car appeared at the end of the alley. It must have waited in the shadows for the *wakagashira* to leave. Still holding hands, Kate and I rushed to it and got in. Neither of us said a word until we were safely home.

Once inside, I bolted the door shut and turned to face Kate.

'Shit, that *was* him, wasn't it?' I said.

'Bastard. Was he trying to scare us with the silent treatment?'

'Tell me you didn't look at him.'

'No, I didn't.' Her eyes moved from left to right, avoiding mine.

She was lying.

Chapter 27

'IT'S LIKE A prison sentence,' I said, crossing the day off the calendar with a pen. 'Six days to go, can you believe it! This is our last Friday night in Hitano. I really don't want to go to Kujaku tonight.'

'I can't wait to get on the Shinkansen. Then the plane. Six months in Japan has been five months too long,' said Kate. 'I wish now I'd gone up to Tokyo to see Jack, though.'

'Well, I did suggest that. We could've changed the tickets to fly from Tokyo.'

'It doesn't matter. I need the extra cash. I don't want to be scrimping when we travel. Do I look alright?' Kate tied her green and black scarf round her neck, the knot at the back.

All our dressy clothes had been collected by the shipping company that morning. I wore my faded Levi's jacket over a long-sleeved white t-shirt and my grey trousers. Kate wore her new walking shoes, trying to break them in. Kate's black sweatshirt and jeans looked fine, but I had a flash of juddery panic.

'Don't wear that green scarf tonight, Kate,' I said.

'Why?'

'I'm not sure. I just have a funny feeling.'

She tutted and rolled her eyes and adjusted the knot at her neck. 'Freaky hippy.'

'WHY ARE YOU dressed like that?' said Yoshi-san when we arrived at Kujaku. 'This is class place. Jeans not allowed. Take taxi and go home. Get changed.'

The lights went out and the fridges in the kitchen gave a dying sigh before they silenced. Yoshi moved around the room and flicked switches.

'I can smell burning,' said Kate.

The door opened and a small dark shape hustled inside.

'Mari? Kate? Are you there?' Melody said. Kate and I moved towards the voice.

'Has Shima lost power too?' I said.

'The whole building. They need an electrician, so Mama is closing for the night. We can all go home.'

'Okay,' said Yoshi-san. 'Go straight home, Mari and Kato.'

We agreed but walked straight around the corner to the yakitori, had something to eat and a few beers. Kate drank her way through two small flasks of sake as well. She signalled for a third, but Masta wouldn't serve her anymore.

Kate rang Koji from the payphone at the back. 'Wait a minute.' She moved the phone away from her mouth. 'We want to go to Ryu's. Will you come, Mari?'

'I don't know.' I placed one hand on my chest, shook my head.

'Koji and Hiroshi will be there. I'd like to see them. Come on. We can have a goodbye party.' She pouted. 'Please? Come on, show him what he's missing.'

I was in two minds. When he'd turned up at the yakitori with his fiancée that night, it had been a bit of a shock to see him. And with her. There'd be no surprises this time and I was sure I'd be able to handle it. But was it the right thing? Feelings tumbled over thoughts. It would be good, so good, to see him again. But what if he blanked me? What if the fiancée was there? What if she wasn't?

'Okay, I'll come. But let's play it by ear. If it's awkward, I won't stay long.' Sod it. It'd be alright. I didn't have to talk to him; there'd be other people there.

But deep within me, I knew then. A small, cold fish of fear

flip-flapped in my belly. The wheels were already in motion. Maybe the moon was full, or the beer spiked. Or maybe karma just wanted to deal her final hand that night. But the madness had started and I did nothing to stop it.

We left the restaurant, heading for the taxi rank near the station. As we passed the bikes parked there, we looked at each other and grinned. I found one to fit my height while Kate tied her handbag to the basket of the bike she'd chosen. At least I'd be able to leave the bar easily if I needed to. We rode towards Ryu's, singing Japanese karaoke songs.

Kate went in first to make sure the fiancée wasn't there while I waited under the blue and white sign outside. Telling myself it would be nice to see him, I shook my hair out of its scrunchie and let it fall down my back.

The door opened and Ryu came out. 'Mari. My Mari.'

I went without thought towards him. He touched my hair, letting it trail through his fingers. He took hold of the edges of my jacket and pulled me to him. I let myself lean into him and closed my eyes. He felt good.

'So much I want to say, but later. Come inside. Koji and Hiroshi are here.'

He took my hand and led me to my friends sitting at the bar, their backs to the door. Laughter and music fought for air space as people crowded in at the bar, leaving very little standing room.

'Where did all these people come from?' I said.

'Some lawyer got a big promotion and the law firm's celebrating,' said Ryu. 'My two cousins are here to help me. I wouldn't manage on my own.'

He'd never mentioned cousins before. In a way, the fact that I'd never met any of his family belittled our relationship. But then, I'd been the other woman, the gaijin woman.

I sidled in next to Kate, jostled by someone leaving. Ryu steadied the man and led him to the door.

'You okay, Mari?' Kate said.

'It's fine. We're fine.' Probably a lie.

'Whoever he's engaged to is one lucky lady,' said Kate. 'I always liked him.'

She waved at Ryu and he left the customers he was chatting to.

'Yes, Kate? Another beer, already?'

'No, I just wanted to say hi, you know.' She leaned forward on her elbow. 'We're leaving in a few days. I'll miss you.' She batted her eyelashes.

'Thursday afternoon, right?' Ryu looked at me. 'We'll all miss you both.'

Kate picked up her bottle and moved further inside the bar. A few people danced in the tiny space in front of the stage while their friend sang karaoke. Kate joined them.

'Kato,' Koji said and followed her. 'You can't dance here. You don't know these people. Come sit down.'

He put his hand in the small of her back, but she jigged to the music.

Ryu got himself a glass and poured from the house bottle of brandy. He lit a cigarette and pulled up an empty stool next to me. I scanned the shelves, but my personal bottle was gone. A pang of sadness hit me. I wondered who had taken it down. Ryu or his future bride?

'I miss you,' he said. I couldn't look at him. 'Mari.'

'Congratulations on your engagement.' I flicked a glance at him. His face was different; something in the way he held his jaw. 'She looks nice. Are you happy?'

'Parents are happy.' He shrugged. 'I'm not sleeping too well, can't stop thinking.'

'I'm the same, but I'm focusing on travelling, on getting to India. Thanks for your help with the passports.'

'Ohayo said it was Sayuri who decided to return them.'

'I don't understand. Who exactly is she anyway?'

'Her dad's the oyabun; head of the Fukuoka *yakuza*. If she was a son, she'd inherit the title, the business and the power.'

I shook my head. Little Sayuri, Kabuki-masked Sayuri, reduced to the role of secretary because of her sex. If I stayed in Japan for ten years, I'd struggle with the nuances of its culture. And semi-arranged marriages.

'You'll be looking forward to your new life with… what's her name? You never told me,' I said.

Kate shimmied over to us. 'Come and dance with me, Ryu.' She took hold of his arm. 'Come on.' She danced in front of him, leaning forward, both hands on his thighs, as she wiggled her hips.

Koji watched her; his shoulders tensed. I wasn't happy either. I'd seen Kate slide herself over Kujaku and Shima customers and plenty of her students. But Ryu? Where were her boundaries?

'No, I'm working,' Ryu said. He moved her hands off him and went behind the bar. Kate wiggled off to find someone else to flirt with, I presumed. Ryu prepared bills for customers about to leave and tidied the bar. He spoke to his cousins, who nodded.

Ryu sat with me and took my hand. 'Nothing will be the same when you go,' he said. 'Can you stay with me tonight? I need to speak with you.' He raised his hand to touch my face and I stopped it mid-air with my own. I slid my other hand out of his.

'What are you doing? You're officially engaged, Ryu.'

Kate moved between us, asking him to light her cigarette.

'What are you playing at, Kate?' I said, over the music and chatter. I moved off my stool and put my hands on her arms, gently manoeuvring her away from Ryu. Kate lurched at me, knocking into a man just getting off his stool. I grabbed her arm, dragging her away from the bar. 'Give me some time with him, will you? It's probably the last chance I'll get.'

'I want some time with him. You've had plenty. I bet I could get him if I really wanted to.' Kate laughed then.

'Koji,' I said, pushing Kate towards him. 'Can you do something with her? She's really drunk.'

He pushed his glasses up onto the bridge of his nose and cleared his throat. 'Kato come sit here with me. You are not behaving well.'

'Oh, poor Koji, are you jealous?' She pulled the corners of her mouth downward. 'Sad face. Come on, it's only a bit of fun.'

I shook my head in disbelief and huffed out a long, frustrated breath.

Koji banged his glass down and beer sloshed over the side, the bubbles sliding along the bar. He grabbed Kate's shoulder, swinging her round to face him. 'Kato, why are you doing this? Don't act like this, please.' Koji's smile was forced. 'It's not fair to Mari or me. You know I love you.'

Kate swayed to the music, a beer bottle in one hand and a cigarette in the other.

'You only love me because you can't have me. You're not my type, Koji. With your stupid baseball jacket,' Kate slurred her words. 'I always liked Ryu, but Mari got there first.'

I pressed my lips together to stop myself telling her not to be such a bitch. Anger prickled at my core; in some dark place I didn't go to often. No one said a word but we all looked at each other. Ryu shook his head and went to see to a customer who sat further along the bar. Hiroshi and I looked on as Koji got up and tried to put his arm around Kate. She wouldn't let him and shoved him away, laughing. But not in a jovial way.

'Hiroshi, do something,' I said but he shrugged.

'You make me humiliate myself,' Koji said. He slapped some yen on the bar and walked straight out of the door. Hiroshi followed.

'Ryuuu… I want more beer, Ryuuuuu,' Kate crooned.

I closed my eyes. The madness shifted up a gear. Nothing would stop it now.

'No more, Kato, you've had enough,' he said. 'Time to go home. I'll call a taxi for you.'

Glancing sideways at him, I knew what he was thinking when he smiled at me. The need to pull him inside me was strong, and I felt a tug, a pulse. I wanted to be with him, taste his mouth, his skin, one last time. But it wouldn't be right. And I couldn't leave Kate to go home alone in the state she was in.

'You're being a bitch, Kate,' I said.

'Don't reproach me, Mari.' She raised her hand like a traffic policeman stopping the flow of cars. 'Just don't – I feel bad now.'

'You should. And what the hell is all this with Ryu? Find someone else for the night. You don't usually have any trouble.'

'I just wanted to see if he was interested, to wind you up.' She gave a little laugh. 'You know I always liked him. I was glad when you split up.'

Just as I raised my hand to slap her, the music stopped and I thumped my fist on the bar instead, and glasses and bottles jumped and rattled. People turned to look. Time to leave. The evening was ruined anyway and I should go before Ryu closed the bar. I didn't want him to think I was waiting for him, so I asked him for the bill.

'It's on me. Look, wait a few minutes, okay? Send Kate home in a taxi and stay. I want to talk. Nothing else, just talk. Say goodbye properly.'

'I don't know how to say goodbye.' I picked up my cloth bag, picked at the embroidered logo. 'I can't. Come on, Kato, let's get you home.'

Ryu stood, holding the door open while Kate whispered something in his ear. He didn't acknowledge her, his eyes still on me. I turned my back to him and heard the door close. Kate stumbled towards her bike, and I waited while she fiddled with the strap of her handbag, tying it to the basket.

I raised my face to the cool drizzle of autumn rain. That was it, done. The thought of never seeing him again killed me. I pursed my lips, blew out a long breath. Maybe I could stay? One more night wouldn't hurt. I turned and looked at the door. It would be so easy to go back inside, go into his arms, into his bed. Instead, I got on my bike, and cycled to the road. Kate followed and we rode in silence for a couple of minutes.

'For God's sake,' I said, riding beside her along the wide, traffic free road. 'What got into you tonight? You don't behave like that Kate, you just don't.'

'You and Ryu are over so what's the problem? Don't expect me to apologise. I need a wee.'

'Apologise? You? Huh. Find a bush or something and I'll wait for you, but hurry up.'

'No, I'll be fine. It's raining, you go home.'

It wasn't right to leave her so I stopped on the corner, watching over my shoulder. I couldn't believe it when she turned her bike to face the opposite direction.

'Where are you going? There are bushes this way too, you know. Kate! If you go back to Ryu's, I'll never speak to you again.'

Kate laughed, a harsh bitchy sound that opened the door to my anger.

'And you can fuck off if you think you're coming to India with me. I hope you get hit by a truck!' I yelled as she rode back down the empty road, towards Ryu's.

I headed home then. "*Bitch, little bitch,*" became the mantra in time to my pedalling, faster and faster. Rage only powered me so far and by the time I turned the corner at the house with blue flowerpots, I was calmer. Anyway, Ryu would call a taxi for her and send her home.

I was soaked through and shivering with cold. When I leant the bike against the wall, I noticed the bodyguard wasn't there. Perhaps he was out looking for us; the *yakuza* must know we hadn't come straight home. I left the door open an inch. Once Kate was back, I'd bolt it shut. I left my wet jacket on the back of the kitchen chair, had a hot shower, put on my sleep shirt and yukata. I rummaged in the bottom of my holdall, looking for a pair of socks. I filled the kettle, made some jasmine tea, and looked at my watch. If Kate had gone back to Ryu's just to use the loo, she'd have been home by now.

Half an hour later and Kate still wasn't home. I threw up. Something coiled through me, an unleashed snake, shedding its skin and leaving behind a trail of rancid jealousy. I went to the kitchen for a glass of water, drank it down, refilled it and carried it back to my room. Through the open partition to Kate's room, I saw my reflection in the mirror.

'Fucking bitch,' I yelled and then screamed as I hurled the

glass. There was a loud crash, the sound ringing in my ears long after the shards of mirror and bits of broken glass finished raining down.

I tried to sleep, hoping that Kate would come back, but the early hours ticked forward, second by second. Maybe she'd passed out and was asleep on the blue sofa. Maybe he'd pushed her up against the cherrywood screen while he took off his jeans. My angry tears eventually gave way to sleep.

Chapter 28

BROKEN GLASS LITTERED Kate's bedroom floor. I picked up the largest pieces, slammed them on top of each other in a pile of jagged edges. A few shards of shattered mirror still clung to the frame, catching the mid-afternoon light, and throwing it onto the wall in sharp patches of brightness. My fractured reflection looked back at me, and I had to turn away. Had I really done that? Shame coloured my cheeks. With an inward breath, I stood straighter, my fingers curling into my palms. How could she? On my way to the kitchen, I side-stepped drops of blood that had soaked into the tatami matting. A crust of the same brown-red coated the outside edge of my instep. The sound of glass on glass scratched the air as I whacked the pieces of mirror on the work top. When they didn't break, I was tempted to bang them down again and again, until they did. But I'd already caused enough damage.

Standing at the kitchen sink, I slowly filled a bowl with water. Outside, my bike was propped against the neighbours' wall, but not Kate's. Bitch. With a wet cloth, I scrubbed at the blood on the tatami. Damson-dark stains that wouldn't come out. Horrible reminders of a horrible night. I tutted, scrubbed harder, but they wouldn't budge. Sitting back on my heels, I looked at my watch, calculating that if Kate wanted to get to work on time, she'd have to be home soon. Unzipping my holdall, I rummaged for a clean top and threw on my grey trousers. Not bothering with make-up, I grabbed my Levi's jacket off the back of the kitchen chair and left for work early. That way, I wouldn't have to see her. Screaming matches weren't my style, but I didn't trust myself. Halfway down the road, I slowed my pace. It would cause more problems if I didn't wait for the *yakuza* car to take me to the language school. We taught our first classes at midday, and there wasn't any point in arriving early. Of course, I could always jump the next train to Osaka and leave Kate here. That'd serve her right, but I couldn't leave her on her own. It wasn't safe. Our flights were booked for the day after pay day. Just five more days, and we'd be out of this nightmare.

I wanted to speak to Ryu, hear his explanation. I worked out what I wanted to say, practised out loud to get my tone right. Taking the narrow road that edged a rice field, I headed round the corner to the phone box. White, long-necked birds waded through the shallow water, barely disturbing the surface. I pulled open the phone box door with such force, the birds took flight in one synchronised movement. Ramming my phone card into the machine, my hand trembled. I punched in his number.

'*Moshi moshi.* Hello.'

'Ryu, it's me.' I struggled to keep my voice neutral 'Let me speak to Kate.'

'Kate? She's not here. Why -?'

'Has she gone straight to work?'

'I haven't seen her since you two left here last night – well, this morning.' His tone was distant, off-hand.

'She didn't go back to the bar?' My hand dragged at my hair, twisted it up off the back of my neck.

'No. Why would you think that?'

'She turned around and cycled back towards your place. I came home on my own.'

I opened the folding door to let in some air, pressed my forehead against the glass wall of the phone box.

'Mari?'

'If she's not with you...' Ryu was silent a moment too long. 'Ryu?'

'She probably went to see Koji.'

I closed my eyes and leant back against the glass, breathing out a half-laugh. 'I didn't think of that. She was horrible to him last night. I was so sure she was with you.'

'Jeez, how could you think that?'

'I know she was drunk, and the way she was all over you.'

'Doesn't mean I was interested. She'll have one hell of a hangover, I bet. Look, I'll call Koji later, make sure he's alright. Call me when you finish teaching, or after Shima closes.'

'I'll tell them she's sick. Can't risk them finding out that we're running away on Thursday, can I?'

'True. Call me after work, okay?'

Relief was sweet, but fleeting. I grabbed at it, held on to it, determined not to let it fade. Filling my mind with a silent monologue, I walked back to the apartment. Waiting for the car, I convinced myself that Kate had left her bike somewhere and got a taxi to Koji's. That was a good thing; it would've been a shame if she left here on bad terms with him. Maybe they'd finally got together. Kate would probably turn up at school later, as if nothing had happened. Knowing her, she wouldn't apologise either.

JUST AS MY class started, Ueno tapped on the glass wall of my classroom and I went out into the hall, pulling the door closed behind me. 'Where is Kate? Students are waiting.'

'She's sick. I'm not sure she'll be in this afternoon.' The fact I needed to cover for Kate annoyed me. I should've been honest, and said she was with Koji.

'Too much trouble. I don't know why I agreed to have you in my language school.' Ueno-san strode across the hall to his office.

The afternoon dragged, and I kept hoping that Kate would turn up. When my last one-to-one student left, I walked round to Kujaku. Kate always came home the morning after she'd been to a love hotel, and she wasn't that into Koji, so why hadn't she come to work? Maybe she was with Micky or Seiji or Kazu or any one of her lover-boy-students. Whichever way my silent monologue went, I had a horrible feeling. It creeped and crawled under my skin, twining around my bones, and slithered into my mind. Something bad had happened.

Yoshi-san greeted me at Kujaku's entrance. 'Your clothes are too casual again. Where is Kato?' His frown hid his eyes behind his 1970's glasses.

'I think she's sick. She's staying with a friend tonight.' It wasn't a complete lie.

He gave me a stern look and went to the telephone. I sat with the Filipinas and told them a pared-down version of what had happened the night before. Embarrassed by my temper, I didn't mention the mirror.

Later, I sat at the bar in a half-empty Shima. I turned every time the door opened, hoping it was Kate. After an hour, Mama gave me a glass of brandy and soda, and my stomach turned at the smell. I'd drunk twice my body weight in brandy in the six months I'd been in Hitano, had too many hangovers. But it was more than that. Anxiety made me nauseous, made my pulse race and my head feel heavy.

'Mama, I don't feel well. Can I go home?'

'Yes. You don't look good today. Go home, rest. I'll arrange the car to collect you now.'

Back home, I opened the door into the dark kitchen, slipped off my shoes, noticing that Kate's weren't there. Everything was the same: nothing had moved since I'd left earlier. The few shards of glass left in the mirror frame gave a distorted reflection of the yellow streetlight and I pulled the curtains closed. *She's with Koji*, I told myself, *she has to be with Koji.*

The bodyguard sat in his car outside the apartment and I waved on my way to the phone box. The light came on inside when I opened the folding door, shining on my phone-card that was decorated with a photo of a geisha, her bloody red mouth sinister and macabre in her white face. I called Ryu. The phone rang and rang and I tapped my foot on the concrete floor, kicking aside the cigarette stubs with my toe. I pushed open the folding glass door and the light went out as the fresh air came in.

'Come on, come on.'

He answered after the eighth ring. 'I only managed to get hold of Koji an hour ago. He's been doing a stock inventory at his warehouse and worked late. He's still upset. It took him ages to stop babbling so I could ask him. Mari, Koji hasn't seen Kate since last night either.'

The thought I'd blocked with my mental chatter, found its way out of my mouth. 'They've got her, haven't they? That *yakuza* boss she offended got his goons to abduct her. Like a punishment or something.'

'That crossed my mind too. Could be she's with one of her students. Who was that one she hung out with most?'

'Mickey. But never for more than one night at a time. And she always comes home the next morning.'

'What about her friend Jack? Could be she went to Tokyo.'

'I don't think she's gone there. She's left all her stuff and there are no trains in the middle of the night, Ryu.' My voice cracked with tiredness. 'The Nagasaki *yakuza* have her.'

Ryu was silent at his end of the phone. I pressed my fingers against my lips breathing deeply, trying to stay calm.

'Mari don't think the worst. I'll come and get you now. You should stay with me tonight.'

'Yes. No, no... I need to stay here in case she comes back. And anyway, that'd just cause more hassle.'

'Listen, try and rest. Koji and I will pick you up in the morning. We'll call Jack and if she's not in Tokyo, we'll go look for her, okay? We'll drive around; we might see her somewhere. She's probably really embarrassed about the other night and just hanging out with a guy somewhere'.

'You're right. Okay, see you in the morning.'

Maybe Kate had checked into a hotel to sleep off her hangover. That was feasible. And maybe she was aware of what a bitch she'd been and couldn't face me. But Tokyo? Still, it was worth a try and I couldn't wait until morning.

I ran back to the apartment and found Kate's red address book on her little cabinet. Brushing tiny bits of glass off it, I flipped through it. There weren't many numbers in it: Koji's, Ryu's as well as the school's and a few other names and addresses. Mickey's number was there too. I opened the 'W' section, for Woodman. Strange that there wasn't anything under Kate's last name, but then I could talk. I hadn't spoken to my family in five years and didn't even have an address book. Had Kate ever mentioned Jack's last name? Starting at the front, I went through the address book, letter by letter, page by page. There it was. Jack O'Brien.

Back at the phone box, I punched in the number. It rang out so I tried again. Still no answer but, at two-thirty on a Sunday morning, he was probably sleeping or maybe he hadn't gone home. Saturday nights in Tokyo probably finished later than they did in small town Hitano.

I rang Mickey's number and a sleepy-voiced woman answered. Minutes passed and I heard soft noises of movement coming from the other end. When I eventually spoke to Mickey, he had nothing to tell me. He hadn't seen Kate for weeks, except at his English class.

Pulling my Levi's jacket closed, I walked back to the apartment. Ryu was right. We'd find her. Or she'd waltz through the door in the morning, bringing cans of iced coffee, and rice buns.

SLEEP DIDN'T COME and I veered from wakefulness to half-dreams of dragons and earthquakes. By dawn, I knew. The clarity that came with gut-churning guilt meant that Kate wouldn't be coming home. And just like when my sister died, it was my fault. I didn't want to accept what my instinct was telling me, so I didn't let the feeling have any space to become a thought. Instead, I replaced it with a mantra. *We'll look for Kate. We'll find her.*

The silence was so loud in the apartment, it made my skin prickle. While the kettle boiled, I played the mix tape that Ryu had given me months ago. '*Yes, my Love*' caught my heart as I moved the cassette player into my bedroom and put it on the floor. I slipped on my shoes, took a plastic bag into Kate's room, and picked up the remaining pieces of broken mirror, then swept the littlest pieces, like dull uncut diamonds, into the dustpan. A vague whiff of stale smoke made me open the balcony door a couple of inches. Sitting on Kate's futon, I shook tiny pieces of diamond-glass off the blue elephant and picked up the guidebook. I opened it at a page with the top corner folded down. Thailand. Kate had put asterisks next to descriptions of golden palaces, ruined temples, and remote island beaches. Carrying the book with me into the kitchen, I drank my cooling coffee, watching through the window as the wind blew dust and autumn leaves down the road.

The water gurgled from the tap as I rinsed my mug and my shaky body reminded me that I hadn't eaten since Friday evening. I'd get something later, I felt too sick to eat anyway. The boys turned up in Ryu's car just after eight. Koji left the passenger door open for me and got into the back. Ryu touched my hand gently, briefly, and drove around the corner to the phone box. I turned to Koji, his face drawn and paler than usual. By the redness around his eyes, I guessed he hadn't slept either.

'I'm very worried. I'm sorry I was angry,' he said.

'It's not your fault. Let me call Jack. When we know she's okay, we can all go for breakfast.' My voice sounded forced, too light and cheerful as I got out of the car. I prayed that Jack would be at home and picked up the receiver.

'*Moshi Moshi, Jack desu.*'

'Jack, hi. This is Mari. Kate's friend.'

'Hi, nice to speak to you again.'

'Is she there with you by any chance?' I held my breath, waiting for him to answer, although I already knew what he'd say.

'But you guys are off to Singapore on Thursday, aren't you?'

'Look, she hasn't been home for two nights and no one knows where she is. None of us have seen her since the early hours yesterday.'

'Jesus Christ. I've not heard from her since she told me about the run in with the *yakuza* boss. I told her to get out of there quickly, but she wouldn't listen. She said something about waiting for pay day. Shit.'

'Jack, I'm scared. I think they've sent her to Nagasaki.' My legs felt rubbery and I held onto the door.

'Or worse. Jesus, I told her to apologise.'

'We all did. I should've done it on her behalf. I feel like a right bitch now.'

'Probably wouldn't have cut it. Look, go to the police. I doubt they'll be able to do much, but they should start looking for her. I don't know how long they wait before she can be classed as an officially missing person.'

The line crackled.

'You there, Mari?'

'I just really hoped she was with you.'

'Let me know what happens. Ring me any time. I'll leave the Ansaphone on. Watch yourself, Mari.'

My hand stayed on the receiver for a moment after I placed it back in the cradle, the last of my hopes draining away down the telephone line and into a dark abyss somewhere. What I feared was real: the *yakuza* had Kate. I walked back to the car on legs that weren't mine. Both men looked at me expectantly.

'Hasn't heard from her since the *wakagashira* issue. The only other thing I can think of ...' I said, 'is that maybe she didn't want to come home and she's staying in a hotel. She has her passport and plenty of cash on her.'

We drove around Hitano's few hotels, some near the station and some on the road to the new town, just before the bridge. We asked at the reception desks if they had any European guests and Koji showed them Kate's photo. The answer was always 'no.' I left a written message at every desk, just in case. After a few hours, we parked up at the station car park.

'Should we try the love hotels?' I said.

'They wouldn't tell you, even if she was there,' said Ryu.

'Privacy.'

By mid-morning we'd exhausted most of the possibilities in the old town. Ryu yanked me out of the way of a motorbike pulling a trailer full of empty calor gas canisters. Turning into the pedestrianised streets, we headed towards the steps. Masta washed down the cobbles outside his yakitori, getting ready for opening time, with his blue trousers tucked into pale grey rubber boots. His broom swept over a decorated man-hole cover. He nodded as he threw a bucket of water into the street.

'*Ohayo gozaimas*,' I said. Good morning.

'Masta, have you seen Kato? Nobody's seen her since Friday night,' said Ryu. 'We're looking everywhere for her.'

'No, really? I'm sorry to hear this. I'll ask all my customers if they have seen her. I'll ask everybody in the neighbourhood. Leave that to me, you go and look elsewhere. Come back later.' He leant his broom against the ceramic raccoon and rushed off to spread the word. His bandy legs were endearing somehow and I smiled. I could've hugged him. It dawned on me that I'd only ever seen the top half of him, behind his counter.

RYU DROVE ACROSS the bridge over the river. Down in the wide green estuary, narrow, reedy islands slowed the flow of the river as it spilled into the Sea of Japan. The business district was empty. Being a Sunday, the office buildings and the small shops and restaurants were closed. The streets were sleepy and the air still and quiet with Sunday's hush. The green and white sign of the Holiday Inn caught Koji's eye, and we checked with reception, but Kate wasn't there.

Next, we took the coast road towards the port. Cargo ships dotted the horizon, a line of steel punctuation between the green sea and grey sky. I opened the window and let in the sea-air, the shrill sound of gulls piercing my ear drums. The volcanic coastline, rugged and angular with sharp, black rocks, should have been beautiful; a photographer's dream. But that day, it looked ugly, hostile even. Menacing waves crashed against the concrete tide barriers, driven by something other than the wind. A fishing boat rocked side to side, heading out to sea, red and green lights flashing on top of its pendulum mast. Nausea swamped me and I closed my eyes. Kate wouldn't be here. We were clutching at straws.

The terminal thronged with passengers disembarking a ferry from Korea that must have just come in. The stevedores stared, and I was glad Ryu and Koji walked either side of me. The clerk in the ticket office asked her colleagues, even used her walkie-talkie to speak to someone onboard the ferry. But of course, no one had seen Kate.

Back in town, we asked at the sushi restaurants, the cosmetic shop, the café in the department store, everywhere we could think of. As each person shook their head and the day wore on, the heaviness of dread descended on me. What if the *wakagashira* had hurt Kate? I convinced myself I was being over-dramatic, but now the feeling had grown into a thought. If the thought was given too much room, it might grow into the truth.

Lastly, we tried the teahouse in the park. As I got out of the car, I had to put both hands on the door to steady myself.

An elderly couple carrying plastic shopping bags, stopped, and stared. Sweat stuck my shirt to my back. My empty stomach wanted to rid itself of nothing and I retched, spitting bitter bile onto the grass at the edge of the carpark. Ryu put his arms round me and I let him hold me. His hand held my head to his shoulder. I felt enfolded, protected. The lady came and gave me a packet of tissues, patting my hand. She said something to Ryu and he smiled, thanking her for her kindness. I sat sideways in the passenger seat for a while, my feet on the ground.

'It's okay, we'll find her.' Ryu crouched down, his face level with mine.

'I'm scared,' I said, shivering so much that my teeth chattered.

Ryu took off his green sweatshirt and gave it to me. He pressed his lips together and a tiny muscle flexed in his jaw as he looked across the park.

'I think we should go to the police now,' Koji said.

Chapter 29

WE DROVE BACK into town, my eyes darting left and right, hoping I'd spot Kate's blonde head somewhere. Ryu parked his car near the koban.

'We should rest up for a while, have something to eat first. We need to decide what to say to the police about the *yakuza*. It might be tricky. It might take a long time in there.' He nodded towards the koban. 'Or they might send us to the main police station in Kitakyushu.'

Although I wanted to keep looking for Kate, I needed to sit down and at least drink something. Hunger had receded hours ago but my stomach needed something to settle it. Inari rolls would do.

Masta didn't beat the drum as we walked into the yakitori.

'The whole town is talking,' he said. 'Everyone knows a gaijin girl is missing, but no one has seen Kato. I will keep asking and let you know if I hear anything.'

He took our order and the smell of sizzling meat filled the room. I tried to eat a little rice. Sitting either side of me at the counter, the boys spoke across me, quietly discussing what to tell the police.

'We'll tell them everything,' I said. I sipped cola, the ice tinkling in the glass.

'We can't say too much about the *wakagashira*,' said Ryu. 'Or about Nagasaki. Better we don't mention that. Just say that she was drunk and didn't come home.'

'She is English, that will be enough to make them look,' said Koji.

'Are you seriously telling me that we can't mention the *yakuza* in all this?' I slammed my chopsticks on the counter. My shoulders dropped. 'Is it because they might come after you if you report it? Then I'll do it. You don't have to put yourselves at risk.' I stood and walked to the door.

Junichi walked in with the customary three beats of the drum and a loud cry of '*Irashaimasse!*'

'Hey Mari, where you off to?'

'The koban, to report Kate missing.'

'No need, Mari. Have a seat,' he smiled. 'I've got news.'

I returned to my stool, waiting to hear what he'd say.

He dragged up a stool and squeezed in between Ryu and me. I shifted a little to make room for him. The v-neck of his sleeveless jumper was bobbled a little where the collar of his checked shirt overlapped.

'How is my niece, Ryu?' said Junichi. 'Don't look so worried. I have good news. Kate's in Kitakyushu. I saw her yesterday with a guy, in a department store downtown. Then again later, in a café. She's just gone off to spend some time with her boyfriend, before she leaves for Nagasaki, that's all. She'll come back when she's ready.'

'Which boyfriend?' I said. 'She doesn't have one.'

'Sorry, Koji, I know you don't want to hear this. Everyone knows she had lots of boyfriends. Maybe she didn't tell you everything, Mari. Some people like to keep private things private,' Junichi glanced at Ryu with hard eyes.

'Did you recognise the man?' I said. Out of the corner of my eye, I watched Koji's mouth crease in defeat.

Ryu frowned. 'That's not important. Was it definitely her, Junichi-san? Are you sure?'

'There's not exactly lots of Europeans 'round here, you know. Yep, it was her. Blonde hair, small nose. I didn't recognise the guy she was with, though.'

'But he might have been *yakuza*. Didn't you speak to her? I asked.

'*Yakuza* don't take girls shopping, Mari. I waved and she waved back. She wasn't close enough to speak to, but she mouthed *hi how are you* or something. I didn't interrupt them in the café, they looked really into each other.'

'Really? So, she seemed happy to be with this guy? Not like she was forced to be there or something?'

'She was looking through her shopping bags and cuddling into him.'

'I'll kill her!' I clenched my fists. 'Selfish little… She must realise we're all worried.'

'But she is fine. And that is good news,' said Koji.

'It is, and I'm glad she's okay,' I said. 'But how could she be so thoughtless?' Relief battled with indignation. 'Especially after the run-in with the *wakagashira*. But who's the boyfriend?'

Ryu closed his eyes and breathed out a long sigh, tension visibly draining from his shoulders. I reached to touch his hand but drew back. With Junichi there, I didn't dare.

The boys dropped me home just as the dark sky unburdened itself of its heavy load. Fat raindrops poured down, and Ryu slapped on the windscreen wipers. Lightning flashed, slashing at the sky, bleaching the colour from the lead-grey clouds. Thunder roared, echoes of echoes rolling off the mountains, bouncing back and forth. I ran the short distance from the car and pulled my key from the depths of my bag. An orange, white and gold origami fish perched on the washing machine, its mouth wide open, and its tail bent as if swimming upstream. Shaking off the rain, I put the fish in my cupboard with the others. Crazy Dog was usually right with his prophecy. But what was he telling me this time?

Junichi wasn't right. I'd know if Kate had a new squeeze; she'd have told me. She always told me. Leaning against the door, I froze for a moment. How had Junichi known we were being sent to Nagasaki? Perhaps Ryu had told him.

Opening the guidebook, I read about Goan beaches and Laos Buddhist temples, which filled my dreams with lazy, waveless seas of lapis-blue, and golden spires that reached up into sunny skies.

Chapter 30

KATE STILL DIDN'T come home.

Just before the car came to take me to school the next morning, I phoned Jack, leaving a message just to tell him that she'd been seen in Kitakyushu.

My students were left to fend for themselves during my classes; I just couldn't concentrate. After my first class finished, I went to the market to buy some vegetables. There was a block of curry sauce in the fridge. It was easy enough to break off a few squares and dissolve them in hot water to make a thick sauce. If I made a big pot of vegetable curry, there'd be enough for a few days. And for Kate whenever she got home. Hope bred on hope, but it was starved with denial.

'Is she back?' Melody joined me at a tomato stall.

'Junichi said he saw her in Kitakyushu on Saturday afternoon with some guy. He could be wrong, though. I know she had a few little romances, but I can't figure out who it is. Do you know who it could be?'

'With Kate, who knows. She went to a love hotel with one of the Kujaku customers a few times, when you were with Ryu,' said Melody. 'You know the one, very handsome, wears a heavy bracelet.'

That was news. 'He's married. God, what was she thinking? Anyone else I don't know about?' I picked a few ripe red tomatoes from the stall, waited for them to be weighed and bagged. A gust of wind threw dust into the air. I turned my head, my hand over my eyes for a second as a plastic bag floated and spun in the air, then dropped, deflated.

'Akira, he comes into Shima. You know him, he's always in a leather jacket.'

'Really? So, Junichi's right. She obviously didn't tell me everything. I'm going to the police anyway. She's been gone for days. That's not like her and with all the *yakuza* shit...'

'You're leaving soon. She'll be back before then.' Melody's hair was caught by the wind and flew around her head in a halo of light brown. 'Don't make trouble, Mari. She's with some guy, that's all.'

Was I over-reacting? My imagination was always colourful, but to mobilise a police force to look for Kate if she was just with a guy was extreme. Maybe Melody was right. I damped down the fear, like coals of a dying fire, sealing it under a new layer of optimism. It wouldn't be long until Kate was opening the door to our apartment, laden with shopping bags. She'd be full of tales of her new lover and excuses as to why she hadn't been in touch, oblivious to the worry she'd caused. And there'd be no apology.

I went to the phone box around the corner and rang the Consulate. Again, no answer. Half an hour later, I tried again. Still no answer. This wasn't something I could do alone and I needed some help.

UENO LOOKED UP from the papers he was marking as I tapped on his door. His desk dominated the small office and he was lost among the textbooks piled all around him. Closing the door behind me, I moved towards his desk and pulled out the chair. The cream walls were as bland as the rest of the school. The red telephone on his desk gave a splash of colour, like a drop of blood.

I sat, my back to the door, and explained the situation.

'I hear she's in Kitakyushu. I'm sure she'll return soon,' said Ueno-san. His matter-of-fact reaction surprised me. Every tick of the wall clock sounded excessively loud in the otherwise silent room. 'Pay day is on Thursday. She'll come back then. Today is only Tuesday. Let's not worry today.' He rose from his desk and crossed the room to open the door, showing me out. He cleared his throat.

'I'm not leaving. Can you call Sayuri and Mr Ohayo? Ask them to come here so that we can decide what to do.'

'It's not necessary. Miss Kate will come for pay day, guaranteed.'

He held the door open but I didn't get up, twisting instead on the chair to face him.

'You have to call them, don't you understand? Kate is missing. We must do something. Please.'

Ueno-san walked out of his office leaving me there. I took Ohayo's business card out of my wallet. Leaning across the desk, I picked up the phone and dialled Onishi Imports number.

'Sayuri? It's Mari. I need to see you.'

'Come to office, I am here.'

The taxi ride to the Onishi office on the other side of the river felt longer than it should be. Sayuri greeted me at the entrance to the building, its dark tinted windows hiding God knows what. With an impassive face, she opened the door to an office on the ground floor. We sat on the same side of a cheap veneer desk with an inlay of dark green leatherette around the edges. I recounted the story, explaining that Kate had been taken by Nagasaki *yakuza*.

'I thought it best to speak to the *yak*– to Mr Ohayo first and see what he thinks we can do to bring Kate back safely.'

'We know Kato is missing. But you must not go to police. That will make very big problem for many people. We will help you. But don't go to the police.'

'Why can't I go to the police?'

'You have only student visa, not possible to work. You go to prison. Your Filipina friends too, not possible to work. They also go to prison. Their families pay back ticket money. Then they go home with nothing and never back again to Japan. No police. We will help you.'

I stretched my arms forward along the desk and laid my head down. 'Prison? I don't care, I need the police, Sayuri. I need the police to find Kate.'

'Wait here.' She left the room, closing the door softly behind her.

Thoughts gathered in my head. Like fans at a football match, each one shouted, yelled over the others, clamouring for my attention. Maybe Kate was in a dark room, tied to a chair and left alone for the last three days as punishment for offending the *wakagashira*. Or had she been forced into working at some seedy club in Nagasaki? That didn't make sense, we were supposed to go together. I paced around the office for a while, then stood at the window. The sun broke through silver-grey clouds. Blue sky pushed them aside and shadows scuttered across the carpark. If Kate was in a good place in Nagasaki, willing or not, she would have called Koji, Ryu, or even the school. She would have called if she could have. So, maybe she couldn't. Maybe they wouldn't let her. I reeled full circle back to Kate being tied to that chair. My thumbs pressed into my temples, then I ran my hands down the back of my head and leaned back to look at the ceiling. A third possibility was looming in the back of my mind. Its dark mass started pushing forward, gaining ground and strength. I was feeling it so I had to think it. What if? No. Surely, they wouldn't have killed her?

About an hour later, Ohayo and Sayuri came into the office. I jumped up from the chair and bowed.

Ohayo put up his hand to tell me not to speak. 'Leave things to us,' he said, in English. 'We will speak to police; we have good relationship with them. You do nothing. We learn anything, we tell you. For now, you stay home. No school anymore. No working anymore. Sunday, you go Nagasaki.'

'I'm not going anywhere, not until Kate's back home. And... wait, so if you're going to the police then it means your *wakagashira* doesn't have her?'

'No questions,' he said and he left the room.

Sayuri touched my arm. 'I am sorry.'

Chapter 31

THE TAXI DRIVER had to tell me three times that I was home. In a daze, I paid him and got out of the car. I unlocked the door to the apartment. My head was all over the place as I tried to think between the words and work out what Ohayo meant; what it all meant.

Was I reading too much into everything? Maybe Kate really had just gone off somewhere for a few days. The alternative was too awful to accept. I stood in the doorway between our rooms. Bottles of bright nail varnish crowded on one side of the bedside cabinet, holding down her flight ticket to Singapore like mini paperweights. Her blue elephant sat propped against the pillow, its trunk heralding my arrival. I looked through the wardrobes to see if there was anything that might help. A note, a letter, anything. But there wasn't. Tucked under a pile of clothes, I found a torn photo of Ryu. I would have been in the other half, the missing half, but I couldn't think about being annoyed now. I rummaged through her backpack. Again, I found nothing, no clue as to who the guy was. I sat back on the floor, ran my hands over my face.

'Kate. Where are you, Kate?' I said out loud.

If Nagasaki had her, Ohayo had to get her back. *Yakuza* versus *yakuza*. How would that happen? Would this spark another turf war? Maybe it was already part of one. I was out of my depth, swimming upstream, like the origami fish. My head ached; my throat ached. Wiping my eyes, I tried to think.

Ohayo must have already sold my contract if I was going to Nagasaki on Sunday. Would he really make me go while Kate was missing? Could he be so cruel? Probably yes, I knew what he'd done to Cherry. Perhaps Kate was in Nagasaki already? But that didn't seem likely, otherwise he would have said. Ohayo was going to talk to the police, that was a good thing. At least they'd do something. At least now I'd set the ball rolling. I wouldn't go to Nagasaki. They'd have to drag me, kicking and screaming. Maybe that happened to Kate. I shook my head, tried to think clearly. Instant miso-soup warmed me as I sat at the kitchen table, listening to the far-off sound of honking geese, flying south. That's where we should be heading. Oh, God.

All I could do now was wait. Wait and see what the police would say to Ohayo. Then I'd go to the British Consular office in the morning. Exhaustion made my vision blurry. I needed to sleep. Kate's black yukata, a pattern of pink cherry blossoms scattered on it, lay folded on top of a pile of clean washing on the kitchen table. I undressed and threaded my arms through the wide sleeves, wrapped it around me and lay on my futon. After a few deep breaths, I closed my eyes.

I woke, suddenly alert. Turning on my side, I looked at my watch. Three-twenty p.m. And then I felt it. A rush of something, a brush of air as subtle as the breeze from a butterfly's wing. A momentary shift in the light, as if the sun had shuddered, and I knew. The light had gone out of Kate's eyes in that moment. I knew.

For a long time, I lay still, shocked into numbness. It was too late. I'd left it too late.

Hours passed and I rose as the late afternoon sun shone through my window. Was the feeling a memory, an echo from five years before, when I'd known the moment my sister died?

Dressing, I convinced myself that Kate wasn't dead. It wasn't real, I must've dreamt it. I went to the phone box to call Ryu, told him what Ueno had said and about the conversation with Ohayo.

'That's not good. I think they want you out of the way. Sending you to Nagasaki makes me think they know where she is,' he said.

'I'm going to the British Consulate in Fukuoka. I'll report her missing and then Nagasaki will have to send her back. It might take a few days, I suppose, but maybe we can still get our flight out of here.'

'I'll come by tomorrow morning and bring you to the Consulate in Fukuoka. Are you okay on your own?'

'It's awful.'

'I'll close early and come to you. You shouldn't be alone. I'll bring food, I bet you haven't eaten.'

I walked back to the apartment and got the bike I'd stolen on Friday night. Freewheeling down the hill to the station, I let the wind numb my face. Once the bike was returned to where I'd taken it from, I went to the koban.

Taking a deep breath, I pushed the door open. Inside, a uniformed officer was talking to an older, wiry man in a herringbone jacket. They both looked up at me from where they sat behind the front desk.

'My friend is missing,' I said, my chin wobbling. 'Please find her.'

The two men glanced at each other. The older man said something I couldn't hear and stood up. Standing now, the officer gave a short, sharp bow and the older man moved towards the door. With one hand ready to pull the door open, he stood for a moment.

'Don't forget', he said and the officer bowed.

The door swung shut behind me and I tapped my fingers on the front desk while I gave the officer Kate's full name, date of birth, and description. The officer wrote it all down on a notepad, and when I mentioned the incident with the *wakagashira*, he didn't miss a beat.

I WALKED HOME, needing the stretch out, to think. If Kate came home now, it wouldn't matter. If she didn't and I was right about the *wakagashira*, then at least now the police would help. There was relief in that, relief that at least now something would be done.

CRAZY DOG HAD left a black and white paper crane, its wings folded open, ready for flight. I half-walked, half-ran to his house. He looked up at me from where sat on his bench, tying string around the stalks of ripe persimmons. Some already hung from the edge of the roof, drying in the sun. His lopsided smile was tentative, his eyes wary. The dog sat beside his feet and it got up to greet me before flopping down again. Crazy Dog shifted along the bench, making space for me to sit beside him.

'Do you know what happened to her?'

'Gone away.' His face looked older, sadder.

'Where?'

He took something out of his pocket and held out his hand. I took it from him. A pale pink and white origami sakura, each petal of the cherry blossom's folds and creases perfectly symmetrical, stunning in its simplicity. Standing to leave, I patted his shoulder. The only thing I could do now was to wait for the police to find her.

RYU CAME AS he had promised. He knocked on the door and I rushed to open it. He slipped off his deck shoes and reached for me. It was wrong, but I couldn't stop, I needed him. I led him across the kitchen and up the step to my room, pulled the curtains closed. We stood facing each other. He undid the sash of my yukata and moved the fabric away from my body, breathing out sharply as he looked down at me. His hands ran down my back and I felt heat rise in my blood. My eyes met Ryu's.

'You okay? Mari? Don't…'

I nodded and kissed his lips, tasting my tears.

The sex was slow and gentle. My cries of pleasure turned to sobs as I wept for Kate. For us all.

Chapter 32

'It's not something we deal with here,' said Mr Suzuki.

'But you're the British Consulate and she's a British subject,' I said as I glanced around the small room that served as an office.

It was no more than a chunky wooden desk, a telephone, and a grey metal filing cabinet. Three metal-legged chairs lined the wall, their red plastic seats worn and shiny. I'd expected a dignified English gentleman in a Saville Row suit, all cut-glass accent and military bearing. What I got was Mr Suzuki. His belly strained against the buttons of his pale blue shirt and his jacket sleeves were an inch too short. On the plus side, there were no tattoos.

I sat in the chair opposite him and tried to keep my hands still while I told him the whole story. *Keep to the facts*, I said to myself. *Don't get emotional*.

'I'm the Honorary Consul, and this is a Consular office. I deal mainly with trade and business matters. I'm not sure, but for something like this, you should go to the local police, get the report and take it to the British Consulate in Osaka.' He tapped his pen on the desk. 'It's lucky you came this morning, I'm only in this office twice a week.'

'I've been calling, but there's no Ansafone. Look, I can get the report,' I turned to Ryu who sat the side of the room. He nodded, urging me to continue. 'Can I fax it through? It's a long journey up there.'

'I haven't dealt with anything like this before. Let me

double-check with Osaka.'

He picked up his telephone and dialled a number. He spoke in Japanese. Glancing at me, he switched to English and explained the situation to whoever was at the other end of the phone.

'They're checking,' he said to me. A few minutes of silence followed. 'Really? Alright, thank you. Yes, I think so.' He sat up straighter in his high-backed leather chair and put his hands together on the desk, linking his fingers. 'The local police would automatically send the report through. But I'm sorry, no report has come through from Hitano. When did you say you reported Miss Woodman missing?'

'Yesterday.' I felt ridiculous. I leant forward with my elbows on my knees, resting my forehead on the heel of my hand. 'The school wouldn't help, and I didn't trust Mr Ohayo when he said he'd speak to the police.'

'The Consulate has received no notification. Did Mr Ohayo have Miss Woodman's passport number and home address? He'd have needed those to make an official report.'

I shook my head. My eyes swam and I twisted my hair. 'The police officer didn't ask me for those either.'

'It doesn't sound good, Miss Randall, I have to say.'

'No.' I looked up at the framed picture of Queen Elizabeth II in a blue velvet cape, a little crown on her dark head. 'What do I do now? To find Kate, I mean?' My hands shook as I covered my mouth, trying not to cry.

'Start by going back to Hitano and making another report.'

Ryu stood next to me, his hand on my shoulder. He spoke to Mr Suzuki in polite, respectful Japanese.

'Please, Suzuki-san, I request that you take as much information as you can and forward it to Osaka on our behalf. Miss Woodman has been missing now for four days. We need help, official help, because of the *yakuza*. You can see how distressed this lady is. I don't think we have much time to wait and protocol will delay things further. I am asking, will you help us?'

He bowed. I'd never seen him do that before. Mr Suzuki

pulled out a large manila folder from the filing cabinet. He searched through it and found a form.

'I can use this to take some details. Can you phone Osaka later with her passport number, home address?'

WE LEFT THE building and walked in silence towards the carpark. An ambulance drove past, the lights flashed and the siren wailed. The sound reverberated in my skull, like a drill through bone.

There was no relief in the fact that Kate was now officially a missing person. I felt sick, lightheaded. Thought led to thought. There was something I didn't want to admit to, didn't want to voice, but it bubbled under the surface, ready to blow. I bent double in the street, winded. My cloth bag dropped to the pavement. Ryu put his hand on my back, between my shoulder blades.

'It's all my fault. Whatever has happened to her, it's all my fault. I shouldn't have left her on the road that night,' I said. 'I should have apologised for her.'

Groaning, I stood upright and took two paces forward, stopped, turned, and walked back the way we'd come. Ryu stood still, watching as I stopped again, my hands curling into fists. I ran the few steps back to him and thumped him on the chest. A businessman carrying a leather briefcase stopped for a second, and then walked on.

'Because of you. I left her on the road because I was angry with her.' I thumped him with two fists. He grabbed my arms and pulled me close. 'Because of you!'

People passed us. Some openly stared, some obviously looking the other way. Ryu held me to him as silent sobs made my body shudder. He said nothing. Nothing to make me think that I was wrong, and his silence was heavy and condemning.

THE DRIVE HOME was tortured by silence. Eventually, Ryu glanced at me, almost smiling.

'At least now we have reported it properly. The officials can handle it now. If the *yakuza* have got her, then they were watching and waiting for an opportunity. Maybe they planned to take you both that night. Who knows? And if something happened to you, my Mari, I couldn't bear it.'

'But they wouldn't take me as well, would they? I didn't offend anyone.'

He pressed a switch on the dashboard and square headlights rose out of the bonnet, casting their beams into the murky dusk.

'It'll be okay, you'll see. The *yakuza* will send her back.'

Rows of red tail lights blinked as the road curved round the side of a mountain ahead. Traffic moved slowly. My eyes were heavy. Rain swept across the windscreen, the wipers' rhythm a half-beat out of time with a song on the radio.

It was dark when I woke.

'You okay?' said Ryu. 'Tomorrow's Thursday. What'll you do?'

'I can't leave until they find her. It's a week until they send me to Nagasaki.' I shifted in the seat and half-turned to look at him. 'Yesterday afternoon, I had a… dream that she died at exactly three twenty. It was so real. It was like I felt her soul leave.'

'Yesterday? Really? Did you see where, or how she died?'

'No, I just know it was then.'

'Yesterday. It can't be.' He tutted and glanced at me, the muscle in his jaw flexing. 'Don't think the worst, Mari. We must keep hoping.' He turned the car into the parking area at the front of my apartment. The engine purred. 'I'm sorry, but I have to leave you. My fiancée and her family arrive this evening. They'll be staying with my parents for a few days. We have things to discuss.'

He tried to take my hand, but I moved it away.

'Wedding plans? How nice. Well, thanks for your help today.'

I got out of the car and slammed the door, not looking back. He waited until I was indoors before he backed the car out onto the street. Standing at the kitchen window, my chin wobbled as I watched him drive away.

Chapter 33

THE NIGHT DRAGGED and sleep was an elusive elixir, just out of my reach. I gave up, and went through Kate's rucksack again, pulling out clothing and flinging it, not caring where it landed amongst the tiny bits of mirror and diamond-glass that still glittered on the carpet. Not knowing what I was looking for, I hoped that maybe I'd missed something last time. Opening Kate's wardrobe, I found the pile of letters from her family. None of them had a sender's address. It was blurry, but *'SW1'* sat in the red circle of the Post Office stamp on the envelope. Nothing had her passport number on it, but I knew Sayuri would have those details. I'd ask her. Maybe the Consulate in Osaka would have found something out by the time I rang them in the morning. Picking up the small blue elephant, I held it to my face and breathed in the smell of Kate's perfume.

I took my Tarot cards from the cupboard and shuffled them. 'Where are you, Kate?'

Blank. The three cards I'd pulled out didn't make any sense. I felt nothing; saw nothing. Scooping the cards back into a pile, I put them behind my bento box, knocking over the little origami cat.

It was light before I crawled onto my futon and slept. But not for long. I woke to the sound of knocking on the door. Tying the sash of my yukata, I glanced out of the kitchen window on my way to the front door. Sayuri stood in the street, talking to a policeman as his two-way radio crackled and trilled. Two dark cars pulled up behind the police car.

There were too many people for it to be good news.

Chapter 34

'YOU FOUND HER? Where is she?' I said. It didn't sound like my voice. My breathing sounded too loud; everything sounded too loud. 'Is she okay?'

A silver-haired detective in a light grey suit chewed gum. I hated the wet, slappy noise it made.

'I'm Superintendent Takeda of Kitakyushu Police, Fukuoka Prefecture,' he said in Japanese as he flashed his badge. 'This is my colleague, Detective Saito.' The younger man gave a small sharp bow. 'They found her in a rice field's irrigation ditch. About twenty-seven kilometres outside town, next to the by-pass to Kitakyushu,' he said. 'I'm sorry you lost your friend.'

His colleague moved around the apartment, scribbling in a hard-backed notebook. I stood in the kitchen and looked down at the pattern on my yukata, noticed the gold edge on some of the flowers. Everything went grainy. There was something I wanted to ask, but my mind blanked. My mouth was too dry for speech, my tongue too thick. I looked at Superintendent Takeda. *I'm sorry you lost your friend*. I shook my head as the truth sunk in.

'No,' I said. 'No...' My legs wouldn't support me and I slumped onto the kitchen chair. Someone pushed a glass of water into my hand. Time slowed down, giving everything a heavy, surreal quality.

'Mari, you need to dress. You must show them your passport.' The voice seemed to come from Sayuri. I heard her words, but my brain was slow to register them. A hand under my elbow helped me stand and led me to my room. Someone moved the kitchen table and the partition door closed behind me. My hands trembled as I pulled on my grey trousers and Ryu's green sweatshirt and tied back my hair. Digging in the bottom of my bag, I found my passport and stood in the middle of the room. I didn't know what to do. Sayuri knocked and slid open the partition. She stepped up into the room, the detectives following behind her.

'I must leave. They will ask questions, but I cannot stay.'

'Sayuri, please – '

'Your Japanese is good, so you will be fine.'

Superintendent Takeda took the lamp off the low table and placed it on the floor. He moved the table from the side of the room into the middle and sat on the floor behind it, his back to Kate's room. After he placed a lined yellow notepad and two pens in front of him, he motioned for me to sit opposite him. I sat where the table had been and leaned back against the wall under the window. He reached across and took my passport from my hand. His colleague walked around, making notes in his book. Standing in the doorway between the two rooms, he looked at the broken mirror, the clothes and belongings strewn across the floor. He bent and spoke to his superior in a hushed tone. I heard the word *kagami*, mirror. The Superintendent glanced behind him, into Kate's room. The sound of chewing gum smacking against his teeth made me wince.

He turned back to look at me, his eyes narrow. 'So, tell me about the mirror.'

I tried to explain what had happened but I couldn't speak properly. The younger detective brought me some water, and I needed both hands to hold the glass steady. Takeda watched me; his eyes hard.

'There's a little blood on the floor, boss,' said the younger detective. He pointed to the stains across the tatami.

'It's mine. I cut it on the broken glass,' I held up my foot to show the fine line of scab still visible.

'We'll need a blood sample from you. Why are you here?' Takeda asked. 'Why did you come to Japan?'

'I came to teach English. We both did.'

'On a student visa?'

He showed me the page in my passport.

'I can't read it – too much kanji. I only found out a few days ago that we weren't allowed to work. They told me... they said if I went to the police, and you found out about the visa, you'd send me to prison. And the Filipinas.' The words came out weak and breathy.

'We're not interested in that right now, we're not immigration.'

Someone had opened the kitchen window and the autumn breeze blew gently through the apartment. Shivering, I wiped both eyes with my fingers and straightened up. I had to get a grip.

'Where? When did you find her?'

'A rice farmer, Mr Ito, found her. This morning he saw a lot of money blowing across his fields. He collected it up, ready to take to the koban.' He scratched his forehead and pressed his lips together. 'And that's when he found her in the irrigation ditch. He called it in at eight a.m. this morning.'

'How?'

'It's hard to tell. We'll known when we have the results of the autopsy.'

'Oh.'

It was all I could say.

It had been the same on that Saturday Elena died. *Oh*, I said. My mother slapped my face, called me a cold and selfish bitch. She said it was my fault because I was supposed to look after Elena. *Dad*, I said. The embrace I craved; the problem-solving-bear hug was withheld as my father turned away from me. *Dad*. I needed my dad now.

'Murdered?' I said to the detective. My shoulders shook as the crying started again.

'We can't say yet,' said Takeda.

'Planning on going somewhere?' said the younger detective, Saito, pointing at my holdall on the floor near the cupboard door.

'Kate's flight ticket. It's on the cabinet.' Pulling my cloth bag towards me, I reached inside for my own ticket and gave it to Takeda. Saito stepped into Kate's room. 'Can you give me her elephant? We were supposed to be flying to Singapore tomorrow.' I sobbed, loud noises that came from deep inside me.

'We need to leave her things as they are for now. So, how do you know Miss Woodman?'

'We met here. Are you sure it's her?' It was a stupid thing to say. We were the only Europeans this side of Osaka, of course it was her.

'Her passport was next to her body,' said Takeda. 'And the money, but we don't know how she got there. So, please, if you can, tell me what happened the last time you saw her.'

'It's the *wakagashira*. Can you ask Ohayo and Mama from Shima? They'll tell you. It's all to do with the *yakuza*.'

The detectives said nothing and continued to write in their notepads. Hadn't they heard me?

Hours passed; I think. Time lost itself, became an unmeasurable, intangible entity. Takeda asked questions and I answered, telling him everything from the beginning. There were words I couldn't remember or didn't know and I had to refer to my dictionary. I told him about the car that followed us, about the hostessing job and the Filipinas. I told him about Ohayo and his tattoos, and the warning the day we went to the mountains, about Nagasaki and the *wakagashira*, and that Kate and I had planned to escape before we were sent there.

'Mari. Can I call you Mari?' asked Takeda. His eyes were softer now. 'You call me Takeda-san, okay?' He smiled. 'I understand you're upset and I'm sorry, but we need you to come to the police station and make a statement. It seems you were the last person to see Miss Woodman alive and you are a key witness. We have other inquiries to make and we will have more questions for you. We'll send a car for you tomorrow morning. Is there anywhere you can go now? You need to leave the apartment.'

'Where can I go?' Ryu. No, not there. 'I don't know.'

'The Forensic Team are coming from Fukuoka. They need to take fingerprints et cetera. We'll find somewhere for you. Come to the Hitano koban for now and we'll get a doctor to take that blood sample, okay? And after we've taken your fingerprints, we'll let you call your family.'

They helped me gather my things, put it all into my already half-packed holdall. Takeda-san handed me my Levi's jacket and opened the front door.

SOMEONE FROM THE koban must have called Sayuri because she came and took me to the Filipinas apartment above Kujaku. She gave me a key to the front door and my pay packet. And Kate's.

I was walking underwater. Everything happened in slow motion, nothing was real. Imee put clean sheets on the bottom mattress of a bunk bed and smoothed the cover. She took my hand and led me to the bed. Silently, I lay down, back to the wall and curled my legs towards my chest.

The other Filipinas, even the ones I didn't really know, came one by one to offer kind words and prayers or tried to make me eat. Myla sat on the floor beside me, brushing my hair.

'Someone must stay with her,' said Sayuri. 'She looks okay, but she is not. She has a shock.'

'I'm not losing pay because Kate was stupid,' Melody said. She fluffed up her peroxide-damaged hair. She put on her make-up in front of a small mirror on top of a chest of drawers that sat between the two sets of bunk beds. 'At least they found the body. Not like with Cherry. You can't do what they did and expect to get away with it.'

'The police haven't confirmed Kate was murdered,' said Imee. 'Don't talk like that. I'll stay.' She sat on the edge of the bunkbed opposite me, wiped her eyes and sniffed. 'I'm happy to. Mari would do the same for me.'

There were no windows in the room, just ten inches of open

fretwork across the top of the door. It allowed some light in from the opaque glass window on the other side of the narrow corridor, and the half- light made everything yet more dream-like. On my way to the bathroom, I passed four rooms, all the same, each with two sets of bunk beds. They reminded me of train sleeper cars. At the end of the corridor was a payphone under a small open window. Clothes, shoes, and make-up lay everywhere. Untidy piles of laundry waited to be ironed in the kitchen and rubbish bags full to bursting sat on the stairs waiting to be taken out. The lack of natural light and fresh air was stifling. It must have been hellish during the hot and humid months of summer. I didn't want to stay there, but I was too exhausted to leave. My legs were shaky and my head spun.

BACK IN IMEE'S room, I sat on the bed, my elbows on my knees. My stomach rumbled. I couldn't remember the last time I'd eaten.

'I know I shouldn't be - but I'm hungry,' I said.

'It means you choose to live, you choose to fight and survive,' Imee said. She moved across and sat next to me, placing her hand on my arm. 'Don't worry about Melody, you know what she's like.'

We sat for a while in silence, holding hands.

'That night, I even said I hoped she'd get hit by a truck or something, and now she's dead.' Another bout of crying took over my words.

'Don't blame yourself, Mari. I'll go to your favourite place, the yakitori and get some food, okay?'

She wouldn't take the money I tried to give her. When she got back, I was still in the same place, I hadn't moved.

'Masta wouldn't let me pay. He says he is sorry for your loss; he likes you both very much. Here, I got you some cola as well, it's got sugar so will give you some energy.'

'I don't even know his real name. Masta – Master of the shop. Can you believe that? We went there so many times and I don't know his name.' For some reason, that released a new wave of tears. 'Imee, will you ring Ryu and tell him they found her?'

Imee went down the corridor to the old-fashioned yellow payphone. She was back a minute or so later, biting her lower lip.

'The police are there, asking him questions. I spoke to a woman, I'm so sorry. Sorry for Kate, sorry for you and Ryu. It's all pretty bad for you.'

'Do you remember that night when I couldn't read her cards? I said she had no future.'

'*Diyos ko po.*' She made the sign of the cross, sat on the bed opposite me. 'I remember.'

Chapter 35

IF I SLEPT, it was fitfully. '*I shouldn't have left her,*' echoed in my head, torturing my heart. Dreams of dead Elena mingled with dreams of dead Kate. The hushed voices and soft movements of the girls as they came back from work comforted me in the early hours. It had been light for ages when a blurry-eyed Myla shook my arm.

'Police.'

The younger of the detectives from the day before, the one who spoke about the kagami, the broken mirror, came with a uniformed lady officer to take me to the main police station just outside Kitakyushu. Four storeys high, it had a concrete, flat-roofed entrance porch that jutted out towards the carpark. Two small trees in ceramic pots stood guard on either side of the double doors. Someone had tried to make the place look welcoming, and failed. Not that I knew much about police stations, besides what I'd seen on TV.

Takeda-san met us and walked me to the first floor. He wore the same silver-grey suit but without the tie. A little grey stubble showed on his chin, and I guessed that he hadn't been home. Uniformed officers passed us and bowed briefly to him.

'Are you the boss?' I asked.

'I'm second-in-command. My superior runs the whole Prefecture, but this police station is under my leadership. Hitano doesn't have a specialist team so that's why I'm involved. Mari, we need you to identify Kate's body.'

I stopped at the top of the stairs, shaking my head. Each finger curled and uncurled around the cold metal handrail. God, this was real.

'No, I can't see her dead.'

The memory of seeing Elena's dead body seared through me. Serene and peaceful, she lay lifeless in a white wooden box, her pale hands folded over each other. Too still for a fifteen-year-old. A candle burned in the corner of the room at the funeral home and I licked my finger and thumb, squeezed the light out. I didn't want it to distract Elena's spirit, to call her back.

I didn't want to see Kate. Dead Kate. No, I couldn't.

'It might help you say goodbye,' Takeda-san said. I shook my head. 'I understand. We can ask someone else. Then she'll be sent to Fukuoka for the autopsy.'

'Hasn't that been done yet?'

'The British Consulate has to have permission from her family first. And what about you, have you contacted your family?'

I shook my head as they ushered me through an open plan office with half a dozen desks. Phones rang and officers rushed around or typed furiously at electric typewriters. Two word processors sat side by side along the far wall, their screens glowing black-green while uniformed girls tapped away at their keyboards.

Takeda-san showed me into a grey, windowless interview room. It reminded me of the cop shows I'd loved as a teenager - *The Streets of San Francisco, Starsky and Hutch* and more recently *Miami Vice*. The bare grey walls seemed hostile. My reflection looked back at me from what I presumed was a two-way mirror. The younger detective pulled out a grey chair and I sat at the grey table.

Takeda-san put a cassette tape into the machine on the table and switched it on. He stated their names and mine, the time, and the date.

'The investigation of Kate Woodman's death,' he said.

I pulled Ryu's sweatshirt more tightly around me, my arms

folded. Investigation? A cold sensation ran through my core. Did they think I'd killed her? My hand shook as I took the plastic cup of water from the younger detective.

'Mari, we've asked for an official translator, but the nearest one's in Osaka. It's Friday and the weekend, but someone will be here on Monday.' He tapped his pencil on the table and smiled at me, his chewing gum visible at the side of his mouth. 'Your spoken Japanese is excellent and you're doing fine.'

'Can't Mr Suzuki from the Consular office translate?'

'He's not officially registered as a translator, Mari. At some stage, you'll need to sign statements and I know you don't read very well. So, we'll deal with all that on Monday. Firstly, we have the results of your blood test. It matches the blood in your apartment and is a different type than Kate's.' He gestured to his colleague. 'Detective Saito, please start.'

Saito cleared his throat and swallowed a small smile. He was like an eager puppy as he opened his notebook; he couldn't wait to ask questions.

'We spoke to your neighbours and they told us there was an argument in your apartment the night you say your friend went missing,' he said. 'What did you and Kate argue about?'

'We didn't have an argument, but she was being difficult and I got annoyed. That was at the Art Bar, not at home. I came home on my own. I told you all this yesterday.'

'We need a clear understanding of what happened, how the mirror got broken, why her things are all over the room,' he said. 'Why did you argue?'

I went through the events of that night again. My voice faltered when I told them I'd left Kate by the side of the road and I couldn't look at them when I told them that I hadn't reported her missing for four days. 'Have you spoken to the *yakuza*?' They were the bad guys, not me.

'Did you do something to her? Is that why she left the apartment?'

'She wasn't there. She didn't come home. I was on my own.'

'Your neighbours say they heard shouting, an argument. Who were you shouting at?' He leaned forward, and one hand tapped out his words on the desk. 'Why were you shouting at her?'

'I don't remember any shouting.' My brow furrowed as I tried to remember, but surely, I hadn't made that much noise.

'If you don't remember shouting, how is it you can remember breaking the mirror... you say, yourself?'

'I threw a glass. I was angry. I thought she'd gone back to Ryu's. I've told you all this. Why are you treating me like a –' Fumbling with my dictionary, I looked up the word for 'suspect' and pushed the dictionary across the desk, my finger on the word. I had no energy to try and say it.

'So, you were angry with her over your boyfriend. You were shouting at her and the argument got violent. Maybe you shoved her against the wall and that's what broke the mirror. Did you get violent with her? Did you push her into the mirror?'

'No. I didn't do anything to her. I just left her on the road and cycled home. The *yakuza*. It was the *yakuza*.'

I looked at the ceiling, tried to blink my eyes dry. Consciously, I uncurled my shoulders and tried to breathe deep. This couldn't be happening.

'But in anger you broke the mirror?'

'The mirror, the mirror! You keep talking about the mirror. She's dead, it has nothing to do with the mirror.' I slapped my hands on the table. 'It's the *yakuza*, the *wakagashira*, I told you.' I pressed the heels of my hands into my eyes. 'You really think I did something to her? How? What did I do to her then?'

'Mari, we have to ask these questions,' Takeda-san said.

'I'm sorry. I'm... I want to know how she died. Did she drown in the irrigation ditch?' In the two-way mirror behind Saito, my reflection distorted my features. My skin looked distorted and shiny. Then I realised, my face was creased, and tears wet my cheeks.

'We won't know until the autopsy results come though.' Takeda-san loosened his tie and unbuttoned his collar. 'What I can tell you is that however she died, it isn't obvious.'

'Boss?' The way the Saito said the word, it sounded more like a warning than a question.

Takeda-san dismissed it with a wave of his hand. He leaned forward, his elbows on the table, his fingers folded together. 'The rice was harvested about a week ago and there was only a little rainwater in the irrigation ditch. At this stage, we don't know a lot. She was fully clothed, but barefoot.' He chewed loudly on his gum for a moment and I raised my eyebrows at him. 'Trying to give up smoking.' He shrugged.

There was a knock on the door and Saito opened it. A Forensic Officer stood in the doorway; said they were finished in the apartment. Saito sat opposite me and flicked through his notebook, while the Officer spoke to Takeda-san.

'So, you didn't argue, and you broke the mirror yourself?'

'Yes, *Kagami-san*, Mr Mirror. I've told you. I was angry with her and I broke the mirror. I was a bit drunk. And maybe I shouted 'bitch' or something, I don't remember exactly.'

The door closed and Takeda-san sat down, gesturing for Saito to continue.

'You don't remember what? Breaking the mirror, or shouting, or if she was in the apartment?'

I gripped the edge of the table, the metal cold under my fingers. Why didn't he listen to what I told him? Why did he twist everything I said?

'Please, you don't remember…?'

'Shouting. Kate wasn't there. I don't remember if I shouted.'

'We'll come back to that. So. You broke the mirror. You like breaking things. And stealing things.'

'The bikes. We only borrowed them. We were going to put them back before we left Hitano. I already put mine back.'

The detective nodded, wrote in his notebook. 'Can you think of anyone who would want to hurt Kate?'

'I told you, the *wakagashira*. Have you spoken to the *yakuza*?'

'What about your friend Koji. She made him lose face so that he left your boyfriend's bar with Hiroshi, correct?'

Kagami-san flipped the pages in his notebook. It wasn't possible to think of him as Saito anymore.

'Yes, but Koji wouldn't do anything like that. Kagami-san. You're up the wrong tree again. He wouldn't hurt her, he loves… loved her.'

The past tense; was, did, liked, loved. Empty, leaden words.

'Would Hiroshi want to hurt Kate on his friend's behalf. Can you think?'

'Think? All I do is think, it's all I've done for the last six days. Trying to think where she is and why she doesn't come home. Didn't come home. No, Hiroshi wouldn't do anything like that.'

'Let me ask you about Ryu Tamaki. Your first thought was that she had gone back to see him. We have witnesses that say she was acting very suggestively towards him that night. It would have been hard for him to resist,' he said.

'Ryu said she didn't go back there. He wasn't interested in her.'

'Perhaps. But she made it clear that she was available. She had many boyfriends, didn't she? Seems she was extremely popular with men.'

'She's just… young. I don't know what to tell you. She liked to have fun.'

I felt ashamed of Kate's promiscuity. It'd be bad enough at home, but here in Japan it was so much worse. I felt heat flood my cheeks.

'Maybe Mr Tamaki didn't resist her advances, it seems a lot of men couldn't. And then afterwards, he felt guilty. After all, he's just got engaged.'

'No. What, you think… and then he dumped her body in a rice field? No. That's ridiculous. You've already spoken to him?' I looked across at Takeda-san, sitting at an angle on his chair, one leg crossing the other.

He shrugged. 'Carry on.'

'No, wait a minute, I know you spoke to him last night. What did he say? Did Kate go back there?'

My heart beat too fast, throbbing so hard in my temples that I could feel it in my eyes. The metal edge of the chair dug into the back of my thighs as I leaned forward.

'Excuse me for asking,' said Kagami-san, 'but have you and Mr Tamaki had sex since his engagement?'

'What's that got to do with anything?' My face burned and I shifted on my chair.

'Just answer the question,' Takeda-san said.

I took a deep breath. 'Yes, he was with me the night before we went to see the Honorary Consul.' My finger traced a scratch on the metal table. I knew what the Japanese thought of foreign women. Kate had proved them right. But not me, I wouldn't be tarred with the same brush. Ryu and I were in love, it was different. Even so, shame rippled through me and heat flushed up my neck. The police knew Ryu was engaged. I did too, so what did that make me?

'We know he was with you two nights ago. Your neighbours told us his car was parked outside your apartment all night. So, he likes sex with foreign women. We know about his Filipina girlfriends too.'

'It wasn't like that. We were in a relationship for months.' I spoke quietly, feeling another flush of embarrassment across my cheeks. *Filipina girlfriends*? Plural? 'That doesn't mean he'd have sex with Kate and then kill her. If he felt guilty because he had sex with someone after he got engaged, why didn't he kill me?'

Kagami-san rubbed his chin. 'Perhaps he tried to resist her, and she got hurt in some way. It's a possibility don't you think? His bar and apartment will be checked by the forensic team. We'll know soon enough. We're holding him for questioning down the corridor.'

'You are so wrong. I know him, he couldn't do something like that. I'm telling you, it's the *wakagashira*. Why don't you believe me? I need a break. Can I see Ryu?'

'No, we haven't finished with him yet,' Takeda-san said.

'Tell me, did you follow her back to Ryu's? You've told me you were angry and jealous. I think you followed her back there and caught them together. And you attacked her,' Kagami-san said.

'What? I told you, I went home.'

Vomit hit the back of my throat but it didn't come up. My whole body was shaky and I rubbed my hands on my trousers. Concentrating and speaking in Japanese for so long made my head ache.

'Three witnesses told us that you got violent with her in the bar before you left.'

'I just pushed her away. She was being an idiot with Ryu. I just pushed her.'

'You found them having sex and your anger turned to a jealous rage. You fought. '

'No.'

Kagami-san stared beyond me at the wall, stayed silent for a while. Then he looked at Takeda-san and smiled.

'When you realised you had killed her, you coerced your boyfriend into helping you get rid of the body. You took the body and dumped it by the side of the road. That's what happened, isn't it?'

'No.'

'That's why you told Ueno-san that Miss Woodman was sick. You pretended she was still alive. You were about to leave, weren't you? We have your plane ticket. That's why it took you four days to report her missing. Unlucky for you that the body was found before you left.'

'No.' It sounded so plausible. So obvious. Now I understood why I was a suspect.

The young detective leaned forwards, elbow on the table. 'Let's see what Forensics turn up.'

I shook my head, my face wet with tears. Takeda-san smacked his gum against his teeth. Standing, he motioned to his colleague, and they left the room.

My head swam and I needed to lie down. I wanted to sleep for the rest of my life. All the questions were making me feel like a crazy person. There were only so many ways to say the same thing. They were trying to make me say something, catch me out. But I had nothing to hide. Rubbing my temples didn't help my aching head.

The detectives came back, bringing vending machine coffee in plastic cups. They asked about our friends, where we went and what we did. Kagami-san asked about Kujaku and Shima.

We broke for a late lunch. I sat on the saggy orange sofa in the open plan office. An officer brought me a bowl of yakisoba fried noodles and removed a pile of box files from the sofa. Hungry but feeling sick at the same time, I picked at the matchsticks of carrot and green pepper with the chopsticks. The detectives sat at a desk in the middle of the office, slurping and sucking up their noodles. The noise made me even less hungry, I put the bowl on the floor and against Japanese etiquette, stuck the chopsticks in, like antennae.

My ears buzzed and the heaviness in my head made me dizzy. I couldn't focus properly, like I was on the edge of a deep sleep that didn't come. Uniformed and plain clothed officers came and went, carrying files and making phone calls. No one paid me any attention. I wanted to stop the world. Pulling the cushion down from the end of the sofa, I lay my head against it and put my feet up.

A VOICE CALLED my name. *No. Please, leave me alone.*

'I let you sleep for an hour. You looked like you needed it,' said Takeda-san. 'But now if you're ready?' He turned and spoke to Kagami-san, and the young detective nodded, sat at a desk, and pulled a file towards him. 'Just you and me, Mari. Okay?'

Takeda-san walked me over to the interview room. Here we go again. He had an A4-sized book under his arm and put it between us on the table. The Japanese lettering on the red hardback cover was that illegible mix of all three alphabets. Takeda-san switched on the tape recorder.

'Four forty-nine p.m. on Friday, 26th October 1985. This is

Fukuoka Prefecture Police Department's book of known *yakuza* members,' he said and pushed it toward me. 'Look through it, see if you recognise anyone.'

'A whole book?'

The *yakuza* were big, but it shocked me that the police had a whole book of their mugshots. A hardback book at that, not some cobbled together poly-folder. I brought the book closer and opened it. Every page showed nine head-and-shoulder photographs of different men, vertical lettering beside each one. Slowly turning the pages, I recognised the *wakagashira* on the first page but wanted to see if there were any other faces I knew before I spoke. On page six there was a face I'd regularly seen in Kujaku, but I'd never spoken to him, and didn't know his name. It was the man with the chunky bracelet. Kate had done more than just talk with him, but that wasn't something I'd tell the detectives unless I needed to. Another photo caught my attention but I wasn't sure if I knew the man. I turned a few more pages.

On page thirty-one, Ohayo's pock-marked face looked back at me and Washan appeared a dozen pages on. I spent a long time looking at a photo on page fifty. How had I not known? I tapped my finger on the photo of Junichi, then swiped the book off the table onto the floor, just as Kagami-san opened the door. He didn't enter the room, just stood at the door, mouth open and eyes wide. Stepping inside he handed Takeda-san a file, turned on his heel and left the room like it was on fire.

'Lying bastard. He knew all along.' I spoke in English, banging my fists on the table. 'He lied when he said he'd seen her. And Ryu's marrying his niece.'

Takeda-san picked the book up and put it back in front of me. 'Stay calm and take your time. Be sure.'

From the beginning, I turned the pages again. 'This one.' I tapped the photo of the man I knew was responsible for Kate's death, the *wakagashira*. Turning the pages quickly, I pointed to the photos of Ohayo, then Washan. 'And him. Junichi. Is he really one of them?' Ryu wouldn't be involved with a *yakuza*.

I looked through the whole book, at each photo on each page, ran my finger along the rows, checking carefully. Every page held nine possibilities of treachery and betrayal. Turning the last few pages was torture but finally, I was done. Closing the book, I pushed it across the desk. My neck was stiff, and I ran my hand under my hair, looked at the ceiling. I wiped my face with the back of my fingers and pulled a tissue from my bag. Thank God, Ryu's photo had not been there.

'It's not all white shirts and tattoos,' Takeda-san said. 'There are plenty of low-key players, especially in the finance sector.'

He asked more questions. Exhaustion made my body weak and my mind fragmented. I looked down at my hands, but they didn't look like mine. A metallic taste jarred my teeth, and I couldn't take much more. My head pounded and I squinted against the glare of the florescent strip light. Kagami-san came in again, bringing documents for his superior to sign.

Takeda-san looked at the papers he'd just been given. 'Kate's been identified by Mr Yoshinori Nakamura from Kujaku Club and is on her way to Fukuoka for autopsy.'

At least that would provide some answers. A white-faced woman with messy hair stared back at me from the mirror. Something tempted me to poke my tongue out, but I didn't. There might be someone on the other side, watching me, judging me.

He pulled down his shirt sleeves and buttoned the cuffs. 'Would you like to go back to your apartment now? Our Forensics Team have finished there.'

'Ryu. Can I see him?'

'He's still being interviewed.'

Chapter 36

THE POLICE CAR dropped me home and drove away. The need to see Ryu, to be held in his arms, was strong, but I had to accept that wasn't going to happen. I'd ring Koji later, see if he wanted to meet up. I needed to be with people, didn't want to be alone.

It took me a while to go inside and I paused with the key in the apartment door. Taking a deep breath, I pushed it open and slipped off my shoes. There was something oily on the door handle. I tried to rub it off, but it just spread further. A fine layer of grey dust covered everything: the partition doors and all the hard surfaces. Forensics dust. Grabbing a bucket from under the sink, I put it under the hot tap. While it filled, I looked across at the wooden house, and a curtain moved.

Only a week ago, our clothes had been collected by the shipping company. Just a week ago, we'd gone to Ryu's for an impromptu leaving party. Today we should have been in Singapore. All the planning Kate had done, all that time she'd spent reading that bloody guidebook. She'd told me about hilltribes and National Parks, royal palaces and chains of Philippine islands where the diving and snorkelling over coral reefs was spectacular. And now she'd never get to see any of it. Like Elena, there'd be many things she'd never do or see. My insides twisted. Both lives cut short because of me.

Water spilled over the top of the bucket. I turned off the tap and squeezed in cherry-scented washing up liquid. Cleaning off the fingerprint dust was a mechanical, methodical job. It was good not to have to think as I wiped everything down with wet cloths. Grey dust covered the white mirror frame in Kate's room. Soap suds slopped over the side of the bucket as I put it down. I sat on the floor, pulled one of Kate's t-shirts to me, held it to my face and breathed in her perfume. It was almost dark. The stillness of the evening wrapped me and comforted me as I folded and carefully repacked all Kate's belongings. Once I'd cleaned the mirror frame and the doors, the room was less disturbing. I wiped my eyes and sniffed, placed Kate's little blue elephant on the top of her backpack and started to slide the partition door. I stopped. We'd never closed it. Not once in the six months we'd lived there.

CURTAINS TWITCHED AS I passed neighbouring houses on route to the phone box. Word was out then; everyone must know the gaijin girl was dead. I stopped in the middle of the road and stared down the driveway at one house and the curtain quickly dropped. Nosy gits. They'd never even said hello. When I lived in London, I hadn't known my neighbours either.

'Koji, it's Mari,' I said down the phone.

'Are you okay? What did the police say?'

'Can we meet somewhere?'

'Come to my house. I can't drive, they have taken my truck, I don't know when they will bring back. Can you take taxi?'

I wrote down the address phonetically on the last tissue from the packet, and half an hour later, I arrived at a house up in the hills. A gravel pathway led off the road to the house which had two carved stone lanterns by the entrance, shining out a golden welcome. Koji's mother and father greeted me at the door with bows. They patted my shoulders, showed me into a room where Koji sat on a hard-backed chair. I didn't know he lived with his parents. How little I actually knew about this man who loved my friend. He nodded as I sat beside him at the highly polished cherrywood table.

'The bad thing,' Koji said in English, placing his glasses on the table, 'The most bad thing is last time I saw her, I was angry. I can't forgive myself. They asked me many, many times if I hurt her.' He looked at me.

I had never seen him without his glasses, never paid any attention to how nice his eyes were. He looked different. His untidy hair was the same and he hadn't shaved. But the way he sat, all hunched up, made him look winded, smaller, diminished. Presumably, I looked the same.

'I know.'

'They ask me what I did to her. It was terrible. And she is dead. They ask if I did it. They ask if you did it, then they ask if Ryu or Hiroshi hurt her. My friends, they ask if my friends killed my beautiful Kato.' His eyes filled with tears and I blinked away my own, my hand on his arm.

His mother brought in a lacquered tea tray laden with a butter-coloured earthenware teapot and small bowls. She placed dishes of rice crackers and plain cookies on the table, poured the tea and sat the other side of Koji, opposite her husband. We sat in silence at the table, sipping sharp green tea. My mind was blank. I felt blank and hollowed out.

'Did you see Ryu at police station?' said Koji.

'They wouldn't let me. They were still interviewing him when I left.'

'They are taking time with him.' He looked at his watch. 'He will phone when they finish.'

Koji's parents invited me to stay and I gratefully accepted. I didn't want to go back to town, I needed to be with someone, and I wanted to be there when Ryu called. When the phone finally rang, I followed Koji into the hall as he answered it. I stood with my fingers pressed to my mouth, listening. There were long silences punctuated with '*Hai,*' and finally '*Arigato gozaimas*'.

'They will give back my truck. I can collect now and also take Ryu home. I know you want to see him, but better you stay here.'

He spoke to his parents and his mother came and stood next

to me. Taking hold of my arm, she patted my hand. His father put on his jacket and headed out to the car.

'Don't rush back. You should stay with him. He must be feeling crap. Tell him…'

I stopped. It was stupid, inconsequential to want to tell Ryu I loved him.

Chapter 37

DAWN DRAGGED ITS feet slowly through the remnants of the night, took its time coming and I was up and dressed long before it was light. Not that I'd slept. Still in Ryu's sweatshirt, I sat on the doorstep overlooking the valley, my hands cupped round the warmth of a tea bowl. I felt removed from the drama, removed from reality. Lights dimmed in the valley as the soft grey-blue of early daylight took over. I stretched my legs out, leaning back against the door frame.

'There you are,' said Koji. 'Ryu and I went to all-night bar and I came home a few hours ago. They closed his place. The Forensics team will go there tomorrow. He's gone to his parents' house.'

'Is he okay? Did the police say anything about the *yakuza*?' I stood to face him.

'He is not okay. No one is okay. Police not say anything. All I know is everyone is questioned. All Kujaku members, students, everyone. The Filipinas say they don't know Kato. They only know she is your friend. I think they have been told to lie.'

'God, Koji, I don't know what to do.'

'There is nothing to do. Rest, Mari, stay here. My mother is here but I must go to work.'

Chapter 38

TIME DID THAT slowed-down thing, making the day drag on and on. Finally, the shrill sound of the phone had me on my feet. Koji's mother came and told me it was Takeda-san.

'Good afternoon, Mari, the autopsy report is back. I'm sending a car for you now.'

I RAN UP the steps of the police station and into the office. Kagami-san and Takeda-san were huddled over a desk, but both looked up as I approached them. They spoke quietly to each other, turning away so that I couldn't hear. Shifting from foot to foot, I waited, wanting to know what the report said. Takeda-san gathered up papers and documents, putting them into a thick, green, cardboard folder. He opened the door to the interview room and beckoned to me. I followed him inside and sat in the same chair as the day before.

'You don't look well, Mari. Did you sleep?' he said.

I shook my head.

He sighed and scratched at the side of his mouth with his middle finger. 'So, we have the autopsy report back. It's tricky. It doesn't tell us exactly how she died. It tells us how she didn't die.' He sat opposite me, his chair at an angle to the table.

'I don't understand.'

He opened the folder and took out the report. 'It rules things out, see?'

He showed me a sheet of paper, but I couldn't read the wording. Typed headings and paragraphs filled one side of the paper. On the other, corresponding boxes were manually marked with ticks or crosses.

'Kate wasn't strangled, she didn't drown, she wasn't stabbed, she had no fatal illnesses, no infectious diseases, she wasn't poisoned.' said Takeda-san.

All I heard was *she didn't drown* and everything else he said sounded like white noise. Thank God, she hadn't drowned. It would have been too much if Kate had died the same way as Elena.

'Sorry, tell me again.' He read the report to me again. 'So, they did something to her? A lethal injection or something?'

'Nothing showed in the blood tests. Let me read on. There were some bruises and her left shoulder and arm were broken. There's a head injury, possibly caused by the impact of falling, or being thrown, into the irrigation channel from the road. All of that happened before she died. The embankment is about four meters above the rice field, it's a steep drop.'

'They must've missed something.' I paced the room.

'Mari, please sit down.'

The request was mild and calm, but I sat back on the chair, placed my hands flat on the table. Aware that I was hyperventilating, I tried to steady my breathing.

'It's the head injury. Accidental death.'

I banged my fist on the table. 'Accident? No, it wasn't.'

'There are a couple of things that don't fit,' said Takeda-san. 'She had only been dead for two days when she was found. Although she had no shoes or socks on, her feet were clean, so she hadn't walked anywhere. We need to find her shoes. They could tell us where she was for those three days before she died.' Takeda-san spoke gently, watching me.

'When did she die? When exactly?' My shoulders tensed, I leaned forward and waited for his answer. He scanned the report.

'Time of death is recorded as Tuesday between two and

five pm.'

'Oh, my God.'

A shudder started deep inside me and ended at my fingertips. I'd been right. Kate died at three-twenty. There was a tightness in my chest, and my breathing was rapid. Kate had been alive for three days after she went missing. Three days when someone could have been looking for her. Three days that could have saved her life. Three days that I did nothing.

'They're working on her clothing now, to see if there's anything that could give us an idea of where she was for those three days. There's a bulletin going out on National TV tonight, asking for information. Someone might have seen her. Mari? Mari, did you hear me?' Takeda-san looked at me. 'Do you need some water?'

I nodded, my teeth chattering. He opened the door and almost collided with Kagami-san. The two men spoke to a uniformed officer, and then Takeda-san grabbed his jacket off the back of the chair and all three left.

Chapter 39

WHEN TAKEDA-SAN CAME back into the office over an hour later, he brought with him the smell of cigarette smoke. Probably Seven Star. It wafted to where I sat on the sofa, trying not to sleep. He slammed his files and notebook down on the desk, making me jump.

'Sorry to have left you like that.' Takeda-san opened the interview room door and we went inside, taking up our usual positions at the desk. 'They brought in Keiko Watanabe, who you know as Mama. I wanted to interview her myself.'

'Did she have anything to do with it? I mean, she was there when Kate offended the *wakagashira*.'

'Her story tallies with yours about the evening when he demanded an apology. She was less than complimentary about you and your friend. She's disturbed me so much I had to have a cigarette.' He shook his head, his eyebrows raised in disbelief. 'Right, we have questioned and interviewed many people and we've taken many statements. But so far, we've got no answers.'

'But the *wakagashira*, it was the *yakuza*,' I said.

'I know you think it's an obvious conclusion, but it's early days and without evidence, we can't do anything. You know who killed her, even I know who killed her, but that isn't enough for a conviction and with the *yakuza*, it's tough.'

'You can't prosecute them?'

'There's no suspicious cause of death. There's no physical

proof that anyone did anything to her. And we have no idea where she was for those three days.' Takeda-san looked saddened by what he was telling me.

A thought stung me with its spiteful barb. I didn't know the Japanese word for it, so looked it up in my dictionary. One syllable in English, and two in Japanese. A small word that held enormous consequences. My body tensed, ready to react.

'Was she...' I cleared my throat. It wouldn't change anything, but I needed to know. 'Was she raped?'

'No.' Takeda-san shook his head, half-smiled and tapped his pen on the table. 'There was no evidence of sexual activity. You know, Mari, I have three children, a boy and two girls. My daughters are the same ages as you and Kate,' he said, unwrapping a piece of chewing gum. 'The older one is married and the younger, well, she's studying in Australia. If something like this happened to her, far away from her family, my heart would break. I feel bad for you, alone here. This case feels very personal to me. We'll get to the truth. We're only two days in. Hopefully, someone will come forward once the news bulletin goes out this evening.'

'Someone must know something. Are they all too scared to speak out against the *yakuza*?'

'That's usually the case. We need to look at the possibility that it was an accident - that she was simply knocked off her bike. But twenty-seven kilometres is a long way from town and there's nowhere she could've been heading. Your apartment and Koji's house aren't that side of town, Ryu's isn't either, so it doesn't make sense that she was even on that road. There's nothing out there – just a few houses and rice fields. Probably wouldn't have been much traffic around at that time of night, but if she had got lost, took a wrong turn and somehow ended up there –'

'So, she angers a *yakuza* boss, who threatens her twice, and coincidentally has a fatal collision with a car? Twenty-seven kilometres out of town on a road she doesn't know?'

'I'm trying to find out what happened, Mari. There'd be

more injuries if she'd been hit by a car, but we must rule out that possibility. Her bike hasn't been found. Nor has her handbag or shoes.' Takeda-san scratched at the corner of his mouth. 'It doesn't make sense.'

'She always tied her bag's straps to the basket in case it fell out. It used to annoy me. It took ages because of her long nails.'

'We'll wait and see what witnesses the bulletin brings in. A blonde European girl on a bike, at one or two in the morning isn't a usual occurrence here. If she was on that road, someone would have seen her. *If* she was on that road. I don't think she was. The fact that the bike and handbag weren't with her, but her passport and the money was, makes me think someone put her there.'

'*Yakuza*. Takeda-san, they said they're sending me to Nagasaki tomorrow. They can't make me go, can they?'

'Long term, I can't do anything to help you with that. You have a contract with the school, and they have a deal with the *yakuza*. All I can do is tell them that you need to stay in Hitano for the time being, until the case is closed.'

'But I thought the student visa -'

'No one is interested in that. And you do need to stay until the case is closed. Hopefully, we'll have some new leads tonight.' He looked at his watch. 'It's already five o'clock. I think you've had enough for today. Go home and get some rest.'

The door opened and a female officer gave Takeda-san two transparent plastic evidence bags, a thick stripe of red across their tops. He placed them side by side on the table in front of me. One contained Kate's gold ring, the letter 'K' engraved on the oval surface, the other her green and black scarf. My breathing stopped on a sharp inward breath; my hands covered my mouth. I remembered telling her not to wear it.

'You know, I felt the exact time she died. Or I dreamt it.' My eyes filled up. 'It was three-twenty on Tuesday. Can you take me to the morgue? I want to see her.'

Takeda-san didn't react, and the silence was loaded for what seemed like forever.

'The Certificate for Cremation was issued at the same time as the Autopsy Report. They cremated her this morning.'

'You cremated her? Why?' I spoke too loudly. My head was spinning and I heard blood rushing in my ears. I slid off the chair onto the floor. The last thing I heard was Takeda-san calling for help.

Chapter 40

THE FLOOR WAS hard under my shoulder. I wasn't sure where I was, the way it sometimes is when waking from a deep sleep. Then I opened my eyes. Takeda-san crouched on one knee beside me and Kagami-san stood next to him. A lady police officer, a bottle of water in her hand, bent and told me a doctor was coming soon. They helped me off the floor and half-carried me to the orange sofa. Still dizzy, I lay my head down on the arm and someone lifted my legs onto the sofa, covering me with a blanket. What was happening to me? My body wasn't working like my brain wanted it to. I felt disjointed from myself, fractured from reality, broken, shattered. I felt like the mirror.

The doctor arrived and checked me over.

'You're very dehydrated. I'd like to give you some IV fluids. At the hospital.'

'No hospital,' I said. Hospitals were full of sick people, scared people, grieving people, and that antiseptic smell made me feel sick. I wouldn't go; I needed to stay there, at the police station, in case new information came in. My eyes were heavy and I closed them. 'I just need some sleep.'

'It's too much for a young woman to bear alone,' Takeda-san said to the doctor. 'She's in a foreign country with no family around her and her friend just died. No one is helping her. The British Consulate can't get here until Monday. And her bosses want to send her to Nagasaki on her own. It's barbaric.'

'The best place for her is in hospital. I can rehydrate her and make sure she rests,' the doctor replied, taking packets of rehydration salts from his medicine bag. 'But I can't force her to go. Make sure she drinks these in two litres of water over the next few hours. And rest. She needs rest. Tell her to take this tablet tonight. At least she'll get some sleep.'

'Mari, you really should call your family. Maybe your mother or someone can come?'

'My mother hates me; she hasn't spoken to me for five years. She won't come. No one will come.' My chin trembled. She'd say it was all my fault or that it should've been me that died. That's what my mother would say. She'd said it all before.

A POLICEMAN COLLECTED my bag from Kujaku before taking me back to the apartment. It felt like somewhere I'd lived years ago. It didn't seem possible that it had only been two days since the police came into the kitchen to tell me that Kate was dead.

After showering I wiped the condensation off the bathroom mirror. Deep shadows spread under my eyes in a pale face that didn't look like my own. Was Takeda-san on the level? Why cremate her so soon? It didn't add up. In the kitchen, I opened the fridge. Empty. It would be nice to have some inari rolls. It would be nice to be with Ryu. God knows what mess the forensic team would make at the bar tomorrow. I held the sleeping tablet the doctor had given me in the palm of my hand for a moment, then swallowed it with some water. My futon felt good as I crawled onto it. Exhaustion and the tablet took me into a deep, dreamless sleep.

SOMETHING PRESSED ME down on my futon. Someone. He was heavy, I couldn't get him off. With his hands around my throat, I choked. My eyes felt too big in my face, pressure was building up behind them. *Wake up, Mari. Wake up.* I grabbed at his hands, tried to get them loose, but my arms felt like rubber and I struggled to breathe. My legs were too heavy to kick, weighed down with a wet blanket of fear. *Wake up, Mari, wake up.*

It was hard to see in the semi-darkness, but the raspy sound of his breathing made me think that something covered his mouth. My fingers scrabbled at his face, pulling the fabric away. Spikey stubble grazed my fingertips. He sat back and his grip loosened. He let go of my throat and grabbed my wrists, pinning my arms above my head. Raspy breaths turned into coughs as I gasped huge gulps of air. *Wake up, Mari, wake up!*

Sitting across my hips, one knee either side, his full body weight pinned my pelvis to the futon. It hurt. He said something in Japanese, something I didn't understand. I tried to fight him off, tried to twist and turn under his weight, tried to dislodge him. He lost his grip on my wrists and I pounded and punched at him. My voice wasn't loud enough as I tried to shout. He covered my mouth with one hand and I swallowed the hollow sound of my scream as it bounced back. Then, a dim flash of something metal in his hand as he shifted his body so that he was raised up on one knee. The other knee came down on my ribs. I couldn't get out from under him. *Wake up!*

He raised his hand and brought the knife down just as I rolled to one side and my right arm came up in front of my chest. I smelled blood. The knife slashed at me again and again, and somehow, I grabbed the lamp from the table and hit him over the head. Then he was gone. He lunged through Kate's room, climbed over the balcony and I was alone.

Groggy from the sedative, I lay on the futon, thinking I'd woken from a nightmare. It had been so real. Nausea swamped me as I got up, hot with panic. Breaths juddered out of my dry mouth, sounding loud in my ears. My whole body shook with each beat of my heart and I thought it would explode. The room spun and I leaned against the window for a second or two to steady myself, struggling to breathe as pain ripped through my side. Slap-slap. Something thick and wet dropped onto the tatami mat. Slap-slap-slap. I stepped across the room, switched on the light. My right forearm was covered in thick, red blood, my flesh sliced open, wide, and deep. Funny that it didn't hurt, that I felt no pain. There was so much blood. It took a while to realise that someone had tried to kill me.

Adrenaline took over and I ran out of the apartment and up the outside staircase. I tried to keep my arm against my body, tried to hold my side. Warm blood saturated my yukata and the metallic smell stung my nose. With my other hand, I banged on the upstairs neighbour's door. I rang the bell, but no one answered. Running along the narrow balcony, I banged on the other door, and the light inside switched off. On the way back downstairs, my bare feet slipped on my own blood.

'Help me, please!' I stood in the street. No one opened a door for me. 'I'm going to bleed to death, please help me.' I sank to my knees, my arm on my thigh. Blood flowed off my leg and into the ground around me. No one came to help.

I staggered to my feet, made it around the corner to the phone box and dialled 119 for an ambulance. My legs crumbled under me and I slid down the glass wall. I sat with my knees drawn into my chest, my head bowed, trying to make myself small, invisible, but I knew there was no safety, no sanctuary inside the cubicle. The emergency service lady asked for my address, but my mind went blank. I couldn't remember how to speak Japanese. Shaking so much that my teeth chattered, I struggled to speak.

'Superintendent Takeda-san,' My words juddered. I said it again.

And everything went hollow and dark.

Chapter 41

I WOKE, HOOKED up to an IV and a monitor that beeped and flashed. My right arm was wrapped in bandages and rested in a thin cotton sling. Odd, but I wanted my mum and dad, my sisters. It hurt too much to cry and my sobs turned to gasps of pain. The sound brought a nurse to the bedside. The woman smiled, checked the monitors, and wrote something on a chart she clipped to the end of the bed before she left the room. She came back with a doctor who did the same checks.

He pulled a chair up to the bedside, looked at me and smiled. 'I'm Dr Yuji Hayashi. You've certainly been through it, haven't you?' His English was tinged with an American accent.

'What?' The *happened* didn't materialise, it was too painful to speak.

'The police will speak to you as soon as you feel you can answer their questions. But first I need to tell you what's been done for you. There's a ten-centimetre diagonal laceration across the inside of your forearm which needed twenty-eight stitches. There are internal stitches too. I'm sorry, it'll scar badly; it's an awkward shape, like a curved 'Y'.' He drew the letter in the air with his forefinger. 'Probably two different cuts merging. It was difficult to pull the tissue together, but I did my best. Can you wiggle your fingers for me?'

What cuts? I didn't know what he was talking about, but he must've been right. My arm was a lead weight, a separate entity that my brain couldn't connect with. I forced my fingers to move. The room spun and I felt sick.

'Good,' said Dr Yuji. 'You're lucky there was no damage to your ligaments. There are also four other, smaller lacerations on your arm which needed stitching.' He handed me a carton of fruit juice and a straw. 'You have two cracked ribs which is why it hurts to breathe. There's bruising around your neck, so your throat is going to be sore for a few days. The broken capillaries around your eyes should fade in time. Your airway wasn't crushed, and your attacker missed cutting a main vein by a centimetre. We could have been looking at a very different outcome.'

'Leave,' I half-croaked, half-whispered. I didn't want to stay longer than I had to. I was ok, wasn't I? I'd already forgotten what the doctor had said. Why was I there?

'Miss Randall, you were so distressed and agitated when the ambulance brought you in, I had to give you a general anaesthetic. I needed you to keep still while I repaired your arm. You've had a blood transfusion too. You've been here since two o'clock on Saturday morning.' He looked at his watch. 'So around thirty hours. When you woke after surgery, you were screaming and thrashing around. Your broken ribs could've punctured your lung so we sedated you. That's wearing off now, but you'll feel groggy for a while. I'm sorry but you're not going anywhere. You need to stay here for another twenty-four hours.'

The door opened and the nurse came back in with a bowl of soup and some rice on a tray. I looked at Dr Yuji, as understanding seeped into the edges of my mind. My eyes widened and my heart raced.

'The police guard is here to protect you.'

He motioned to the uniformed officer standing outside the door. He smiled that kindly doctor smile. Then, I remembered what had happened. I couldn't breathe and pain crushed my chest. The nurse grabbed an oxygen mask and tried to put the elastic strap over my head, but I fought her off, thrashing and kicking, every movement flashing pain through my ribs and my arm. I tried to pull the canula out of my left hand but my bandaged arm was too heavy, too clumsy.

Dr Yuji leaned over me, held me down by my shoulders. 'Look at me. Look at me. Breathe… stay calm, you're safe. Breathe, Mari. That's it… just concentrate on breathing, okay? That's it, breathe… breathe… just breathe.'

The strength went out of me and I flopped back on the bed, taking shallow gulps of air through the mask the nurse held over my mouth. I looked at Dr Yuji, my breathing slowing as he talked me down. What the hell was happening? I couldn't take much more.

Chapter 42

Soft pink cocooned me. The curtains, sheets, the armchair by the window, everything baby pink. A nurse brought in a jug of water in her pink and white striped uniform, like a sugared almond. I wondered why it had to be pink. Why of all the colours in the spectrum, everything had to be pink. Kate's sakura-pink, cherry-blossom-pink. And pink was Elena's favourite colour.

I wiped the vomit from my lips. The room still spun and a cold sweat made me clammy. Dr Yuji apologised, saying he should have known I'd react badly to the painkillers and anaesthetic because I had so much red in my hair. The anti-emetics kicked in and after a while, I managed to sit up.

The pink and white striped nurse helped me into the en-suite shower. I had to stand with my back to the water while she held my bandaged arm out of the cubicle to keep it dry. She spoke to me in short soothing words, making me feel like a child. The hot water felt good and I leaned back, letting it cascade over my face, hiding my tears. The nurse dried me with white fluffy towels and put me into a clean hospital gown. She rubbed my hair dry and reattached the IV to the back of my hand. I leaned on her arm as she pulled the IV stand with her and led me back into my room, to the window that looked over a grassy area below.

'Good to see you up and about. You had me really worried.' Takeda-san came into the room, two paper carrier bags in one hand and my cloth bag and shoes in the other. The sugared-almond nurse took them from him and placed them on the floor next to the chair. I stood there, tears flowing, tiny noises coming from my throat. Takeda-san held me then, like a father would hold his injured daughter.

'It'll take more than a thug with a knife to kill you off, Mari Randall. You fought the doctors and nurses like a tiger before they sedated you. I dread to think what you did to your attacker.'

'Ryu?' I whispered.

'Nobody is allowed near you, I'm sorry. Only medical staff. And me. And when anyone else is in the room with you, the door must be open so that the officers can hear what's going on.' He motioned to the chair. 'My wife bought some essentials you might need and I went to your apartment for your clothes and things. Your black bag with the rest of your belongings is in the car.' He sat me back on the bed. 'Mari, I know you can't speak very well, so I will ask you simple questions. You can answer me with a yes or no.'

Pulling a silver Dictaphone out of his inside pocket, he placed it on the bedside cabinet, moving the pink plastic water jug out of the way. The nurse helped lift my bare legs onto the bed and Takeda-san averted his eyes. She covered me with the pink waffle blanket, bowed, leaving the door ajar as she left the room. Slowly, gingerly, I leaned back against the pillows. Takeda-san slipped off his jacket and pulled the sakura-pink armchair away from the window, turning it to face me. He sat and leaned forward, his elbows on his knees.

'Do you know who attacked you?'

'No.' A whisper.

'Male?'

'Yes.'

'It's too much of a coincidence that you've been attacked so soon after Kate's death. But then, you openly accused the *wakagashira*. Forensics came up with nothing from your apartment or your yukata. Just some black fibres that probably came from his clothing. Did he speak?'

'*Shizukani*' My voice didn't come out properly.

'*Shizukani shite?* He said that?'

Nodding, I reached for my bag and fumbled one-handed, trying not to knock the canula until I found my dictionary. Takeda-san looked up the word and showed it to me. *Be silent.*

He spoke to the policeman by the door, who nodded and disappeared. Sitting down again, he rested his elbows on his knees, the fingers of both hands linked together. I waited for him to speak. He was lost in thought, sighing every now and then, moving around in his seat as though he was uncomfortable. A few minutes later, he got up and looked out of the window, his hands on his hips. Eventually he turned to me.

'The British Consulate should come from Osaka tomorrow but, Mari, we have to get you out of here, get you somewhere safe.'

'Guard?'

'There should be two of them. The other one said he was going for a cigarette over two hours ago. He hasn't come back. Something doesn't feel right. One guard or two, they told you to be silent. They'll try again.'

One look at Takeda-san's face and I understood the seriousness of what was happening. I didn't know if I could take much more and closed my eyes, willing myself not to cry.

'I can't.'

'Now, Mari! Get up and get dressed. I'll get you medication from the doctor and sign you out. My officer is bringing the car to the back entrance, we'll go out through the basement. We have to leave as soon as possible.'

Questions turned my thinking this way and that. My head reeled. Could I trust him? What if he worked for the *yakuza*? Maybe he bribed the other officer not to come back?

I looked at him, my eyes narrow. He looked back at me, the same way.

When the officer returned, Takeda-san went to find the doctor and I tried to dress. The pain made me feel sick and I couldn't even take off the hospital gown. I tipped everything out of my cloth bag, looking for my scrunchie and Kate's blue elephant tumbled out. Takeda-san must've put it in there.

There was a knock on the door, but I was too scared to open it. The nurse came in, wide-eyed and nervous. She unhooked me from the IV, took the needle out of the back of my hand and helped me dress. The door was ajar, and I could see Takeda-san, standing with his back at an angle to me, holding the handles of a wheelchair. The nurse left and Takeda-san came in with a white paper bag which he tried to shove in my hand. I took a step back.

'Painkillers, antibiotics, sedatives and a letter to take to a doctor when your stitches are ready to come out. Mari, we must go. Now.' He stood in the doorway, waited for me to move. 'Do you trust me?' His hand reached for mine.

I nodded, took his hand.

And I did trust him. Because of the blue elephant.

Chapter 43

MADNESS. I LAY on my good side on the back seat of the police car with a scratchy brown blanket over me.

'Stay down as long as you can,' Takeda-san said. 'I need to stop at the police station first. I don't want anyone to see you.'

I didn't have much choice; it wasn't as though I could move easily. Every time the car braked, turned, or sped up, it was agony. Fear made me more aware of my body. My hands and feet were cold, my face hot. My brain was numb though. Rational thought was impossible. Fear and pain were all there was. It was painful to breathe and with the heavy blanket over my head, it was near impossible. Pain seared my side as I moved a bit so that I could at least get some air. The door by my head opened.

'Mari, we're leaving Kitakyushu now, okay? Stay down until I tell you.'

'It hurts,' I whispered, but he hadn't heard. The door closed.

A muffled exchange of words continued outside the car and then the driver's door opened and someone got in. The engine turned over and the car started moving. The soft thlunk-thlunk of the indicator told me we were turning. That sound heralded pain as the car turned and my body's centre of gravity shifted. My ribs felt like they were ripping into my lungs, tearing into my soul. No one spoke and I hoped to God that it was Takeda-san in the driving seat.

The sedative I'd taken before I got in the car kicked in and I floated, almost sleepy, but the jolting of the car in traffic caused pain enough to keep me awake. Somehow, I managed to move onto my back and bent my legs. In that position, it was harder to breathe and with gritted teeth, I turned onto my side again. My shirt rode up at the back and the vinyl next to my skin was cold. I tried to focus on that uninjured part of my body, but my mind was liquid, slipping and skating all over the place.

We stopped. The driver's door opened, then mine. I glanced up from under the blanket.

Takeda-san looked at me, his hands on his knees. 'You alive in there?' he asked. 'Come on, let's get you out. We're changing cars.'

How? I tried to push myself up to a sitting position, but it was too painful. Takeda-san opened the door by my feet and crouched down. He held my ankles, gently pulled my legs towards the door, and leaned into the car to help me sit up. With my feet on the ground, I sat for a while, trying to catch my breath as pain stabbed everywhere. Takeda-san gave me a carton of juice and another painkiller. The tiny tablet hurt my throat. I wanted to cry, but I didn't have the energy.

A man in grey trousers and a white shirt handed Takeda-san the keys to a brown Toyota parked in front of the police car and pulled my bags out of the boot. Takeda-san walked me to the Toyota, one arm round my waist, the other under my left elbow. The sky was early-afternoon blue, and the autumn leaves of the maple trees gleamed golden in the sunlight. Smells of pine trees and wood-smoke wove themselves into the wind and drifted through the mountains. I wished I was the wind. Then I could go anywhere, weightlessly, painlessly. It was only then that I realised, I had no idea where we were going. Not that it mattered.

'Sit?' I moved inch by inch into the back of the car.

'For a while. You can lie down if a car passes us.'

The man bowed as Takeda-san said goodbye and started the engine. We drove through the mountains for an hour or so. The medication made me slip in and out of awareness, the pain keeping me the wrong side of sleep. Flashes of colour peeked through the trees. The advertising signs of a town in the valley below.

Takeda-san looked at me in the rear-view mirror. 'Shall we stop for a while? I can get us some coffee. Are you hungry?'

I nodded. The road wound down the hillside and we drove through fields of persimmon trees towards a small town. Takeda-san parked in a far corner of an almost empty carpark. He went into the modern low-rise shopping centre. A few minutes later, he was back with a bag of snacks and a blue cotton sunhat. He opened the door and tried to put it on my head, but it didn't fit. He went back to the shop, returned with a black baseball cap. It fit much better, but I struggled to reach up and tuck my hair inside it.

'Here, let me.' With one knee on the backseat, he stuffed my hair down the back of my sweatshirt so that it was less visible.

'Papa-san.'

He smiled and patted my hand. On the way out of the car park, he stopped at the vending machines and got four cans of hot coffee. Three hours or so later we arrived - wherever it was.

Chapter 44

THE OLD WOODEN house sat in the middle of terraced rice fields that formed deep watery steps down the mountainside. Gingko and maple trees glowed red and gold in the autumn afternoon. Takeda-san said it was his sister Asa's house. We were halfway to Osaka, a long way from Hitano, a long way from anywhere.

Asa stood at the door of her house, her arms folded, and her silver hair pulled back from her round face. She wore loose charcoal grey trousers and a tunic of the same colour. Farmers' clothing.

'I saw the car coming. You've made good time, brother. Welcome, Mari. Come, come.'

There was none of the formality I'd expected and got used to. Asa put her arm around my waist and held my hand. She showed me to the bathroom and gave me a lace edged towel. Scented water steamed gently in the ofuro, the deep sided square bathtub, tempting me to get in fully clothed and let the hot water wash over me, soothe me. I heard Takeda-san talking to Asa, but couldn't make out the words so I stopped trying.

I looked at my reflection in the mirror for a long time. My eyes looked greener against the pink-rimmed lids and my hair was a knotted mess. When had I last combed it? My clothes felt dirty; I'd been wearing them for days. Four blue bruises striped my neck on one side and thumbprints stood out like love-bites on the other. Under my sweatshirt, the reddish swelling on my left side felt hot. Holding on to the side of the ofuro, while my head turned and reeled, I fought the urge to cry.

When I came out, I followed the sound of voices into the main room of the house. The shoji partitions to the outside were open, and the low sun of late afternoon streamed in. I gingerly moved outside onto the wooden platform that ringed the house. Stepping down, I stood for a moment, catching my breath. Terraced fields clung to the mountains and a small village lay low in the valley. It hurt like hell, but I walked a little way around the outside of the house, listening to bird-song. I wanted to move my body. It felt alien to me, maybe because of the medication. Sharp nobbles of tiny stones dug into the soles of my bare feet as I walked on the path. My legs shook and I stopped and leaned against a cherry tree, holding my ribs. I tried to raise my knee, to look at the sole of my foot. It was too painful. Papa-san watched me from the doorway of the house. He stepped down and walked towards me.

'Papa-san?' I whispered as he took my arm and I leaned against him. 'Her shoes?'

'Let's get you inside. I'm still trying to find out. Nobody knows anything. Nobody saw anything. Nobody is saying anything. The *yakuza* deny any involvement and we have no proof of anything. Mari, they're closing the case.'

'Why?' I struggled to speak and to breathe. 'No evidence?' Every word hurt, like I'd swallowed broken glass. Or pieces of broken mirror. 'Why cremate?'

'Standard police procedure. Here in Japan, once the death certificate is issued after autopsy, so is the cremation order. If there had been a suspicious cause of death, the certificate wouldn't have been issued. The fact that there wasn't meant they had to issue it. Her parents agreed to it, so that her remains can be flown home.' His hand rubbed across his chin, over his face to his forehead. 'I've never had a case like this. She was only twenty-two, the same age as my youngest daughter. The whole situation...' He let out a long sigh. 'Come inside now, Asa has made food. I'm starving.'

Asa smiled warmly and rushed to help me up the step from the garden. Her rounded body was sturdy as she took my arm and led me to the low table. Involuntary noises escaped me as I bent to sit on the floor. I managed a few sips of the miso shiro soup and a mouthful of rice. It hurt to eat. It hurt to breathe. Asa pushed back the sleeves of her tunic and took a piece of the aubergine that she had cooked with soy and garlic. She cut it up into tiny pieces as if she were going to hand feed a kitten, then slid the dish towards me, watching from the corner of her eye.

Takeda-san laughed. 'My sister is very good at looking after sick animals, Mari. Years ago, she hand-raised a new-born deer we found by the road. And there's always stray dogs and injured cats. I remember a goat once.'

Asa flicked her hand at her brother, hit his arm. 'Who was it who brought me these sick animals? And now you bring me a sick girl. Hmm?' She took hold of my hand.

My chin trembled. I didn't think I could cry anymore. But there were still tears.

Asa tilted her head to one side and tucked a stray strand of hair behind her ear. 'It's okay. You lost your friend and you lost your love, and someone tried to take your life. It's too much for anyone.'

Excusing myself, I tried to get up off the floor. Takeda-san stood behind me, lifting me by my elbows. Standing at the front of the house, I wondered where I was, where this place was. It was so quiet, no noise except the crickets and a soft trickling sigh of a stream somewhere. A man, dressed in jeans and a checked shirt, walked slowly towards me, eyeing me, his hand behind his back. I backed inside the house, holding my ribs.

'Papa-san.'

He and Asa jumped up and ran to the door.

'It's my husband, Tetsu. Just my husband,' she said as the man came along the path with the handful of pak-choi he had cut from his fields.

He stared at me but said nothing.

'Don't mind him. He's the silent type.' Asa put her arm round my waist. 'Come, child, come.'

TAKEDA-SAN MADE CALLS from the phone in another room, then spoke at length to Tetsu and Asa. The car keys jangled in his hand; he was ready to start his journey back. I didn't want him to go. It felt safe with him there.

'The British Consulate know you are here. They'll contact you about your flight.'

'Leave?' I gasped for breath, razor blades of words ripping at my throat. 'No, Papa-san.'

'In a few days, you'll be in Singapore. You'll be safe here until then. Nobody could even guess you're here. They'll phone you to make the final arrangements.'

'We don't know… what happened.'

'Mari, we do know.' He looked at me, his eyebrows creased. 'Ultimately, she died. They put it down to the head injury. But how that happened… there's not enough to convict the *wakagashira*, so there's nothing more to be done. It's not my decision but the case will be closed.'

'Not leaving.' I shook my head.

'Try and understand, it's safer for you, long term. Once you're out of Japan, there'll be nothing to fear. Kate's bones and ashes will be sent back to her parents. We have them in Hitano morgue until the Consulate come for them.'

'Bones?'

Asa explained the ritual of Japanese cremation. Only the flesh is burned and the bones, once removed from the ashes by the family, are put into an urn and taken to the cemetery. It sounded horrendous. I couldn't think about it.

We walked up the path to the car parked at the roadside and he opened the door. Asa stood next to me, holding onto my arm. It was sweet; this lady, whose silver head only reached my shoulder, tried to support me physically. Tetsu put two boxes of vegetables into the boot of the car and stood, holding the door open.

'You... so kind.' I took a step towards Takeda-san. My cheeks were wet. 'Don't go.'

'I have to get back. You and I have been together every step of the way since they found her. Go to Singapore, stay safe and live your life well.' He put one arm round my shoulders in a brief hug. 'I'm sorry that I can't bring someone to justice for what happened.'

'Thank you.' With my bandaged arm across my ribs, I stood to attention, raising my other hand, and saluted him. 'Papa Takeda-san.'

He laughed and drove away, his hand waving out of the window.

Asa led me back inside the house, to the room that I would be sleeping in. Thick bamboo beams, floor to ceiling, dissected the white walls. A small window looked out over the rice fields to the mountains. She'd already laid the futon out on the tatami mats. They smelled of late summer sunshine. It made me think of the first time I'd seen a tatami. Before Ryu, before Kate. I pulled the blue elephant out of my cloth bag, held it to my face and breathed in Kate's perfume.

By the time I'd had a bath, Asa had washed Ryu's sweatshirt and my other clothes and hung them on a bamboo frame at the rear of the house. She gave me a yukata and a pair of white tabi house socks to wear. My holdall sat by the wall, and my cassette player next to it. I found my cassette tapes and dug out Anzen Chitai. Their name translated as *Safety Zone*. If I could've smiled, I would have. I slotted the tape into my Walkman. The sad melody of '*Friend*' did nothing to soothe me, but dosed with medication, I fell asleep.

Chapter 45

THE AUTUMN DAWN was misty and cold under a colourless sky. A drizzle of soft rain formed little pools on the gravel path. The mountains had lost their contours and looked like cardboard cut-outs, layered over each other in shades of pewter. The wind smelled of the sea and brought red and gold leaves to my bare feet.

Of course, I didn't know where I was so I had no destination in mind, I just walked. My jeans and Ryu's sweatshirt clung to me and the wind tumbled my hair. I must've looked like a crazed witch, a mad Medusa. Walking until I was wet through, I trembled with cold, but it wasn't enough; I still didn't feel alive.

Asa stood in the doorway, her hands in her trouser pockets. She came out into the rain, hunched her shoulders, and folded her arms across her chest.

'You'll get ill. Get those wet clothes off and have a hot bath. Crazy girl, going off like that. How can I help you if you don't let me? Soup, I'll make you soup, you must be hungry. You slept for thirty hours straight.'

'I can't feel anymore.' My voice was whispery and croaky. I blinked away tears. I'd walked barefooted, but it didn't hurt enough. My ribs didn't hurt enough. My arm didn't hurt enough. 'I can't feel, I want to hurt more.'

Standing in the doorway, I shivered, dripping rain and tears. The urge to scream with anger and rage faded. I didn't have the energy.

'It's not that you don't feel anything, child. It's the opposite, hmm? You are feeling too much. Your feelings are overwhelming you.' Asa came to me and pulled at the hem of my sweatshirt. I raised my arms one at a time, like a child, and the wet clothes were taken off me. 'Your brain can't process it all. Your body and your mind are not aligned at this time, how could they be? Give yourself time. You will find balance again.' Asa pushed me gently towards to bathroom. 'Get warm in the bath and when you finish, we will talk more. Your voice sounds better today. And I want to change that dressing on your arm. It shouldn't have got wet in the rain.'

After showering clean, I stepped into the deep straight-sided wooden bathtub. With my bandaged arm wrapped in a thick towel, I leant it on the rim of the bath, hoping it wouldn't get any damper. The hot water steamed with sweet fragrance. I picked up a pink packet of salts from a small shelf.

'Sa. Ku. Ra. Sakura.' I read the symbols and the word stabbed me. 'Oh, Kate.' I sighed. The main reason Kate had come to Japan was to see the cherry blossom, the sakura. My eyes burned.

The ofuro had a built-in seat and as I slid my hips forward a little, the water covered my shoulders. Warmth spread through my body and tension ebbed away. For the first time in weeks, my emotions were still as if I'd switched them off, or had entered some void where no thoughts were allowed. Sitting in the perfumed water, I trickled my good hand along the surface, watching the steam rise. I closed my eyes and for a few moments, felt nothing and thought nothing.

When I finished, Asa helped me dress. She'd already lit the small wood burner and made a breakfast of miso soup, fried tofu, and steamed rice. I ate a little before I put down my chopsticks. The bowl of soup created swirls of steam that moved like the sea. Asa watched me intently.

'Come, eat more. You cannot heal your soul if you don't take care of your body.'

'I don't care. I don't deserve… ' Even so, I drank tiny sips from the soup bowl. Holding the bowl, I remembered the afternoon in the teahouse. 'Can I call Ryu?'

'Don't you think it's best left the way it is?'

'I just want to hear his voice.' I tried to clear my throat.

'That won't help either of you. Your beautiful heart needs to let him go, Mari. Let him get over this tragedy and move forward with his life, and his marriage.'

'You don't understand.'

'I understand too well. I was in love with a boy when I was seventeen. My parents did not agree, his parents did not agree. I thought I would die without him,' she said. She cleared away the dishes and came back with a bowl of warm water and a large plastic box. 'I prayed and meditated and nothing helped to fill that hole in my heart. I decided to become a nun for a while. And then one morning, not long after, I was helping my mother in the orchard and I saw Tetsu. And I knew he was my destiny. I entered the Buddhist nunnery then, and four years later, I returned and we were married. He waited for me, all that time. That was thirty-three years ago.'

Asa held my arm and unwound the damp bandage. The gauze stuck to the wounds; the blood dried to black. She bathed them in warm water until they peeled off, cleaning away the dried blood. Examining the wounds closely, she nodded, and put on a clean dressing.

'What if Ryu is my destiny? And I am his?'

'Then none of this would have happened. Destiny is pushing you apart, not drawing you together. Can you see that?' She touched my hand. 'All done. Your cuts are healing well.'

The phone rang and Asa went into the other room to answer it. When she came back, she tucked the plastic box under her arm and took the bowl back into the kitchen.

'My brother. You'll leave two days after tomorrow.' she said over her shoulder.

'So soon? I'm not ready.'

'You are welcome for as long as you like, but it's not up to me.' She added two logs to the wood burner, and the warmth did nothing to soothe me. 'The Consulate are involved now. My brother will send your Kagami-san and another detective. They'll take you to the consulate in Osaka. A hotel's been arranged for you for that night and your flight leaves Sunday morning. They'll escort you the whole way, so that you're safe.'

The phone rang again, and this time it was the British Consulate for me. I took the call and listened as the male secretary to the Ambassador explained what would happen.

Asa sat at the low table, pouring hot tea into tall handle-less cups. A square plate held two ripe persimmons, the green leaves on their stalks curling inwards. Asa peeled the fruits, slicing them into wedges. I didn't want to eat them. Their sweet smell was cloying, and I remembered the one I'd seen in Hitano, smashed to pieces on the hard ground, slowly rotting in the heat. Looking out of the small window at the side of the room, I watched as mist floated soft and silvery across the yellowing rice fields. I ran my hands across my face and turned to face Asa.

'The police have asked them to help get me out of Japan, because of the *yakuza* They've been arranging for Kate's... remains to be sent home.' I felt like I'd lived a whole life in those last few days.

'Here, drink this,' said Asa.

She presented the teacup in both hands. Pain flashed everywhere as I sat on the floor.

'I dreamt, or maybe I felt, the exact time she died. Three-twenty in the afternoon. I felt her soul go.' I sipped the tea slowly, letting the warmth soothe my throat. Thinking back to that moment brought a new wave of emotions that left me shaky and worn out.

'It can happen when a soul leaves a body.' Asa smiled. 'That's a rare and beautiful thing. Mari, you won't believe me, but this will get easier. Maybe years later, maybe next week, but one day you will find acceptance and understand that what has happened isn't your fault. You'll accept that it was her ending and not confuse it with yours.'

'It's my fault. I shouldn't have left her. I can't imagine a day without this pain, this guilt.' I put my hand over my heart. 'Her poor family, they must be devastated.'

'My eldest son Himuro lives in Yokohama, my youngest Masako in Osaka. I miss them every day, like my heart is waiting to beat properly again. How terrible life would be if something bad happened to them. But we cannot control such things. We must accept that other people's destiny isn't ours. Sometimes it dovetails, sometimes it doesn't. Accept that what happened to Kate was her destiny. Acceptance is the balm that heals all wounds.'

'Acceptance is the balm that heals all wounds,' I repeated her words. 'I wish I could feel it.'

'You will. When you're ready.'

'When I was seventeen, my sister died. It was my fault.' And I told her the whole story.

Mum had taken the twins to visit Uncle Saturnino in Acton. Dad was, of course, at work. Elena had been home from hospital for three days, after having her appendix out. She had me running around for her all morning. Her demands were simple enough. *Mari, plump the pillows, Mari, change the TV channel, Mari, get me a cold drink. Mari, get me a sandwich. Mari. Mari. Mari.* I was irritated and tired of playing nursemaid. When she asked me to help her shower, I refused and told her she could manage by herself. And she could, she was just being a pain. Leaving Elena at the bathroom door, I went downstairs and rang my boyfriend, twisting the curly cord of the receiver round my fingers. *Mari. Mari.* Now what? Upstairs the overhead shower ran splish-splash in the bath. *Mari. Mari.* I shouted then, told her to shut the fuck up. I said I was sick of her, that she had to stop bothering me. Turning on the TV in the lounge, I watched a Doris Day double-bill on BB2. I loved the romance of the 1950's films, loved the full skirted dresses.

After about ten minutes, Elena stopped calling my name.

The light changed, as if the sun had shuddered, and I should've gone to check on her, because I felt something was wrong. But I didn't, I stayed downstairs watching TV.

When my family came home, Dad in tow, I was sitting on the sofa, reading an NME magazine, half watching videos on MTV. Mum and the twins went straight upstairs to see Elena. That's when the screaming started. Rushing upstairs behind Dad, we found the twins wailing by the bathroom door, entwined in each other. My mother sat in the bath, under the still running shower, cradling Elena's wet body. She had fallen in the shower, knocked herself out and drowned in three inches of water. And it was my fault. I shouldn't have left her alone in the bathroom. I should've checked on her. Maybe I could've saved her.

By the time I finished telling Asa, my face was wet and I needed to blow my nose.

'My brother said he thought there was a problem with your family,' said Asa. 'Can't you go home?'

'How can I?'

'Pain either alienates people or binds them together. And it's easy to put the blame on someone else. Perhaps your mother blames herself, after all, she is the parent. You are your mother's child too.'

'But it's happened again. I left Kate on her own after we'd argued. I even wished her dead. And then she died.' My hand flew to my throat. I'd spoken too much.

WHEN THE RAIN subsided into a misty dampness, we walked to edge of the nearest rice terrace and looked down over the hillside. Ready for harvesting, the rice plants were tatami-coloured. The trees still held the rain, and the dark red and orange leaves had the sheen of patent leather. Across the valley, the tops of the mountains were lost behind low cloud.

Asa lit incense and placed it in the ground. Its smoke twirled and floated upwards before the wind whipped it away. She put thin cushions on the damp ground next to a brass bowl. As she helped me to kneel, I bit my lip against the pain. Asa struck the bowl with a thick wooden stick and took my hand.

'*Namu Amida bu,*' chanted Asa, in a low monotone. She repeated the phrase over and over so that the words ran into each other. When she paused to take another deep breath, she struck the bowl. The metal chimed like a bell, its resonance filling the air across the valley. '*Namu Amida bu.*'

I joined in the chant on the third round and the rhythmic sound soothed me. My heart was calm as we chanted the words that honour the dead.

Chapter 46

JUST AFTER BREAKFAST on Saturday, I watched from the doorway as a brown car made its way along the road that hugged the mountain. Asa cut the last sedative in two and gave me the remaining half wrapped in a tissue. Swallowing was easier but I'd need more than half a sedative. The journey to Osaka would take longer than the one from Hitano, and that had been bad enough. And being cooped up in a car with Kagami-san for hours wasn't my idea of fun.

'Look, Mari.' Asa patted my arm as the car slowed down and I squinted against the morning sun as the driver got out.

'Papa-san!' I took a few steps towards him.

Takeda-san put his arm round my shoulders in a one-armed hug. He stood me back, holding me at arm's length. Frowning, he shook his head.

From the doorway, Asa called, 'Brother, you visit me two times in one week. I am happy and blessed. Come in, there is food.'

'I decided to see this through myself. I don't trust anyone else.' He moved his chewing gum aside while he spoke. 'No one knows I'm here, except my wife.'

'I'm glad it's you and not Kagami-san. I don't like him.'

'You terrified him. Poor man, it was his first case, straight out of the police academy.' He looked at me closely and smiled. 'You look terrible. I wish you could stay here longer.'

'Me too. But it's good to see you, Papa-san.'

Asa led him inside and served his food while I gathered my things together. There wasn't much; a second pair of jeans, my sunflower skirt, and few shirts and t-shirts. I wrapped toiletries in a plastic bag and put half a dozen cassette tapes into a small plastic box. My bento box of cosmetics wasn't there nor the origami animals. That saddened me, I'd like to have kept them. They must still be in Hitano with my Tarot cards. I didn't want them anymore. Not after Kate's blank reading.

Asa stepped into the room, holding a long piece of pale grey cloth with a silver thread through it. She moved towards me, looping the soft cotton scarf round my neck. 'To hide your bruises.'

Saying goodbye to Asa wasn't easy. She embodied the peace that I needed, the safety and sanctuary. I tried to absorb it into my blood, into my bones, so that I could carry the feeling with me.

'It's time?' said Asa, looking at her brother. 'I will miss you, child. Thank you for coming here, to my house.'

'It's me who should be thanking you. You've helped me so much.'

'It was my privilege to help you. Sometimes giving can be a greater gift than receiving.'

She pressed a six-inch piece of cardboard tubing into my hand. Inside was a scroll of rice paper parchment. I tipped it out and unrolled it. Japanese ink-brush calligraphy graced the paper. Two large, black hiragana symbols. My name; Ma Ri.

I smiled. 'You did this? It's beautiful. Thank you.'

'I wanted to give you something. The square red stamp at the bottom,' she pointed to the kanji character, 'means *joy of the truthful soul*. This round one, *insightful heart*. You have both, Mari.' She handed me an unsealed oblong envelope, showed me the sheets of folded paper inside. 'Blank paper, for when you decide to write to your mother.'

I bowed to Asa. A long, respectful bow. And I meant it.

Chapter 47

TAKEDA-SAN AND I drove in comfortable silence for a long way. The car radio hissed, losing its signal in the forested hills, then crackled to life with music. The trees wore their autumn colours now, celebrating the end of summer, enjoying a last chance to show-off before the onset of winter.

'Where are we?' I said.

'Near Okayama. Honshu. We'll be in Osaka in about three hours.' Takeda-san said.

The land levelled out and the car slipped onto the straight dual carriageway.

'There was a girl, Cherry,' I said. 'She lived in our apartment before we got here in May. All her things were still there until Sayuri got someone to take them away. She was Ohayo's girlfriend and then she disappeared. Do you know anything? Was she reported as a missing person?'

'Your friend, Imee, reported it when we interviewed her about Kate. We're looking into it, but these things are never easy. Not with the *yakuza*.'

Another dead girl. No doubt they'd get away with that murder too. Who'd have thought things like that could happen in a small town?

'What's happening in Hitano?' It was out of my mouth before I could stop myself.

'Mama has gone missing. That evil woman hasn't been seen

for days. We're looking though. And when she turns up, I'll find something, anything, to put her away. But there's nothing new regarding Kate.'

'And our friends, my friends? Did you see Koji?'

Ryu's name would not pass my lips. It was stuck somewhere on the other side of acceptance.

'Not since I brought you to Asa. I rang your other friend when I got back to Hitano to tell him you were safe, waiting for the Consulate to get you out of Japan. Someone smashed up his bar the night you were attacked. Set fire to his car as well. He's paid the price, so they'll leave him alone now. He said he'll get a good pay out from his insurance policies and rebuild.'

'Will they leave him alone?' I felt sick. Was there no end to this? Ripples in a dark lake, my curse touched everyone around me.

'Believe me, if he wasn't engaged to Junichi's niece, it would have been worse for him.' He shot me an apologetic look. I nodded. 'His business will recover.'

I turned my head, looked out the side window and tried to process the thoughts that crowded in, knowing that I had to accept the part I'd played in all of this. All this had happened because of my relationship with Ryu. But wait, I had to go further back. A hard knot of truth stuck in my chest like a shadow on my soul. If only I'd understood the nightmares I'd had in Sydney. I wished I'd trusted my instinct and never got on the plane. What had I done? If I hadn't come to Japan, none of this would have happened. How was I supposed to live with that? Guilt spasmed across my belly.

'Stop the car,' I said. 'Quick, stop the car.'

As soon as Takeda-san braked, I opened the door and vomited onto the road. The watery bile tasted bitter, and underneath was the tang of guilt and the sourness of self-loathing.

TAKEDA-SAN WALKED WITH me up the steps of the Consulate. It gave me no comfort to see the Union Jack flying from a high mast by the entrance. Persian rugs covered a dark wood floor in the dim and musty entrance hall. We sat on a leather Chesterfield beneath a mounted picture of Queen Elizabeth II, flicking through recent editions of The Economist that lay on the glass table.

A door closed somewhere and footsteps echoed across the hall. Takeda-san and I stood.

'I'm Edward Kington, Secretary to the Ambassador. Sorry to keep you, it's a busy time.' He shook Takeda-san's hand and then mine. 'We spoke on the phone.'

He was young. Maybe not much older than me. The manila folder slipped from under his arm and he steadied it with his other hand, then gave it to me.

'Your hotel and flight details. All arranged, but you will have to sort payment yourself. I understand you have… enough funds? Good.' He acknowledged my nod. 'I will accompany you to the airport from the hotel tomorrow morning.' He pronounced hotel as *otel*. It sounded pretentious, like something people who were pleased with themselves would say. 'This isn't something we usually do, but because of the attack on your good self, Takeda-san here has asked us, on behalf of the Police Department, to help you.'

'Great, thanks.' I stood holding my escape from Japan in a manila folder. It felt too light, too insubstantial. 'Kate -'

'Ah, your friend. Not clever, insulting a *wakagashira*. Her family have been contacted and her remains will be flown home. If there's nothing else? I really must get on. See you at nine tomorrow morning.' And he was gone.

ON THE STREET, Takeda-san asked directions to the hotel and after a quick cup of tea, I knew I should let the man go home. He must be exhausted; all that driving. He'd gone above and beyond to help me. I'd never forget that. We walked to his car.

'Another goodbye then. Can I ask you a favour? Would you look in on Crazy Dog. The man who lives near -'

'I know who you mean.'

'Would you take him some coffee, and biscuits? And just one last favour?'

Takeda-san unwrapped a piece of gum and shoved it between his teeth 'Go on then. I know what you're going to ask me. A message?'

'If you don't mind, will you tell him... tell him *not to forget the willow tree.*'

He smiled and pulled me into a one-armed hug. 'See you, English daughter. Write to your mother.'

'See you, Papa-san.' I saluted and watched him drive away, my eyes welling up. My arms wrapped round myself, I pulled my sweatshirt tighter, standing there until his car was swallowed up in traffic and I couldn't tell which one it was anymore.

Chapter 48

Edward Kington looked at his watch. The people ahead of us in the queue at the ticketing desk took their time, but there was no rush; my flight didn't leave for a few hours. Announcements for departing flights came over the P.A. system in Japanese, followed by English. Kington shifted from foot to foot and tutted. If he said how busy he was one more time, I'd smack him.

'Look, I'll be okay from here. You really don't need to stay. I know you don't have time and I can sort out my ticket.'

My teeth clenched, my lips felt like plastic and I knew the fake smile didn't reach my eyes. I wanted him gone. After all the weeks of planning to leave Japan, the day had finally come, even if the circumstances had changed. This departure should have been the first step in an exciting journey. So much had happened, so much had been gained and lost. I wanted to be alone to feel, to think, and Kington drove me nuts as he tutted and huffed.

'Well, if you're sure? I could do with getting back to the office. We have a meeting this afternoon with the Japanese Minister for Trade. I'll wish you a safe journey, then. And good luck.' He shook my hand and hurried away into the crowd.

I breathed out. When it was my turn, I moved my black holdall between my feet, and leaned on the counter, travellers' cheques ready to pay for my ticket. Gingerly, I hoisted my cloth bag back on my shoulder. The movement sent flashes of pain through my ribs.

'Good morning, can I help you?' said the lady in the red Japanese Airlines uniform

I hesitated. She asked the question again.

'Actually, no. Sorry.'

I bent slowly, picked up my holdall and turned away. Oh Lord, what was I doing? I walked around the check-in desks and past the cafes and newsagents stands, checking that no one was watching or following me. Coffee: that was a good idea. It was ages since I'd had a decent coffee. I sat at the entrance of the café, breathing in the rich smell before I took a sip. It tasted bitter, like burned rubber. Disappointed, I put the cup back onto the saucer. It didn't really matter, I had other things to think about.

I PULLED THE grey scarf over my head so that it hid my hair and sat for over an hour, pretending to read the guide book and watching out of the corner of my eye for anyone paying me too much attention. Ideas whizzed around my head as a plan took shape. I was going to find out what happened to Kate. And then I was going to make sure that whoever killed her was prosecuted. Just how I'd achieve that wasn't clear, but I had an idea where to start. Another stroll around the check-in desks and I was sure I wasn't being followed. I found the lift that took me from departures to arrivals and walked straight out of the airport.

THE TAXI TOOK me to a small modern hotel close by. Check-in was quick, but I tapped my foot impatiently while they took a photocopy of my passport.

'Three-twenty?' I said. No way. I pushed the key fob back towards the receptionist. 'I can't have a room with that number. Can you give me a different room?'

If they thought I was crazy, I didn't care. I was gaijin anyway, so what the hell. In the lift, I looked at myself in the smoky mirrored walls. My reflection was colourless. That's how I would need to be from now on; colourless. In room two-ten, I put my bags down and deadlocked the door shut behind me.

Chapter 49

THE LETTING AGENT put down the phone. She stared at my neck, and I adjusted my scarf to hide the bruises.

'I think you will like the apartment. Just one room, kitchen, and bathroom,' she said. 'It's cheap, it's close to the subway, and there's an indoor market nearby. I've agreed with the landlady that you will rent it until the end of the year and then month by month.'

'It sounds ideal. I've got the first two months' rent in cash.' I slid the envelope over to her and picked up the tenancy agreement I'd just signed.

'Your landlady is my aunt. She recently bought the apartment as an investment. This is kind of unofficial, as it's short term. I'm just helping her out and I won't put it through the books.' She gave me the key to the apartment and a receipt for the cash. 'I think you need someone to help you.'

'I had to leave him,' I lied, fiddling with the scarf at my neck. 'He hurt me.'

She only nodded, but her sympathy was tangible. 'I understand.'

FROM THE TAXI window, I saw a city that boomed: new high-rises towered above the trees and there were construction sites everywhere. Cars filled the lanes of the dual carriage ways, and I didn't see one bicycle. Neon advertising signs hung off every floor of every building. Huge billboards and banners lined the streets, offering all the trappings of a luxury consumer-driven life.

Such a contrast from the rice fields and small-town atmosphere of Hitano and wherever it was that Asa lived. I didn't know if I'd done the right thing by staying, but I wasn't ready to leave.

The taxi parked outside an apartment complex in a suburb of Osaka. My hands full with two large carrier bags, the driver carried my holdall up three flights of outside stairs and left it in front of my new front door. I huddled into my Levi's jacket in case anyone was watching. Opening the door, I walked straight into a kitchen so small, there wasn't room for a table. The apartment smelt clean, of newly dried paint and new carpet. White laminated cupboards lined the wall opposite, next to a sliding door, and a small stainless-steel sink sat in a tiled worktop, under the window at the side of the room.

I opened the door and stepped out onto the narrow balcony. The green washing machine took up most of the space but there was just enough room for a clothes horse. There was a sadness in knowing I wouldn't be finding any origami animals. The block of flats stood in a semi-circle of identical modern blocks that surrounded a car park. In a children's playground across the busy road that separated the complex from smaller buildings, a mother pushed her child on a red roundabout. Straggly trees surrounded the playground. Their few remaining leaves hung on, fighting against a winter that advanced fast this far north. Cold, I came back inside and opened the door to the capsule bathroom. One piece of moulded fibreglass, it had a built-in ofuro bath and enough space to stand and shower. I loved that. The loo was separate, with a small hand-basin and a large round mirror on the wall above it.

Being in a big city like Osaka would keep me safe. That was my assumption, my hope. No one in Hitano knew I was there. Takeda-san, the Filipinas, no one. Not even Ryu. They'd all think I was in Singapore by now. It was easy to hide the truth from them. But the *yakuza*? I would have to be very, very careful.

'THIS'LL DO,' I said and added the key to my Hello Kitty keyring.

The keys to the Hitano apartment and the rooms above Kujaku were still on it. One day, I would throw them away, but not yet.

I opened one of the carrier bags, and took out a man's khaki parka and a long woollen scarf, a pair of gloves and a woolly bobble hat. Camouflage. And a pair of scissors. In front of the bathroom mirror, I parted my hair down the back of my head and pulled it over each shoulder. The chestnut waves almost reached my elbows. All my life, my hair had defined me. At primary school I'd been called ginger-nut. As I grew older, it had darkened, but people still assumed that the red tinge to my brown hair meant I had a temperament that matched. If I did, it was probably down to my Spanish blood.

The scissors were poised to cut, but I couldn't do it. In the last few weeks, I'd seen a different person every time I looked in the mirror, but to do this? I tried to hide my hair under the golf cap Takeda-san gave me, piling it on top of my head. The hat wouldn't stay on. I tried plaiting my hair and tucking it up inside. The bobble hat I had bought was too small as well. It wasn't going to work. I flung the hats on the floor, stamping my feet. My breath caught as pain jolted through my ribs. There was only one thing to do.

Pulling my hair over my shoulders again, I positioned the scissors, building up courage. I had to do this. A twelve-inch hank of hair silently wafted to the floor. Dragon breath. Each time the scissors rasped through a section of hair more tears streamed down my face. When I'd finished, I looked at my reflection. My chin trembled in a face that was thin and pale, eyes bright from crying. The physical change mirrored everything I felt inside and I would never be the same again. The ragged ends of my hair touched the top of my shoulders and it was just long enough to drag back into a ponytail and tuck up inside the bobble hat. My head felt strangely light.

I took my holdall into the carpeted bedroom and dropped it on the single bed that took up half the space. The zip of the bag had come partially undone, and Kate's elephant poked out. I placed it on the windowsill and closed the curtain across the tiny window. My few personal belongings and clothes were unpacked onto shelves in the single fitted wardrobe. Shivering, my teeth chattered. My first task would be to buy a few thick jumpers and an electric fire. The guidebook stayed in the bottom of the holdall, at the bottom of the wardrobe. It was no use to me now.

Chapter 50

WITH A MENTAL list of the things I needed to buy, I pulled on my parka. Reaching to open the front door, I thought I heard something outside, and I pulled my hand back. Standing dead still, I listened, but there was nothing. It took me another minute or two to open the door. In the end, I had to force myself. I peered round, making sure no one was there. When I felt certain that no one lurked or waited for me, I headed down the outside staircase, keeping my eye on the other walkways of other buildings just in case anyone watched. By the time I got to the road, I was exhausted. Maybe I was being irrational. Unless the *yakuza* had someone follow me from Asa's, they couldn't possibly know I was here. But they may have found out I wasn't on the flight to Singapore, and then it could only be a matter of time before they found me.

The covered market housed small open-fronted shops and stalls under a low concrete roof. Vegetables, tofu, a grocery shop. It might mean trouble if someone worked out that I was gaijin so I had to buy things without getting into conversation with anyone. Shop owners in thick coats and woolly hats ignored me as I walked past, and with a surge of bravery, I bought miso soup, some instant noodles and inari rolls. I looked at the shelves in another grocery shop and jumped a mile when a woman bumped into me. My heart pounded and my head spun as I tried to breathe. I rushed out of the shop without buying the instant coffee I'd gone in there for. There was nothing I could tell myself to make it easier, so I went back to the apartment and waited until two p.m.

It took all my courage to leave the apartment again and head to the subway. But I had to do this, it was why I didn't get on the plane. I walked, head down, and bought a ticket from the automated machine. Hunched and cold, I waited on the platform for the next train.

My reflection looked back at me from the train window, my hat hiding what was left of my most obvious feature. The fur trimmed hood on my parka made me smile, reminding me of a schoolgirl crush I had on a boy when I was fourteen. Colin, or Christopher, or some such, had constantly worn his parka, even in summer, trying to be 1970's cool.

I inched my hat further down my forehead and adjusted the scarf over the lower half of my face, determined not to make eye-contact with anyone, to stay inconspicuous. I'd phoned the office I was headed to the day before to set up the appointment. And now I found it, in a small apartment block in a middle-of-nowhere suburb, eight stops away. In the small front yard, a persimmon tree stood bearing its fruit, ripe and voluptuous among the orange leaves.

The private investigator, Seung-Heon Moon, greeted me with a moist-palmed handshake. I resisted the urge to wipe my hand on my jeans as I stepped over boxes to get to the chair opposite his desk. He was zainichi, the same as Ryu's paternal family. It was partly why I'd chosen his name from the phone book. That and the fact his listing was the only one in Japanese, Korean and English.

'Most of my work is spousal. Cheating husbands, suspicious husbands checking on their wives. That sort of thing,' he said. He sat back in his chair, moving the papers strewn across his desk into a pile, plonking an empty whisky bottle on top. A jumble of boxes, files, and balls of screwed up paper covered the carpeted floor. 'I have handled missing persons once or twice, mainly for insurance companies. I have many contacts in the police.'

'Good. I need you to find out where my friend was for the three days she was missing. If you could find out what happened to her shoes too, and the name of the person who killed her. I need all the information you can find.'

'Leave it with me. It might take some time. Tell me where I can find you?'

'I'll come to you if that's okay. I'll phone you in a week?'

'Two. I should have information for you by then. I must be honest with you. *Yakuza* cover their tracks very well. This might be difficult.'

On the subway ride back to my apartment, I wondered if I was doing the right thing or if I'd thrown my money away. Trusting him was another matter. If Hitano and Osaka were the same *yakuza* syndicate, the Yamaguchi-gumi, there was a possibility that while Moon asked around, someone would find out that I was the one he was asking for. Hopefully, he'd come up with the truth and the police would take it from there. I'd love to stand in the witness box aand point the finger at the *wakagashira*, see him go down for life. I wanted him to rot in a stinking jail for what he'd done. Two weeks was a long time to have to wait to see Mr Moon again. What was I supposed to do until then?

Needing to focus on something good, something positive, I tried to work out my finances for travelling. There was enough money for Singapore to India, but probably not enough for India to England. Mr Moon's time was expensive but if I lived frugally, I'd still get to India. And for Kate's sake, I had to get to India. Remembering the last thing I'd said to her made me feel sick. But there was no way to take back my words.

BRAVING THE MARKET again on my way home, I bought a warm jumper. Still hidden under my hat and scarf, I got a three-bar fire from a tiny hole-in-the-wall shop and lugged it back to my apartment, pain racking through my ribs. Later that evening, I went out yet again and bought half a dozen packs of instant ramen, a bottle of Hennessy brandy and some soda from the konbini near the subway entrance. Commuter-busy, people pushed through the turnstiles on their way home. My body tensed every time someone got a little too close, but no one noticed me. Anonymity was what I needed but it came with an emptiness that made me long for the past, for the carefree days before Elena died. Cold had got into my bones, but the rain had finally stopped. Raindrops clung to the telegraph wires, catching the street-lights' amber glow, reminding me of the fireflies that had danced across the rice fields of summer.

The phone box lured me, I walked straight past, proud of my willpower. Then I doubled back. I didn't even need to try and remember Ryu's number; my fingers knew the sequence by heart.

'*Moshi moshi*, hello?'

'Ryu, it's me.'

'Mari? How are you? Where are you? God, I miss you.' He laughed softly and my heart came back to life.

'I'm good. I'm in Singapore and it's wonderful.' I closed my eyes, imagining the warmth of him, the smell of him. 'How's everything?'

'My Mari, it's… different. Takeda-san is still probing, you know, even though the case is closed. He's trying to take Ohayo down. And still looking for Mama.'

'I hope he finds whoever killed her. Hanging wouldn't be good enough.' I wanted to tell him that I was in Osaka, tell him about Mr Moon. It was there, ready to spill out of my mouth, but I didn't say it. 'It's so good to hear your voice.'

'Yours too, I –' In the background, I heard a woman's voice.

'Ryu, my card's running out,' I lied. 'Bye.'

My stitches pulled as I replaced the receiver and I walked the short distance to my new apartment.

For the last few days, my arm had felt tight. It was almost two weeks since the attack. My stomach lurched with the memory of what had happened, leaving me light-headed and breathy. The stitches needed to come out, but it probably wasn't a clever idea to go to a hospital. They'd ask questions; they were supposed to. And who might they tell?

I had to do it myself, but I needed a drink. The nail scissors and tweezers that I'd sterilized in boiling water gleamed under the kitchen strip light, placed on a piece of sterile gauze on top of the draining board. Pouring brandy into a glass, I added soda. The smell took me right back to Hitano. Sadness dragged up from my belly, through my chest, and I waited for the booze to kick in. My scars were visible reminders. How would they look in thirty years? Would I still feel the same? Probably. I'd carry the guilt, shame and sadness with me forever.

It was fiddly, my left hand fumbled with the small scissors as I snipped at the black stitches. Snip. Just next to the knot. Snip. Snip. Nausea rose, I breathed deep, hoping it would pass. Snip. Twenty-eight times snip. I felt something move inside my arm every time. The scar was thick and red, the cut stitches sticking out along each side like a caterpillar's legs. I needed more brandy and drank straight from the bottle, grimacing as the harsh liquid burnt the back of my throat. I tugged at the end of a stitch with the tweezers. The thread came away with a pulling sensation, and I nearly threw up. The next few came out fairly easily, but by the time I'd taken out a dozen stitches, sweat beaded my top lip and trickled down my back. There was no choice but to finish what I'd started. The next stitch wouldn't come away and I had to pull hard a few times. There was a tiny tearing sensation and blood pooled in the hole it left. I leant over the sink and vomited. The pain in my ribs made my head spin, and I thought I'd faint.

It took an hour to get rid of the remaining sixteen stitches. I poured brandy over the bloody little holes as I went. Then I started on the other, smaller cuts. One by one, I snipped and pulled the stitches out, stopping frequently to vomit and, towards the end, dry heave. I wrapped my unstitched arm in a clean bandage, lay down on the bed as the room lurched and finally went dark.

Chapter 51

FORCING MYSELF TO go out every day was something to focus on, anything to get me out of that tiny prison cell of an apartment.

Sleep was impossible. Some nights, the darkness was too much, and I was afraid it would never end. With no Japanese homework to do, no Kate to talk to, and no Ryu to be with, time was cold and empty. I lay in bed under the thick quilt as soon as dusk stole the light from the sky, scared to put the lamp on in case anyone watched from outside. I dozed, but the sound of doors closing somewhere in the building, or footsteps on the stairs. made me wide-eyed and panicky. Six metal forks stood in a tall glass by the front door - if someone came in, I'd hear them and be ready with the kitchen knife I kept under the bed.

With the quilt pulled up under my nose, I waited and listened. Waited for the *yakuza* to find me. Waited for the first birdsong of morning, for that specific change in the darkness. Waited for that blue-grey light between night and day that heralded the arrival of the safer hours.

LATE ONE NIGHT, I heard a noise on the balcony. I held my breath and moved my head off the pillow so I could hear better. Someone was out there, scraping and scuffling. They'd found me. I wondered if Mr Moon had told them, or maybe I hadn't been careful enough and someone had spotted me. Blood surged through my ears and pounded behind my eyes. I reached for the knife and slid silently out of bed, moving across the room. The knife handle was heavy and I adjusted my left-handed grip. Fuck them, I'd go down fighting. And then I heard it. The flapping and the cooing, and I realised it was a pigeon.

I cried, great sobs ripping through my body in time to the shots of pain that ripped through my ribs. This was no way to live. They would've found me by now if they were going to. Had I created my own prison? I grabbed the brandy bottle and poured a large one. It soothed me, calmed me, and made me feel brave. I had another, and told myself that I, Marianna Randall, was not going to live in fear.

AFTER THAT, DRINKING too much became a coping mechanism. It started with a gulp or two of brandy to steady my nerves before I left the apartment each day. When I came back, I needed a gulp or two to calm me down. And by the evening, I needed a lot to numb the horror of everything. Listening to my cassettes, I sat on the floor drinking and writing letters that I never posted, and poems that tore my heart to shreds. I dug out the photo of Ryu and me at the teahouse and talked to him. Brandy-soaked words that didn't matter now. Conversations with Kate were a regular feature and I lost count of how many times I asked her to forgive me. When the tears took over, which they always did, I dragged myself onto the bed and let the alcohol take me into the darkness of non-feeling.

ON THE FOURTEENTH day, I woke, my breath like dragon smoke in the cold apartment. My head pounded as I pulled my parka on over my pyjamas, stuffed my cold feet into shoes, and went out to the rubbish bins with nine empty brandy bottles in two carrier bags. A woman wearing a blue anorak ignored me, thank God, as she emptied her rubbish into the bin. I hesitated, ashamed by what I was about to throw away. That was it. No more. I was losing my grip on reality. Living in a haze of booze wasn't going to achieve anything.

I FELT WRETCHED as I sat on the subway heading to Mr Moon's office and knew I probably stank of alcohol. Madness. The madness had started that night, just a few weeks ago when we walked out of Kujaku and didn't go back, the night Kate had gone missing. Madness. It flowed in my blood like a physical disease, and I could feel it burning through my soul. Maybe today would be the end of it. Maybe today the circle would close. And even if it didn't, I had to do something to stop the madness before it dragged me under.

Chapter 52

ON MY WAY to see Seung-heon Moon, I passed a TV shop. A dozen or so TVs in the window showed the same news programme. Greenpeace's ship, *Rainbow Warrior,* had been bombed in New Zealand. They'd been protesting against the French government's nuclear testing on Mururoa Atoll in the Pacific.

I remembered back to August, when Ryu and I had watched TV coverage of the fortieth anniversary of the bombings of Hiroshima and Nagasaki. I was sickened, upset by the archived wartime footage they showed. School history lessons told us about the atomic bomb, about Enola Gay. It happened long ago and far away, but I'd understood the implications. My stance on nuclear arms was strong and living in Japan brought it closer, made the horror more real. Watching as school children lay a thousand paper cranes at the cenotaph in Hiroshima's Peace Park, Ryu told me that it was dedicated to the more than 200,000 souls thought to have perished. On a stone chest under the arched cenotaph, the inscription read:

Let all the souls here rest in peace, for we shall not repeat the evil.

And evil it was. The world had to disarm. It had to. As I walked to Mr Moon's office, I thought about souls and death and nuclear bombs. And Ryu's grandma, how hard it must've been for a woman alone in post-war Japan with a half-American baby. It made me realise how small my problems were, how small my existence was. I was just one tiny person in a huge world. So what if I hated myself for what I'd done – or hadn't done. That was my problem. That was nothing in comparison to what Kate's family must be going through. But the guilt I felt didn't go away.

MR MOON HAD been busy. He'd tidied his office, and had an air of satisfaction about him. He motioned for me to sit down in the chair opposite his desk. He smiled, his teeth small and crooked.

'Before we start, I have a proposition for you,' he said.

'What kind of proposition, Mr Moon?' I said, my tone wary.

'I have two grandchildren.' He took a framed photo off the wall and handed it to me. 'They study English in school but need some extra help. My son can pay you an excellent rate, for say, a few hours a week?'

'Yes, okay.' I had expected a quite different proposition.

'And so, let me tell you. I have found out a few things. They might be of interest,' Moon said. He opened a file on his desk and tapped his fingers on it.

'Have you found out where Kate was for those three days?'

Moon shook his head. 'I have someone in contact with the pathologist who carried out the autopsy. The woman is teaching a course in Tokyo. She will return to Fukuoka in the middle of December. She has promised to get in touch.'

'Another month? What if she doesn't call back?' I leaned forward. Time dragged already, and waiting another four weeks would be torture. As it was, I was already halfway to crazy.

'My contact says she has information.' He pulled out a piece of paper from the file. 'The pathologist told my contact this - "*I am happy to help. I can't give any details now but there is something your client should know.*" So, we wait.'

'Has someone actually asked the *wakagashira*? I got the impression that the police didn't even question him.'

Moon sucked his teeth and wagged his finger. 'Alright, alright, let me see. Maybe I can find out.'

As I left the building, it crossed my mind to give up there and then, but I had to be patient. Time. I had plenty of that. And time marched autumn towards a bleak winter. The persimmon tree's leaves clustered around its narrow trunk and the breeze chased them across the path that led to the street.

THE FIRST LESSON with Mr Moon's grandchildren went well. I sat on the floor in the kids' bedroom and helped them pronounce the English alphabet. Easy money. The parents asked me to come back twice a week for two hours at a time. They told me that as only English grammar was taught at school, conversation practice was essential. On my second visit, they asked if I would like to teach some of the neighbours' children. By the end of that week, I had lessons lined up every weekday after school and into the evenings. Within a few days, Saturdays were full as well. I had nothing else to do. And the money would be good for travelling, whenever that would happen. But it was bigger and better than that - I'd been thrown a life-line. Something to focus on.

The families welcomed me into their homes, happy not to have to pay expensive city language schools for a native English speaker to teach their kids. It wasn't really teaching; I just helped them with their English homework and got them to talk about something that interested them. I fell into an easy routine for the next month or so; teaching in the afternoons and evenings, going from apartment to apartment, and waiting, always waiting for updates from Mr Moon.

I received a message from him via his grandchildren. He wanted to see me and I rushed to his office. Our meeting was over in two minutes. The pathologist had changed her mind, wasn't sure she should speak out. Probably too scared. Mr Moon said he was following other leads and would keep me updated. I had no choice but to wait even longer.

ONE EVENING, THE mother of a little girl I taught invited me to stay for dinner, and for once I accepted. I didn't want to be alone. Not that day. The lady created divine-smelling food in the kitchen while I helped her daughter with her homework. It felt good to share a meal with someone, in an apartment warm with life. We ate at a low table with a heater underneath, a fireproof quilt pulled over our legs. They held bowls to their lips and flicked rice into their mouths with chopsticks. I'd never perfected the art of eating with chopsticks to that level and still dropped a little rice. Of course, my kind hosts didn't pass comment.

Once the meal was over, I made excuses about needing to get back, even though it was still early evening. The company and the kindness were suddenly all too much and emotions threatened to surface. Funny how they caught me off guard now and then, always at a time I least expected it, when Elena, Kate and Ryu had been absent from my mind for hours. '*Hey,*' they said "*Hey, we're still here. Remember us. Remember what you did.*'

I got off the subway a stop early, to walk, just to kill another twenty minutes. The hairs rose on the back of my neck as a cold sensation ran through my already frozen body and I huddled into my parka. In a doorway, a shadow lurked. Whoever it was didn't move as I passed. Crossing to the other side of the road, I checked behind me, but there was no one there. My footsteps echoed in the empty street, bouncing off the windows and doors of the closed shops. Every few steps, I looked over my shoulder to make sure no one was following. The only sound of life came from the open fronted Pachinko parlour. Players in puffer jackets and anoraks sat huddled in front of the vertical gaming machines as multicoloured lights flashed, garish and harsh. The electronic noise was oddly soothing as I passed by.

Osaka's winter was cold, and it well and truly echoed my mood. I felt as bare as the trees that waited for spring. All I did was wait. Wait for news of Kate's murder, wait for the *yakuza* to find me, wait to feel alive. I'd lost sense of who I was. Now I was only part of Kate's story, of Ryu's story and I'd forgotten my own. I would have given anything to be with Ryu, to be held by him, to feel him breathe and taste his mouth. Did he wonder how my days were without him? Trudging through the frozen streets, I felt hollow, I couldn't remember ever feeling so lonely.

Something dark had swallowed me and I didn't know if I'd ever be free.

My boots crunched on ice crystals that sparkled under the street lights as I headed home, making me think of glittery Christmas cards. A white Christmas was something I'd dreamt of as a child. I bought into that romantic image with love, laughter, and roaring fires. So different from the beach barbies and back yard pool parties I'd grown up with in Sydney. My few years in England hadn't given me that perfect Christmas card experience, either.

At the konbini near the station, I bought a bottle of Siglo red wine and a box of Pocky chocolate sticks. When I came out of the shop, the air was full of feathery snowflakes. I pulled off my gloves and twirled slowly, face to the sky, hands out to catch the snow. Happy Christmas, Mari.

I stopped at a phone box. I just wanted to hear Ryu, wish him a Happy Christmas. My phone-card was decorated with an old wood-block print from a hundred-and-fifty years ago. The huge wave's white crest curled into menacing fingers, a snow-capped Fujiyama looked on helplessly, waiting for the devastation. I tapped in Ryu's number, but hung up when a woman answered.

Chapter 53

My appointment with Seung-Heon Moon was arranged for December 29th and I prayed he had something to tell me. The three-day New Year's holiday was coming up, and I didn't want another delay.

Nerves made me jumpy, and the eight-stop subway journey was endless. Walking from the station to the apartment block, I dug my hands into my pockets to keep them warm and turned onto the path that led to the entrance of Mr Moon's building. The persimmon tree was naked of leaves now and its gnarly black branches held a few hard-to-reach orange orbs. Next to the skinny trunk was a lone fallen persimmon, cracked open, its velvety flesh exposed to the frigid wind. In a way, I felt the same.

I sat on the edge of the chair in Mr Moon's office with my hands hooked under my knees.

'I learned something interesting. The order to close the case came from the Chief of Police. For all of Kyushu, not just Fukuoka Prefecture. Most highly ranked policeman. He shouldn't have been involved in anything procedural. Especially not a murder. But he ordered the case to be closed. He hurried the issue of the Death Certificate. And therefore, the one for cremation.'

'So, it's a cover-up because it's *yakuza*.' I stared at the space above his head. 'So that's it. The w*akagashira* gets away with it.'

'I can learn nothing more.' He pushed a thin envelope across his desk. 'A refund. I have not found out as much as I hoped.

Also, I mistakenly overcharged you. And there's someone here to see you.'

Turning as the door opened, I expected to see Takeda-san or maybe Ryu. Sayuri entered the room, releasing her hands from leather gloves as she undid the buttons on her black woollen coat. I stood, my mouth open, sweat already sheening my palms. There was nowhere to go. Moon stood by the window, Sayuri by the door. My eyes flicked from one to the other, waiting for one of them to attack me. I had no way of getting out of the apartment. My heart thudded and my lips were dry.

'Mari, how are you? I come to talk to you. Please, sit.'

'What about?' My tongue felt thick.

'The Yamaguchi-gumi think it's time you leave Japan. No one will hurt you, but you must leave. Today.'

'And if I don't?'

'No choice, Mari.

'Was it you, Moon?' I glared at him. 'Did you tell them I was here?'

'When they contacted me and asked, I could not lie. I'm sorry, but you must understand my position.'

Sayuri stepped further into the room. I glanced behind her to see if anyone else was there, gauging whether I could make a run for it.

'It is nice you care for your friend, but nothing for you to learn. You are making much trouble. So many questions not good for our organisation. My father say, *please go now*.'

'His *wakagashira* killed Kate. I want him to go to the police, to confess.'

'Not our people, not our family. My father questioned all our members. You know we have code of honour. You are mistaken.'

'And what your people, your family did to me?' I touched my forearm. 'That's honour?'

'That person acted alone, out of respect for his *wakagashira*. He was punished in appropriate way.'

My head swam but standing there, opposite tiny Sayuri, the

female face of the Hitano *yakuza*, the oyabun's daughter, I knew I'd failed. Kate's death was covered up and I could do nothing about it.

'Here is ticket to Singapore.' She held it out for me and I took a step towards her, snatching it out of her hand. 'For tonight. First, we go to your apartment and take your things. Then we help you to airport. Will you go nicely?

My shoulders slumped, the fight leeching out of me. I had to give up now. 'Yes, I'll go,' I said. Walking away was all I could do; all I'd ever done. And I hated myself for it.

Chapter 54

My THAI VISA was about to run out and I needed to get to Bangkok. From Singapore, I'd travelled overland through Malaysia for a month and fallen in love with Thailand. Probably because that had been Kate's focus for our trip, not India like mine. Two months travelling had been wonderful, and I'd visited every place Kate had earmarked in the guidebook, except for the Philippines. I wasn't sure if I'd extend my Thai visa and travel to the north of the country, or head off to India. I walked through the train carriage and found my seat. The girl in the seat opposite mine was Japanese. For God's sake. I looked around for a spare seat, but there wasn't one. Hopefully, the girl wouldn't talk to me. As I stuffed my holdall under the seat, she looked up and inclined her head. Without thinking, I half-nodded back, then averted my eyes.

An attendant came to take the meal order, his clipboard the colour of cherries. The Japanese girl struggled to understand him.

Feelings I'd buried deep stirred and the sleeping dragon woke. I twisted my hair round my finger, breathed out a long sigh. It wasn't realistic to avoid Japanese people for the rest of my life, but I didn't want to interact with this girl, with her almond-shaped eyes and her black hair and her Japanese-ness. An odd feeling coiled in the dragon. In a way, I wanted her to suffer, wanted to take revenge on the whole Japanese nation for Kate's death by denying this girl a meal. In my mind, I heard Kate saying, *"Not your problem. Bloody idiot.."* But it wouldn't be right not to help the girl. It wouldn't be right to let her go hungry on an overnight journey to Bangkok. I'd had plenty of kindness from strangers, it was only fair that I help her out.

'He's asking if you want to eat. Chicken and rice,' I said in English.

The girl looked at me but shook her head. She didn't understand. I closed my eyes and sighed. It wasn't my problem. I ran my fingers across my forehead, tutted and blew out a breath. I repeated what I'd said, this time in Japanese and regretted it instantly.

The girl's face lit up with a big smile. Now she'd probably want to chat, probably ask me why I spoke Japanese and why I had a scar on my arm. She nodded to the attendant. There, job done, Mari.

'My name is Kimiko Hamada. You speak Japanese well. Where did you learn?'

'Japan.'

I pulled my Walkman out of my bag, popped in a pirated tape of Bruce Springsteen I'd bought on the beach and focused on looking out of the window. The train sped past villages and jungle as the skies darkened over southern Thailand.

The attendant was back, arms full of clean bedding. I stood up to let him push the two seats together, making the bed. When he finished, he pulled another bunk down from the wall, tucked in the sheets and blankets. I threw my cloth bag on the bunk and climbed up, glad to get away from the girl.

I WOKE AT dawn and stood by the door, ready to get off the train as soon as it arrived at Hualalumpong station in Bangkok. The bartering game with the driver of a three-wheeled tuk-tuk took ages. In the end I probably didn't get the best deal, but I wanted to get away as quickly as possible, in case Miss Japan was hovering. Last thing I needed was for her to ask to share the tuk-tuk. The driver took me to a backpacker area, just off Khao San Road where I rented a second-floor room in the first guest house I found. I opened the windows that looked out over houses separated by trees and overhead electric cables. Sitting by the window on a white plastic stool, I absorbed the city view. The ceiling fan whipped up a breeze in the humid air that wafted smells of ginger and garlic into the room from the street below. I liked it already.

Bangkok balanced real life and tourism perfectly. Small guesthouses with ground-floor cafes flanked the street I was staying on, and narrow alleys led to homes. Motorbikes leaned up against the walls and children played or chased chickens away from doorways.

In the early morning light, I sat on a low wall by the river, watching the wide waterway and all its traffic. Long narrow boats, full of people or produce, flew in both directions and in the distance on the other side, temples with tall spires gleamed golden in the sun. Sadness tinged everything and it was hard to be positive. My heart was heavy that day, my sadness overwhelming. I went back to my room, and back to bed. Arms wrapped around myself, I let the tears go. Once I started, I couldn't stop and my pillow was soggy and wet beneath my face. For the first time in years, I was homesick. Elena was always in my thoughts and often I missed my dad. My sisters and Uncle Saturnino too. But missing my twin sisters was worse that day, their thirteenth birthday. Did they remember me as their kooky older sister or as the monster my mother had no doubt turned me into?

DAYS PASSED AND I began to explore the back streets. I stood on a corner, watching a processions of student monks, cloth bags hung on bare shoulders, their burgundy robes offset by the brass bowls they carried. Women came out of doorways and placed food items wrapped in banana leaves into the bowls. Sometimes they gave a ladle-full of rice or a plastic bag full of something in a rich-looking sauce. The monks bowed and moved on to the next street. It touched me, soothed me, to see such generosity.

Turning a corner, I entered a market that filled the street. Vendors sold all manner of clothing, kitchenware, and fabrics. Hawkers wheeled their mobile carts until someone stopped them, asking for their food. The smell of barbequed meats and noodle dishes filled the air. Then, I saw it. Green and black paisley fabric, like Kate's scarf. Crossing the street, I went to the stall and bought two meters of it. The vendor must have thought I was nuts when I put the fabric to my face and cried.

SLEEP LEFT ME earlier than usual one morning. It wasn't yet light, but the sounds of the streets below told me that the city was preparing for the day. Wandering in back alleys might not be the best thing to do in the dark, so I walked to the river and sat on the steps by the ferry stop. A riverboat came in and people got off, scuttled up the steps on their way to their jobs, reminding me of my commute to work by ferry in Sydney. The riverboat man offered me a ticket.

'Wat Arun? Ten baht.'

I climbed aboard with a few Thai people and the boat whizzed down the river. After a few more stops to drop and pick up passengers, Wat Arun loomed on the opposite bank, the tall tower of the stupa stabbing the sky. The boat glided to a halt and I walked up the steps, straight into the temple complex.

The sun rose slowly and the soft light from the east reflected pearlescent off the pieces of porcelain and coloured glass that covered the main stupa of the temple. It rose high into the dawn sky. A seven-pronged golden trident, perched right at the top, caught the first rays of the sun, and looked like a flame. Four smaller stupas stood at each corner of the main area, and behind them, a white-walled monastery. The green-tiled roof was edged with orange and the corners tilted up to the sky. I circled the stupa, ran my hand along the intricately inlaid surface, feeling each ridge and crevice on my fingertips. It must've taken a lot of people a long time to create this.

I pulled my cloth bag on my shoulder, walked up the pathway towards an ornate, gilded building. Without a barrier or gate, I thought it must be okay to be there, but I wasn't sure. The peace was tangible and the soft rhythmic chanting of monks somewhere close by reminded me of Asa. Warmth flooded through me as I remembered her. I turned to go back to the stupa and a line of bald, burgundy-robed monks came past, their brass bowls glinting in the morning sun. One of them signalled to me to follow and I walked behind them.

An older monk in mustard-coloured robes stood at the doorway, next to a sign that said '*Ordination Hall*', and smiled at me. 'Welcome to Wat Arun, Temple of Dawn. Let me show you around.'

'I don't want to intrude,' I said. 'It's so peaceful here.'

'You have timed your visit well. Please, come.' He extended his arm to show me the way.

As we strolled through the complex, the monk explained what each building was for and I felt privileged to get such an insight into a working monastery. The monk spoke of their charitable works and how they existed on donations from the community.

'Did something happen to you? That scar on your arm… you keep touching it.'

My emotional dragon woke again, and I could feel the tears about to spill. The monk led me to some steps which were in shade from the already scorching sun.

'My friend was murdered five months ago. The man I love is marrying someone else. My sister died. It's hard. I feel so sad. All the time.'

I sat on the steps with my arms wrapped round my knees. The monk adjusted his robe and sat a little way apart from me and nodded. 'Are you religious?'

'No, but my family are Catholic.'

'Ah. Did you know His Holiness Dalai Lama met with Pope John Paul the second a few months ago? That would have been an interesting meeting, I think.'

'When I go to India, I want to go to Dharamshala, to see the Dalai Lama,' I said.

'His home is a little further north, in McLeod Gange. Let me tell you something. Buddha teaches many things that can help a person in this life. One thing that might help you is the concept of impermanence, of inevitable change. We become attached to things, to people, and suffering comes to us when we are separated from those things and people. Separation is bound to happen because nothing stays the same. Life moves on.'

'Live for the moment,' I said. A tiny orange bird fluttered to a stop on the edge of a stone fountain, scooped the water into its bright yellow beak. It looked at me, almost quizzically, for a long time before it flew off. 'How does that help when someone dies?'

'All things come into being and all things dissolve. Like the waves of the sea, all existence is fleeting. No thought, no physical or emotional feeling, is permanent. A person's life is the same. It's a series of moments, ever changing. The cycle of birth, living, death and reincarnation –'

'Samsara,' I said. 'My sister and Kate were too young to die. They hadn't had the chance to live their lives yet.'

'So, if you can accept the changes that death brings, you can accept the impermanence of life and in turn, learn to accept yourself.

'So, accepting impermanence is the key to happiness?'

'No, but it might help you deal with your loss. Remember life is like water, not stone.' I nodded and put my forehead to my knees to hide my tears. I remembered what Asa had told me: that acceptance is the balm that heals all wounds.

When I looked up, he had gone. On my way back to the ferry stop, I put a large wad of baht into the collection box.

Instead of going back to my guesthouse, I travelled upriver. The riverboat crossed from one side to the other and I got off an hour later. A dozen or so tables and chairs on a large wooden deck caught my eye and the waitress-slash-owner gave a polite *wai* as I entered. Breakfast ordered, I asked her for a pen and took out the postcard I'd been carrying around for days. I addressed it to Superintendent Takeda at Kitakyushu Police Station. I wrote my name in Japanese. Just so he'd know I was alive. Maybe he'd even tell Ryu. Then, I took the paper and envelope Asa had given me out of my bag. It was time.

Dear Mum and Dad, I began.

Chapter 55

I sat on a low stool at a street-side stall with a cold Singha beer and a plate of fried prawns, watching the street bustle with locals. Rummaging in my new cloth bag, embroidered with blue elephants, I pulled out the guidebook. People meandered by, scuffing, and shuffling their plastic sandals on the pavement, their carrier bags full of produce. Motorbikes and tuk-tuks whizzed past, weaving their way between cars and pedestrians. I photographed a group of motorcycle taxis that lined the other side of the street, waiting to take pillion passengers anywhere, faster than a car. A grey and blue bus with no glass in the windows stopped a little way down the road. Taller and fairer-skinned than the other passengers, I recognised the Japanese girl from the train. I ducked my head behind the guidebook, pretending to read. It didn't work.

'Hello. We met on the train, nice to see you again.' Kimiko said.

There was no option but to close the book. I gestured to the stool next to me and she sat. 'How are you finding Bangkok?' I said in Japanese.

'It's a quite different kind of city, but I like it. I'm here to learn about Theravada Buddhism for my university thesis. I thought it was a good opportunity to travel and see it for myself. Better than studying in a library.'

'Wow, that must be interesting.' I felt bad that I had misjudged her. 'Where are you studying?'

'Osaka. But I'm from Nagasaki, in Kyushu. Where did you stay in Japan?'

Nagasaki. Osaka. The sharp sounds of the words sliced my heart. Why couldn't she have been from Aomori and been studying in Nara?

'I was in… a few places.' I didn't want to explain. My mouth found it difficult to form the words. She may have seen news about Kate's death on the TV, and I didn't want to talk about it. 'Sorry, I don't mean to be rude but I had some problems there. I'm a bit negative about Japan.'

'Yes, our culture can be difficult for Westerners. But there must have been something you liked?'

'Yes,' I twisted my hair. 'I have some good memories.'

'I'm feeling homesick today, especially because the sakura has blossomed in Kyushu. Do you know sakura?'

'I know it's supposed to be incredibly beautiful, but I don't get why it's such a big deal.'

My eyes closed for a moment as I tried to compose myself, I didn't want to think about Kate and her sakura. After my visit to Wat Arun, I'd started to feel better. The monk's words had touched me, and I understood what Asa had said about acceptance.

'We Japanese have a reverence for the cherry blossom,' said Kimiko. 'For us, it is about more than just the beauty of pale pink flowers. There's a more spiritual connection.'

'In what way?'

'Millions of flowers bloom all at once, almost overnight. Spring brings a new beginning when the earth becomes green and fertile again.' Kimiko signalled to the stall owner and ordered a rice dish. 'Then, in their prime, the flowers fall from the trees to wither and die. They exist for just a few days and accept their fate gracefully. They symbolise the impermanence of life.'

'Sorry.' I stood up, knocked the stool over. 'Sorry.' I paid what I owed, put my bag on my shoulder and ran down the street.

At the post office, I placed a long-distance call to Detective Superintendent Takeda.

The operator put me on hold for ages. There was a click on the line.

'*Moshi moshi,*'

'Papa-san. How are you?'

'Mari! I'm fine. Where are you?'

'Bangkok. I want to come to Hitano. Just for a short visit. Is it safe, Papa-san?'

'It's safe. We've made arrests, but not in connection with Kate's death.'

'That's no surprise,' I said. 'Who's been arrested?'

'Ohayo confessed to strangling Cherry and taking her body out to sea in a fishing boat. We'll never find it.'

A chill skittered through me, even though it was no surprise. If Ryu knew, then he must feel so guilty. If I was honest, it was probably the only thing we had in common.

'What are you up to? No, don't tell me.' Papa-san laughed softly. 'When will you arrive?'

It was Tuesday, and I worked things out in my head. 'On the 10.55am train on Friday.'

Chapter 56

NINETEEN HOURS LATER, I stood at an immigration desk in Osaka airport, while the uniformed official stamped my passport. I entered Japan on a temporary visitor's visa, valid for thirty days, but I didn't plan to stay that long. My legs shook while I waited for my luggage at the carousel. The familiar smell of Seven Star cigarettes hit me as I waited in line for a taxi.

The taxi took me to the same hotel I'd stayed at five months before. It felt like a lifetime ago. I ordered room-service while I waited for the ofuro bath to heat up. Breathing in the almost-sweet smell of the inari rolls, I remembered how Ryu used to feed them to me. He felt close. Being in Japan breathed life back into my love for him, but coming back wasn't about him.

Watching the news on TV, I lay on the bed, propped up by pillows. Jacques Chirac gave a speech on his newly formed French government. Yawning, I changed channels. After some adverts, I watched a short programme, *The Sakura Forecast*. Apparently, Osaka didn't expect the sakura for another week or ten days, but on the southern island of Kyushu it had blossomed already, as Kimiko had said. I had to get down there. I'd join the thousands of people in Hanami, flower-viewing parties and picnics under the trees. I could wait until the blossoms opened here in Osaka. But it would mean so much more to see them in Hitano. For Kate's sake.

Chapter 57

THE VIEW FROM the train was the same as before, but everything looked different. Maybe it was the soft light of spring. Taking deep breaths, I tried to stay calm. It was my choice to come back, but that didn't make it any easier. As the train pulled into the station, passing the sign for Hitano, a wave of nausea flipped my stomach. My hands shook as I reached up to the luggage rack for my holdall. I never imagined I'd set foot in Japan again, but there I was, back where it all happened.

Takeda-san waited at the entrance and he put one arm around my shoulders briefly. 'You got too skinny,' he said. 'And your hair; I can't believe it.'

'I got a bit carried away in Osaka. Anyway, it was time for a change.' I pulled at the ends of my hair, which fell to my collarbone.

'Change. There's been a lot of that here recently. How long will you stay?'

'Until Sunday afternoon. It should be long enough.'

We walked past the bicycles parked at the station and my breath caught in my throat as I thought of the bikes Kate and I stole.

I checked in to a hotel nearby. The receptionist said he remembered me from when I'd come to ask if Kate was staying there. His pity stung. I'd have to stay strong if I was going to do this. I took my holdall up to a fourth-floor room while Takeda-san waited for me downstairs. Standing at the window, I looked down on Hitano. If I craned my neck and looked towards the park, I could just see the pink. *Sakura*. My emotions were all over the place as I looked left, across rooftops, towards Ryu's. Checking my make-up in the bathroom mirror, I ran my fingers through my hair.

'Alright,' I said to my reflection. 'Let's do this.'

Takeda-san smiled when I came out of the lift. 'It's an enjoyable time to be here,' he said. 'The sakura have bloomed. There'll be picnics and celebrations all weekend.'

We bypassed the mall, taking the quieter narrow streets of the old town.

'*Irashaimasse! Irashaimasse!*' Masta beat his drum more than the usual three times. 'Very good to see you again. What a surprise. Come… come.' He came out from behind his counter and took my hand. 'You look so well, Mari-chan.'

He took us to the room at the back and we sat at the low table on the tatami floor. My fingers stroked the soft golden straw and I sighed, remembering the last time I'd been there.

'I have to say, I'm surprised you've come back. This must be hard for you.' Takeda-san scratched the side of his mouth.

'Yes, everything is a memory. It's like being punched in the stomach with a reminder every two seconds. But I have to make my peace with it all.' I sniffed. 'How's Asa?'

'She's became a grandmother for the fourth time, two days ago. She's in Osaka with Masako and his wife, helping out. If not for that, she'd be here to see you.'

'I'll write to her.' I missed that kind lady more than I'd thought possible.

'And did you write to your mother?'

'Yes, from Bangkok.' I cleared my throat. 'I'm building up the courage to phone her. Maybe next week, once I'm in India.'

'Good girl. So, let me tell you everything that's happened while you've been away.' Takeda-san took off his jacket and rolled up his sleeves. 'Mama is in prison. Did you know she ran a brothel?'

'No!' I laughed, shook my head. 'Where, not Shima?'

'A place down by the docks. Not a bar, a sleazy brothel. I've seen places like that in Yokohama, but never expected something so low class here.' His laugh was low. 'After fifteen years in anti-crime, I came here for a quiet few years before I retire. Thought it would be nice and peaceful. Never expected to deal with two murders.' He shot me a look. 'Anyway, we convicted her for living off prostitution money and for employing illegal Filipinas and Koreans.'

Masta brought food and a small flask of warm sake. I poured it into a tiny cup and handed it with both hands to Takeda-san.

'Kampai, Papa-san. I've missed so many things about Japan.'

He raised his cup to me. 'Welcome back, English daughter.' He smiled. 'So, Mama lost everything. Her home had to be sold to pay legal fees and debts, and her businesses closed. When she gets out of prison in seven years, she'll have nothing. I'll never forget the day I interviewed her for the first time. She deserves everything she got.'

'I know. We all hated her. She was only ever nice to me once, the day after...' I cleared my throat. 'The day after Kate went missing. I think she knew all along.'

'Probably.'

'So, Kujaku is closed as well? And Imee and the girls, are they still here?'

'All sent back to the Philippines. Most of them had tourist visas except for the singer, Melody Song. She had an entertainer's visa and she's now working in Tokyo until the end of her contract. Her Korean husband came from Busan, looking for her. They see each other once every three months.'

Melody Song. What a great name for a singer. No doubt she married the guy for his name. She was cold and calculating enough, but it surprised me that she'd never mentioned a husband. People only revealed what they want people to know. I knew what keeping secrets was like.

'There's more. Ohayo presented his little finger to the *wakagashira* moments before we arrested him. He'll serve life, Mari. Onishi Imports has been closed and your friend Sayuri is working in the *yakuza* headquarters in Fukuoka. She's getting married in a few weeks.'

'As is Ryu if I remember correctly. His wedding is planned for sakura season.'

'Yes.' After a moment, he put down his chopsticks and sighed. 'His to-be-wife's uncle arranged for you and Kate to be sent to Nagoya when Ryu wouldn't stop seeing you.'

'What? They said it was because of Nagasaki *yakuza*. But it was Junichi?' My mouth hung open. For a moment I was furious. If Junichi hadn't interfered, I wouldn't have planned to leave. That awful farewell party would never have happened, and maybe Kate would still be alive.

'Yes, there was a problem with Nagasaki; they wanted you to work as hostesses in a strip club. Not a good place. Junichi wanted them to be kind to you – he liked you – but he wanted you out of the way before his niece got back from Italy, so he asked for you to be sent to Nagoya instead. He moved money around so that Nagasaki could be paid off. But then Kate insulted the *wakagashira*, and they decided Nagasaki could have you.'

That's why Junichi had made that comment about Kate spending time with her boyfriend before going to Nagasaki. My flash of anger faded; there was no place for it now.

'But the *wakagashira* gets away with what he did, Papa-san.'

'I know. But his card is marked and I am waiting. I'll get him on something. I will. For your friend's sake. For yours.' He put his hand over mine. 'You are a force to reckon with, Mari Randall.'

'How is Ryu?'

Takeda-san shook his head. 'He's a good man. After you left, we spoke many times and I'd say we've become friends. Tell me about your travels. I got your postcard.'

'I will, but first I need your help with something. I want to do something for Kate, go to where she died. Would you ring Koji and Ryu, and the man who found her? Maybe we can all go there together?'

DETECTIVE SUPERINTENDENT TAKEDA-SAN needed to get back to the police station in Kitakyushu and he said he'd phone me later.

His wife and daughters wanted to meet me and had invited me to their home for dinner. It wasn't polite to arrive empty handed, so I went to the shopping mall to get some wagashi sweets and a bottle of whisky for Papa-san.

By the escalator to the upper floor, a stand displayed boxes of coloured origami paper. Thinking of Crazy Dog, I bought some. I needed new underwear so headed upstairs. Taking a selection into the changing room, I tried them on. I hadn't seen myself in a full-length mirror for months. It wasn't that I'd tried to avoid them, just that backpackers' digs didn't have that kind of luxury. My fair skin didn't tan well, but my bottom was a shade or two whiter than my back. I bought a set of undies in pale sakura pink lace; tiny fabric flowers decorated the edges, and ribbons formed the bra straps and tied the knickers at the sides. Frivolous and feminine and somehow very Japanese.

The underwear made me think of Ryu. I'd only just started to breathe out properly, to rationalise everything. I wanted to see those damn flowers and somehow say goodbye to Kate. Ryu couldn't figure in all of this, and I shook my head, trying to dislodge him from my mind. Had he got over me easily? Planning his wedding must have helped, and that would be happening soon. Or it may have already happened. I'd find out when I met up with everyone. How would my heart feel then? Stupid question.

Needing to kill time until dinner, I tried to keep occupied so that I didn't give in and phone Ryu. Walking through the old town, I found myself standing at the end of a familiar street. It was quiet, too early for the bars and clubs to be open. A woman with a long-handled dustpan and brush swept the street outside the takoyaki stall. She glanced at me, and carried on sweeping as I walked past her. I stood outside the building, looking up at the opaque windows. All the signage was gone. No more Kujaku, no more Shima. No more Kate.

On impulse, I took my keys out of my bag. The key still fit the street level door, and I turned the lock. The air smelt stale, but that was to be expected after nearly half a year. I climbed the stairs and opened the door to Kukaju. Empty and dusty, it looked smaller than I remembered. And Yoshi-san? What happened to him? Abandoned, Kujaku had an air of sadness. Even the engraved peacock on the door looked sad. I went downstairs and found that Shima's door wasn't locked. Inside, I flicked at the light switch, hoping for some light in the gloom, but the electric had been cut off. The stage creaked as I stepped onto it. I remembered Kate singing karaoke, and the nights we'd danced and laughed. This place had so much energy, and it was sad to see it empty and neglected.

'Kate,' I said. Blinking back tears, I sat on one of the stools. Good memories and bad ones filled my head, but the guilt was still there. 'I'm sorry.'

AFTER I DROPPED my shopping at my hotel, I jumped into a taxi. Butterflies flitted in my belly during the short ride up the hill, past the house with the blue flowerpots, and through the rice fields. As the car approached the house, the man stood from his bench, and the dog barked. Opening the taxi door, I asked the driver to wait.

Crazy Dog smiled and moved the flight goggles on his forehead, rubbing the red marks where they'd dug in. On the bench were two cans of coffee and a plate of inari rolls. We sat in our usual companionable silence, the dog between us at our feet. The sweet cold coffee was always a favourite, as were the inari rolls, but it all tasted better that day, sitting there with him.

With a little bow of my head, I gave him the box of paper with both hands. He moved the hessian that covered the doorway aside and took it inside the house. A moment later he came back out, cupping something in his hands. Crazy Dog extended his arms and I took the two origami butterflies from him. There we were, Kate and I, immortalised in coloured paper by this gentle, damaged man who knew things. I caught a tear on the back of my finger, just under my lashes, and smiled at Crazy Dog. He looked at the taxi, and back at me and I understood it was time to go.

Chapter 58

THE PARK BUZZED with people that fresh spring Saturday morning. Cherry trees lined both sides of the pathway, and the air was laced with the blossom's subtle fragrance. Fragile flowers dusted the branches like pinkish-white icing sugar. Walking along the path, I pulled the collar of my Levi's jacket up against the breeze and dodged people with pocket cameras as they took photos of each other. A group of teenaged girls, wrapped in coats and scarves, made peace signs with their fingers as a friend snapped away. It was still early, but people were setting up picnic tables and spreading rugs on the grass. They chatted and unloaded food and drink from bags and cool boxes. Kate would've loved it.

Koji was waiting for me outside the teahouse, his hands shoved into the pockets of his red puffer jacket. I waved.

He smiled and walked towards me. 'I can't believe you are back. Wow, you look different.'

'Good to see you, Koji.' I put my hand on his arm.

'It was big surprise. Takeda-san called and told me you are here.'

'Thanks for coming. I wasn't sure you would.'

We went into a tatami-matted room. Red lines of warmth radiated from electric bar heaters at the far side of the small space. The shoji screens would stay shut until the days of warmer weather. We sat on thin cushions and drank tea from grey bowls.

'I miss her, Mari. Every day. Seeing you makes it better.'

'Sometimes, I can't believe it really happened. But then I look at this and I know it did.' I pushed back the sleeve of my jacket to show him the scar. 'Tell me about Ryu. Did he rebuild the bar?'

'Completely fresh style. He is not the same, Mari, he is very distressed. He misses you. Some nights when we drink too much, we talk about it. It's difficult.'

'It's been hard on all of us. The Filipinas, all sent home.'

'Yes. Hiroshi is there now. He missed Myla and one day last month he said *I am going to Phillipines, I am going to marry Myla.* He is coming back soon. She is already married and he met her husband!'

'Another heart broken.'

'So many. I'll never forget. Ryu says the same. But he is busy. His cousins both work in the bar now and Ryu is painting. Next month, a large art gallery in Fukuoka is showing his work. There is another exhibition planned in Kyoto, in June, I think.'

'That's fantastic. I'm so happy for him. His paintings are beautiful. He deserves success.' My heart smiled all the way up to my lips. I blew out a breath, serious again. 'I'm scared of how I'll feel when I see him.

'You know his wedding is next Sunday, one week tomorrow?'

'I didn't. Well, I knew it would be this time of year. I hope there'll still be some blossom on the trees for them. He'll make a wonderful husband. What's she like?'

'Chie? Nice lady. If he did not meet you, she was perfect for him. That is something I blame myself for.' He looked at his watch.

'Don't blame yourself. None of us knew how things would turn out. I still feel guilty but I'm finally learning to stop tearing myself apart for what happened. Trying to accept that it wasn't my fault.'

Koji adjusted his glasses and looked at his watch again. Poor guy, I felt sorry for him. It was probably too much for him, being reminded of everything again. I don't know why, but I looked at my watch too. It was almost ten.

'She did love you, Koji, just not in the way you wanted her to. She thought the world of you.'

'Yes, I was in love and she was not, but we were best friends. Glad I knew her. We had happy times, all of us. I will never forget her.'

'I'll come back here one day and find you married with three cute kids.' I smiled at him as he rubbed his eyes behind his glasses. 'Here, you should have this.'

I reached into my bag and gave him Kate's blue elephant. Koji held it tightly to his chest.

'My Mari.'

I stopped breathing, my head whipped round to face the voice, and my hand flew to my mouth.

'I will blame myself later,' said Koji. 'I told him you would be here.'

In a flash, I was on my feet and in Ryu's arms. Breathing in that smell of him, I held him so close that I could feel his heart thump.

'I couldn't wait until tomorrow to see you,' he said. He leaned back to look at me. His eyes looked in mine and he tutted as he tucked my hair behind my ear. 'You're still beautiful.'.

Electricity sparked through me. I turned to speak to Koji, but he had gone. Ryu held me to him again, one hand on the back of my head. It felt so good in his arms, to feel his warmth. In Osaka, I'd been almost mental with grief for Kate and with missing him. Now, I wanted to sink into him; stop the world. Someone coughed politely. Ryu and I moved away from each other as the teahouse man came in to clear the table. Ryu led me by the hand through the door and along the stone footpath. We smiled at each other when we passed the willow tree where he'd first kissed me. His hand dropped mine when we reached the park. People gathered to admire the blush-pink trees and I understood he couldn't be seen to be 'with' me. We were close enough that our little fingers brushed against each other's. It felt like the only thing in the world that mattered.

'I was demented with worry after they attacked you. Why didn't you call me?'.

'Don't be angry with me. Your fiancée was here, you were making wedding plans.'

'She and her parents went back to Osaka that day. Once the police released me, I should have come to you. You accused the *wakagashira*, we should have known something would happen.' He stopped, turning me to face him. His hand reached up and took a fallen petal from my hair. 'I can't believe you're here walking under the cherry blossoms with me.' He smiled that slow smile of his and my heartbeat went wild.

'Neither can I. One minute I was in Bangkok, eating lunch and when I heard the flowers were out, I ran into a travel agency and booked the next plane to Osaka. I didn't even think about it. Just knew I had to come.'

We reached the road and walked along a line of parked cars. He opened the passenger door of his silver Toyota Celica for me. I got in, breathed in that new-car smell, presuming he'd take me back to the hotel. Instead, he drove out of town and towards the hills.

'Why didn't you let me know where you were?' He frowned. 'Why?'

'There was so much I wanted to tell you, but I didn't even know where I was. Takeda-san – I call him Papa-san now – took me to his sister, a house in the mountains somewhere. I wanted to call you, but I was so strung out, I couldn't think clearly. Kate… And I was in so much physical pain.' I blinked away the dampness in my eyes. 'And you were engaged, Ryu. Engaged, and I was trying to let you go. And I blamed myself for what happened to Kate.'

'Takeda-san told me you were safe, but he wouldn't tell me where you were. When you called me from Singapore, I couldn't speak freely and you hung up on me. I was so relieved you were safe.'

'I did call you a few other times, but she always answered.'

Ten minutes later, he pulled up in the car park of The No Tell Motel. His eyes asked me an unspoken question and he reached for my hand.

My eyes flicked over his face, from his mouth to his eyes and back. It was wrong, He was about to get married. This was so wrong. But I opened the car door.

Chapter 59

THE ENTRANCE TO the love hotel was kitsch and cheesy. Red love hearts decorated the walls and sunset prints of couples in silhouette hung over the doors. Hidden by a small folding screen on the front desk, someone took Ryu's cash without saying a word. He paid for five hours.

'I have a perfectly good hotel room in Hitano,' I said.

'I know, but this is better. There's more privacy and you always said you wanted to see inside one.'

Red sheets and a huge heart-shaped cushion decorated a round bed in the middle of the small room. I looked at myself in the mirrors on the ceiling, my laugh husky and nervous.

Ryu sat on the bed and I smiled. He pulled me onto his lap and held me. All those feelings that I'd squashed down for so long, that had been put away, came back stronger than ever.

He kissed my neck and his hand moved under my shirt. As his thumb moved the lace fabric of my bra, I pulled away.

'Ryu –'

His mouth stopped me talking and it was too late. I was lost in him, lost in his kiss and his hands as they took off my clothes. His fingers stroked me until I couldn't wait any longer. He smiled, looking in my eyes as he pushed inside me.

AFTERWARDS, HE LAY behind me, holding me and I felt warm tears on the back of my shoulder. I turned, touched his cheek, and ran my finger under his eyes. This love. My heart filled to breaking point.

'Ryu, don't.'

'I can't believe what you've gone through,' he said. 'Forgive me.' Gently lifting my arm, he examined the scar. 'I didn't protect you. I'm sorry, I should've been there.'

'You couldn't be. You were with your fiancée. Ryu, you're getting married next week; we shouldn't even be here,' I said. 'God, what was I thinking?' Sitting up, I moved away from him.

'Damn.' He pulled me close, hugging me to him. 'You're not going anywhere.'

I relaxed into him, played with his fingers. 'I have something to tell you. Something that might change the way you feel about me.' I took a deep breath. 'I had a sister, Elena. She died when she was fifteen.' And then I told him the whole story.

Ryu didn't react, or interrupt. It was the first time I'd told someone about it without crying. Ryu held my hand and that little muscle in his jaw twitched.

'So that's why you never talk about your family.' He leaned on his elbow, looking down at me. 'It wasn't really your fault, Mari. You were young and headstrong. You still are. Your mom shouldn't have left you with the responsibility of looking after Elena. How could you have known what would happen?'

'I know. Accepting my part in what happened to her, and what happened to Kate, hasn't been easy. Because of me, two girls died.'

'Two girls died,' he said. 'Mari, do you ever think that sometimes things just happen? Things that change everything, things that are just beyond our control.' He held me to him, kissing my shoulder.

'Did you know what happened to Cherry?' I touched his face, the faint stubble that only grew along his jaw-line and upper lip. 'Did you know Ohayo killed her?'

'I knew she'd disappeared, that's all. Look, I don't wanna talk about that.'

Probably best to leave it. After all, he'd been seeing Cherry.

I kissed him, savouring the taste of him.

'When I told Kate why they called us ice-buckets, we laughed so hard, neither of us could stand up.' I knew my smile was sad. 'Did you know she liked you?'

'Yeah. She made it pretty obvious. She called me a few times, asking to meet up. I told her no, that I was with you. She had so many boyfriends, and Koji was crazy in love with her.'

'He used to look at her like a puppy when they did karaoke duets together, it was sweet.'

Ryu nodded. 'Poor kid, she really couldn't sing, could she?'

'I don't remember you doing too much better.' I laughed as he thumped me gently and thumped him back. Our play fight lasted for a few seconds before it turned into something else.

'I can't stop, Mari. I know it's wrong but I don't know how to stop.'

'We had a beautiful summer, Ryu, that has to be enough.'

'It'll never be enough.'

'But that was all we could be.' He pushed deeper into me, holding my hips. 'That was as much as we could be.'

'Yes,' he said, breathless now. 'Nothing can change that.'

'Nothing can change the past. Or the truth,' I said before speech became impossible and pleasure took over.

RYU CAME OUT of the shower, the towel tied low on his slim hips, the line of fine hair leading down from his belly button drawing my eye.

'I'm sorry, I need to go. There's a family Hanami this afternoon,' he said, drying his hair with another towel.

'Picnic party in the park.' My hand touched his arm and he stopped dressing. 'What's Chie like?'

'She's a strong woman. Very measured. I told her about you after they found Kate.' He pulled on his jeans and slipped his bare feet into his deck shoes. 'I know it's wrong, and I didn't plan on bringing you here, but when I saw you...'

I stepped into the shower, my legs still trembling, and turned the water on. Ryu stood, shirtless, in the doorway of the small bathroom, a cigarette in his mouth. He lit it, blew the smoke out, watching me run the soap over myself.

'I wasn't expecting to see you until tomorrow. I thought I'd stop by the Art Bar this evening to see how you've remodelled it. Will Chie be there?'

'She will. I won't be there tonight; I have to go somewhere. You'd like the new décor. It took time to get the bar right and it's very different. It's all summery and green.'

I got out of the shower, still wet, he grabbed my waist, and pulled me to him. 'I renamed it too. Want to know what I called it?'

Nodding, I held his head as his tongue followed a trickle of water that ran down my breast. He licked my nipple.

'The Willow Tree. For you.'

Grabbing his belt buckle, I dragged him back to the bed.

Chapter 60

THE FIERCE WINDS of the night before gave way to a blue-sky day. Flowers covered the ground, a snowfall of blush pink petals. I picked up a five-petalled flower, so pale a pink, it was almost white. A darker pink heart grew stamen like a little coronet, and the small dip in the outer edge of each petal turned them into elongated hearts. I scooped up handful after handful; I'd need a lot more to fill the carrier bag. A woman in a dark green coat walked towards me. Her hands in her pockets, she slowed her pace. Although I wasn't sure what she looked like as I'd only seen her once, I knew it was Chie. We stood and faced each other. I half expected her to slap my face or scream at me or something, but then I remembered, I was in Japan. Even so, my heart pounded.

'I will be there this afternoon, at your little ceremony, to stand by my Ryu. And to watch you leave.'

She carried on walking and I stood there, rooted in shame, a carrier bag full of sakura in my hand.

Chapter 61

TAKEDA-SAN OPENED THE taxi door for me. I smiled at him as I got out. I was touched that he wore dress uniform. He carried his peaked cap under his arm, and his white gloves were pristine. It was a bleak, long stretch of road like any other; a straight ribbon of concrete as far as the eye could see, leading from one place to another. It ran along an embankment, nine feet or so above the dry, empty rice fields that sat either side, waiting for new seedlings that would bring the furrowed earth to life with greenery. I leaned on Takeda-san's arm and walked towards the others. My heart fluttered with nervousness and I was glad of his body to steady me, like a father giving away his daughter on her wedding day.

Ryu walked towards me. He looked good; his black suit, shirt and tie made his skin glow. He bowed at Takeda-san, who ignored him. That surprised me, I thought they'd become friends.

'Chie told me she saw you yesterday, I'm sorry,' Ryu said, raising his hand to touch my face, but I moved away. The smile I gave him was one of those sad half-smiles, but I couldn't speak. I looked down at his black lace-up shoes, a line of punched holes creating the shape of a widow's peak. Like the *wakagashira*'s. My heart filled to bursting. Ryu even wore socks.

A little further along the side of the road, past where Koji's truck was parked, Chie and Koji waited with Takeda-san. It was as close as we could get to where Kate had been found, other than trudging across the rice field.

'Such a lonely place. It was here?' I walked the few meters to where the others stood.

Takeda-san nodded, put his cap on.

A car drew up and an elderly man in a navy-blue suit got out, followed by a woman in a charcoal grey kimono. The high, white collar of the formal underdress caught my eye like a sliver of moonlight on a dark night. Her wide white obi belt had large pink cherry blossoms embroidered onto it. I closed my eyes briefly and then Takeda-san introduced us. Mr and Mrs Ito needed to be there; after all, he had found Kate.

'Mr and Mrs Ito, thank you for coming, it means a great deal to me.' I bowed deeply.

'We were very honoured when Takeda-san asked us to come. We are sorry for your suffering,' said Mr Ito. 'It was a shock to find such a young woman dead in our field. Such a shame.'

I nodded and bit my bottom lip, determined not to let my chin tremble.

'Is it time?' said Koji. He moved close to me, checking his watch. 'It's gone three fifteen… are you ready?' He nudged his arm against mine and we all gathered.

Koji lit an incense stick and placed it in a narrow crack at the edge of the embankment. Nobody spoke. One by one we placed gifts for Kate beside the incense, little things for her afterlife. A packet of Seven Star cigarettes from Koji, a bottle of Asahi beer from Ryu. Takeda-san gave a packet of sakura scented bath crystals; the Itos, a bar of chocolate. I dug in my bag, pulled out a small box of dried persimmons and placed it beside the other gifts. My shoulders shook but I made no sound, covering my face with my hands.

'I know. It's okay, it's okay now,' Ryu said.

He put his arm round me, and I sank into him for a few seconds before moving away from him. Chie pretended not to look. She poured brandy into plastic cups and handed them out to everyone. I admired her composure and wished I had her grace.

Koji raised his glass. 'To Kato. We love you and miss you.'

'To Kato,' we all said.

I went back to the waiting taxi and got something off the back seat. It was wrapped in green and black paisley patterned fabric, the corners pleated and gathered, tied in a loose knot at the top.

'Last night, Mrs Papa-san told me about the traditional way to give a gift, *furoshiki,* so I used this piece of cloth I found in Bangkok. It's the same as Kate's scarf.' I smiled at Papa-san. 'Thank you for this, for everything. Koji, would you?'

He stepped forward, undid the knot, and pulled the cloth away. I held a Perspex ice-bucket from the hotel's bar, filled with the delicate cherry blossoms I'd collected that morning.

At exactly twenty past three, I tipped the flowers towards the concrete irrigation channel. A car passed, and the backdraught threw the blossoms into a high swirl of pink and blush-white. I tipped my head back, looked up to the sky, hands outstretched as the petals rained down on us like confetti. Ice-buckets and cherry blossoms – that about summed it up.

I shook hands with the Itos, who needed to leave to attend a cherry blossom party. Turning to Takeda-san, I stood to attention and saluted him.

'Papa Takeda-san,' I took his hand. 'Thanks for your help with all this today.'

'My pleasure. I hope I don't see you again, you're too much trouble.' He gave me a one-armed hug. 'Forget what happened here. You go, daughter, live well.'

He stood to attention and saluted me. How I didn't cry, I'll never know.

Ryu walked me to the taxi. He held me for a moment and when I pulled away, he blinked away tears. Stepping closer, he looked over my shoulder. I turned and glanced at a black and white police car, parked fifty meters down the road.

'Read this when you're somewhere wonderful, not before you leave Japan though, promise me?' I nodded. 'I'm glad you came back.'

I smiled at him, my eyes drinking in every contour of his face. I put the envelope he gave me into my bag. 'I needed to. For Kate. But mostly for myself. I needed to say goodbye. Let Chie make you happy. Have a good life together.'

He opened the door of the taxi and I slid onto the seat. '*Sayonara.*'

I didn't look back after they waved me off. With a tissue I found in my Levi's jacket pocket, I wiped my eyes. Opening the window to let the wind in, I watched as the rice fields fell away under a watery, early spring sky. Rummaging in my bag, I pulled out my train ticket to Osaka. And my flight ticket.

One way. To Bombay, India.

The Last Chapter

I CHECKED IN for my Air India flight to Bombay, feeling as happy as the cartoon turbaned man in the airline's logo. That day was the right day to leave Japan, and it was the right way to leave Japan. I'd turned the page. Yes, there were still regrets, but I could live with those. Love wasn't enough and circumstances had taken over. But knowing Ryu loved me was enough, it really was. Perhaps he was the prince that had lifted my curse. Telling him about Elena had been so liberating. He hadn't judged me, hadn't treated me like a monster. He'd understood.

There were still two hours or so before I needed to board the aircraft and I sat in a coffee shop, watching people come and go. The heavy perfume of anticipation and promises of the exotic and unknown hung in the air of the departure lounge.

India. I'd heard her siren song for so long and in just a few hours, I'd be there. Peacocks and palaces, I couldn't wait. Kate would be there with me, in spirit, and so would Elena.

Ryu's letter lay on the table next to my coffee. He wanted me to read it somewhere wonderful, and I was almost somewhere wonderful, so I opened the envelope.

My Mari,
Before you read further, remember I love you. Never forget, I love you.
Please understand. Your coming back has changed everything again. You said we can't change the past or the truth. I must do the honourable thing.

Kate came back to my bar that night.

My eyes were dry, but in my chest, my heart skipped a beat or two. My imagination brought Ryu's words to life as I read on, and images played across my mind like a film.

Kate rubbed herself up against Ryu and tried to kiss him. He gently moved her away, laughing. *I'll call you a cab*, he said. He turned to the phone and picked up the receiver. She pouted, promised he'd enjoy it. *You're a nice girl, Kate. But I'm not interested*, he said. She asked him to let her stay with him and rubbed her hand on his crotch. He swung her off, she lost her balance and fell. A sickening thwack. The back of her head hit the counter, her arm knocking the tub of rice crackers to the floor. She lay there, not moving. Ryu crouched over her, panic making his breath ragged. He stood, picked up the phone again, but a moment later replaced the receiver. Kneeling beside her among the rice crackers, he put his ear to her mouth, placed his hand on her chest. No movement, no sound. Leaning back against the fridges with his head in his hands, he tried to think, work out what he should do.

I knew the yakuza would get the blame. I wrapped her in a bed sheet and one of her shoes came off, so I took off the other one and threw them into the sea with her bike. And you know the rest.

My heartbeat was too fast, too loud. My hands trembled and I put the letter on my knees but they were shaking too. I held it in both hands, trying to focus on his handwriting

I swear Mari, I thought she was already dead. Guilt has tortured me for all these months. Knowing what you've been through makes it worse. I want to take your guilt away.

Thank you for coming back, you have given me the courage to face the truth and its consequences. I spoke to Takeda-san last night but no one else knows. He agreed to let me be there for Kate's ceremony and by the time you read this, I will have been arrested.

I beg you, my Mari, forgive me.
Ryu.

It wouldn't sink in. It couldn't be true. I must have misread something. Still shaking, I read it a second time, slowly and carefully. The letter dropped from my hand and I slid to the floor, knocking the coffee cup over with a clatter. Someone ran to me and helped me back onto the chair. I don't know how long I sat there. There were no tears, just a semi-awareness that jolted and stabbed me into a new understanding; I wasn't surprised.

Thinking back over everything, I was disgusted at myself for not realising. It was so obvious now. His cool reaction when I told him Kate was missing, his relief when Junichi said he'd seen her. Ryu wasn't worried about her; he was worried about himself. And when I'd told him I'd felt her soul pass, he was surprised. Not at the fact I'd felt it, he was surprised at *when* it had happened. At that point, he thought she'd been dead for days. Oh, God. Perhaps deep down, I'd always known.

And my dream of the black shoes. My stomach curdled and I tasted vomit in my throat. The shoes that I was sure belonged to the *wakagashira*. The nightmare wasn't about him, it was about Ryu. And I'd known he had those shoes. How many times had I left mine beside them?

In a daze, I went to the loo and threw up. I splashed my face in cold water, letting it run over the backs of my hands far longer than I needed to. Cupping my hand under the tap, I swilled my mouth and drank a little water. The bitter taste remained. I looked into the reflection of my eyes in the mirror. Love really is blind. I leaned on the basin with both hands, my shoulders shaking as I sobbed. Forgive him? He needed to accept what he'd done and forgive himself first, and I knew how hard that could be.

Acceptance is the balm that heals all wounds. Asa was wrong. No amount of acceptance would heal this new wound. Not in this lifetime.

They called my flight over the PA system. Last call, they said.

My legs shook as I straightened up and pulled my bag onto my shoulder. On shaky legs, I walked to the gate and showed my boarding pass.

Ryu's letter was still where I'd dropped it on the floor, stained with coffee and guilt.

Acknowledgments

My thanks go to everyone who has helped me get this book to publication. All my beta readers deserve a round of applause, but especially, Angelina Supranov, Allie Boler, Lyn Ward, and Kathy Calderbank. Your thoughtful comments helped me shape Mari's story.

Special thanks go to Jenny Downing for her keen eye, and to Roy Gray for his advice on publishing. Heartfelt thanks to the very fabulous Harriet Whyatt, and Sue and Keith Philips for your total belief in me and the story I wanted to tell.

And to whoever is reading this; thank you for choosing my book. I hope you've enjoyed it. And that perhaps, in difficult times, you'll find that acceptance is the balm that heals all wounds.

About the Author

Gigi has spent most of her life living and working in countries all over the world. Her passions are writing and traveling. She loves Asia, and India is a favourite destination. Giving up a career in tourism, Gigi qualified in various holistic therapies and worked in yoga retreats in the Mediterranean for twelve years. Currently, Gigi lives in Wiltshire with Isabella, the cat she rescued from the streets of Fethiye, in southern Turkey.

Gigi's second book Sandalwood is set in India and will be available late 2021

Printed in Great Britain
by Amazon